Counting Kennedys

A political thriller

An Assassination Novel

By
MARK LEONARD

Copyright © 2022 by Mark Leonard

All rights reserved under Title 17, U.S. Code, International and Pan-American Copyright Conventions. No part of this work may be reproduced or transmitted in any form or by any means electronic or mechanical, including but not limited to photocopying, scanning, recording, broadcast, or live performance or duplication by any information storage or retrieval system without prior written permission from the author or publisher, except for the inclusion of brief quotations with attribution in a review or report.

This is a work of fiction. All characters, products, corporations, institutions, and/or entities of any kind in this book are either the product of the author's imagination or, if real, used fictitiously, without any intent to describe their actual characteristics.

To the late great Karl Fleming—a great journalist, good friend and a champion for Civil Rights

PROLOGUE

Tuesday April 30, 1968

The Senator was moving fast. He was halfway up the concrete steps that led from the sidewalk to the front lawn when it happened. At one moment there was music coming out of the main tent, the dull under-roar of a hundred conversations. The next moment there was the explosion. Off to our right, the top of Henderson Hill erupted in a ball of flame. The neon Ramada Inn sign sparked and crashed to the ground. Bobby instinctively ducked down below the cement railings on either side of the stairs. I turned back to the car as the window on the front passenger side shattered.

"Christ," said the Senator. "What was that?"

I stood staring at the car window. Rodney was down on the ground. Women were screaming at The Mansion. Policemen and Sheriff's deputies were starting up their whirling lights and sirens.

Then Bobby was grabbing my arms and shaking me. I looked down at him.

"What was that? What was that?" he was asking. I shook my head.

"The Ramada Inn," I said.

"Let's go," he said and headed back for the car. I just stood there. Bobby stopped at Rodney and knelt down.

"Are you all-right?" he was asking. Rodney got up on his knees and nodded his head then he threw up on the sidewalk. Bobby helped him stand. Cop cars were ripping up Sid's lawn as they peeled out onto Main Street, bumping over the curb and skidding down the road.

I was still standing there.

"Does it hurt anywhere? Are you bleeding?" Bobby was asking Rodney.

Rodney shook his head and Bobby led him over to the concrete stairs and sat him on the little curlicue base of the railing.

"Stay here!" Bobby commanded him. Rodney nodded again. Bobby came over and grabbed my right arm.

"Let's go!" he insisted.

I still didn't move. I looked past him at the shattered window of the Lincoln. Something about that window bothered me.

"Where?" I managed to ask.

"The Ramada!" he said. "Do you know how to get there?"

"Yes," I said.

"You drive," Bobby commanded.

By the sheer force of the Senator's will, I found myself opening the driver's door. Bobby swept broken glass off the seat and into the gutter and got in the front passenger side.

He slammed his door and shouted, "Let's go! Let's go!" as if he were a cheerleader at a football game.

The keys were still in the ignition. I remember thinking stupidly, "Why not? Who would steal Bobby Kennedy's car?" I turned the huge engine over, flipped on the lights, hit the blinker and slowly pulled out.

"Step on it!" I looked over at Bobby. His eyes were on fire. His hair was falling across his forehead. He was leaning forward, every muscle tensed, his jaw muscles bulging.

Then suddenly I woke up.

"Let's go," I echoed him and I tromped on the gas pedal and pulled a screaming U-turn in the empty Main Street. The Continental took off like a shot as Bobby slammed against the passenger door.

"Now we're cooking!" he screamed. He was like a maniacal teenager, fierce and focused.

I got to the base of Henderson Hill in mere seconds. Two unmarked cop cars, a city police car and a county sheriff's cruiser, blocked the entrance to the drive that led up to the motel parking lot. The deputy was signaling me to go away, but Bobby was shouting, "Drive around! Drive around!"

I started to circle past the police car when the sheriff's deputy pulled his gun and ran toward me. Oh, man, I thought. Shot by a cop. At least Dad will be proud. I slammed on the brakes. The deputy screamed, "What the hell do you think you're doing?"

"Press," I told him, but it didn't stop him from throwing open the door and dragging me out onto the curb. In the meantime Bobby had jumped out of his side of the car and was screaming "Attorney General! Attorney General!" in that familiar Boston accent.

I stood up when my deputy let go of my shoulder.

Bobby was standing there, nose to nose with a pudgy Port Gibson city cop, and waving what looked like a small wallet.

"Jesus," my deputy said. "Is that Bobby Kennedy?"

"Yeah," I told him.

"What's he doing up here?" he asked.

"Ask him!" I screamed over the roar of the fire up on the hill.

"Let them go!" said Bobby's cop and my deputy stepped back. I jumped back in the car as Bobby slid into the seat and slammed his door.

"Attorney General?" I asked as I hit the ignition.

"I kept the badge," said Bobby. "Senators don't get one."

I jerked the steering wheel to the right and bounced up over the curb and around the police car. The rear of the Lincoln slammed against a concrete light pole.

"I hope this isn't your car!" I yelled at Bobby as we tore up the hill toward the fire.

"Borrowed!" he screamed back. "From your rich Republican mayor!" I looked over at him. He was grinning.

At the top of the hill there was a circle of cop cars around the fire. The fire department hadn't shown up yet. I drove around them and parked on a little rise above the motel so we could see what was going on. Bobby and I got out and looked down.

The explosion had to have been a car bomb. Several other cars, pickup trucks and one semi, had been slammed into each other in a semicircle around the burning ball of flame that could have once been a Chrysler Imperial. There was a gaping hole in the row of hotel rooms and flames were darting out of shattered windows.

The center of the hole was where I had spent my afternoon talking to Pete Decker. The ball of fire was where his Chrysler had been parked.

"Room 146," Bobby said. The firelight bounced off his face.

"Yeah," I said and then, "how did you know?"

"I was supposed to be there tonight. After the party."

CHAPTER 1

The Free Press

Sunday, April 28, 1968

In the spring of 1968 the Vietnam War was at its peak. In the spring of 1968 Martin Luther King was gunned down in Memphis, Tennessee. In the spring of 1968 President Lyndon Johnson told a stunned nation that he had no intention of running for a second complete term. In the spring of 1968 I saved Bobby Kennedy's life.

Bobby Kennedy ran in the Indiana Presidential Primary against Eugene McCarthy and favorite son Governor Roger D. Branigin. I had just finished my freshman year at Northern Indiana Teachers College in my hometown of Port Gibson. I didn't want to be a teacher. I wanted to be a journalist. But my grades weren't great and my mom had worked two jobs to keep me clothed and fed the first eighteen years of my life, so I couldn't afford Indiana University without a scholarship. And as for Dear Old Dad . . . more about him later.

All my life, it seemed, I had been working for the local paper, first as a delivery boy and then a runner for the pressroom, and finally as a reporter mostly working the society beat.

The North Indiana Free Press newspaper office was on Main Street just beyond jogging distance from the house I shared with my roommate, Rick Hamilton, but I never jogged there. I always took my trusty sixty-three Corvair, the one with the automatic lever shift, the one that was supposed to flip over on its back like a puppy wanting a tummy rub when you took any corner faster than thirty miles an hour. Mine never did. It might have had something to do with all the fast-food garbage that weighted down my backseat.

The Free Press was this huge room with about twenty desks scattered behind a long counter that separated the public from the working staff. There were no walls. This was way before cubicles. The place was almost always a noise riot with clacking Smith Coronas, swearing reporters, and only one receptionist trying to answer the phone and deal with the public above the din.

There was a mural covering the back wall painted by this Thomas Hart Benton clone. It portrayed various strong-armed men performing Herculean tasks of industry: riveting steel, chopping down trees, welding automobile frames. All of them blue-eyed, all of them square-jawed, all of them White.

"If you want niggers, go down by the river," Raymond Varnado the owner, publisher and editor of the Free Press was fond of saying. He was an old-fashioned bigot with old-fashioned ideas about most everything. "Nothing worth a crap has been invented since 1916," which just happened to be the year he was born. He thought he was the world's last great innovation.

"I want you to go down to the VFW this morning. They are rehearsing some damn beauty pageant my wife has gotten herself involved in." Mr. Varnado was chewing on his perpetual cigar that he never lit and shuffling through some black and white photos on his huge oak desk, the center of all the journalist activity. He said he liked to "Keep his eye on all the assholes that worked for him." Ben Shields, the paper's printer forever, said Varnado liked being "the hole in the middle of the ass."

"Take some pictures of the girlies and write a blurb so Charlene will keep roasting my weenie on a regular basis," my boss told me.

"Yes, sir," I said and did this little half-salute. I grabbed one of the big box cameras off an empty desk and went back out to my Corvair.

"And don't go bustin' any cherries while you're down there."

He guffawed. If he only knew that probably the only cherry in the VFW would be mine.

CHAPTER 2

The VFW

The VFW was this huge one-story building just a few blocks from the city park. You could see it coming from a long way away because of the American Flag flying on its roof.

Inside was one great hall with a stage at one end. That Sunday it was a beehive of activity with a dozen or so girls and women bustling around, hanging up red, white and blue bunting, and stringing microphone and lighting cable. I recognized a couple of guys from the college drama department putting up electrical stands and lugging lighting instruments up and down ladders. On the stage itself, this built redhead was twirling a baton and wearing a blue spangled bathing suit that was never meant for water.

I looked around for Mrs. Varnado in this swarm of patriotic preparation. I grabbed one of the lighting guys.

"Last I saw her she was heading for the back room. She's probably hoisting a few," he told me.

I turned toward the back of the large hall and that is when I saw the girl. She was sitting on the floor with her legs crossed. All the movement and chaos seemed to swirl around her as if she were their center.

And then there were her eyes.

They looked black. Not as if someone had hit her, but the eyes themselves, the irises looked black. And to emphasize that, she had rimmed them with heavy black liner. And her hair was black and her lips, well, not black but full and soft, no lipstick, just a faded rose red, pushed forward by a strong jaw line that gave here a determined, yet definitely feminine, look. She wore this black, thin-strapped t-shirt that was flecked with odd-shaped sparkles and it dipped well below her magnificent collarbones. Her legs were covered with black shorts and black dancer leggings. No shoes.

A girl in black. Motionless. Calm. The essence of repose. Those black eyes seemingly focused and unfocused at the same time, seeing everything and nothing.

I had never seen her before. I had never seen anyone like her before. I wanted to sit down next to her, hold her, brush her black hair away from her black eyes and touch that incredible jaw line as I bent to kiss those lips.

But I didn't. I had a Mrs. Varnado to find. This girl was obviously here with the beauty pageant. She was obviously one of the contestants. I will have Mrs. Varnado introduce us. Then I'll sit next to her, then I'll brush her black hair away from her black eyes and then . . .

I tore myself away and went into the back room.

The back room at the VFW was the bar, a place where vets could go and start their drinking at nine A.M. without worrying about a boss or a wife intruding on their reverie.

The room was packed. After all it was almost noon Sunday and it was the only place in town the "blue laws" allowed people to drink in public on the Sabbath. I saw Mrs. Varnado leaning against the long shelf on the back wall that served as a second bar. She had a beer in her right hand and the outstretched fingers of her left rested lightly on the hairy forearm of Tony Hargus, a local ex-college-football-hero who sold insurance and was always running for some minor political office and always losing.

Mrs. Varnado was a piece of work, mostly of her own doing. She had orange-red hair and red-red lipstick and wore that aqua eye shadow that looked good only on Gina Lollobrigida. She flirted with every man available and many not available and was known to mess around with more than a few. Even I had been subject to her advances, but I had managed to keep my virginity intact.

Okay, the cat is out of the bag. Eighteen-years-old, 1968, the year after the summer of love, the era of sex, drugs and rock and roll and I was still a virgin. I'm not sure why, exactly. I wasn't bad looking for a tall, gangly kid, six-six, two thirty-odd. And I could talk to girls—I had several girl "friends." I just couldn't—I don't know—I could get the gun sited all right. I just couldn't pull the trigger, especially with Mrs. Varnado.

This was not out of any sense of nobility or loyalty to the boss. Mrs. V had been a prime opportunity to solve my manhood problem. It was just that there was a deep hardness under all her eyeliner and rouge and I had a feeling that if I didn't put the right wrinkle in her bedspread, I would be looking for new employment.

And I loved my job. I really did. I got to be on the inside of the whole world. I got to read the ticker from the news agencies as news broke. Vietnam. Civil Rights.

I was the first person in Port Gibson to know about Martin Luther King's assassination.

I got to hear all the local gossip. I got to know all the inferences, the underside of things, the horrible stories that did not make it in the papers but affected our lives just as deeply. And that job was the heart and soul of what little self-esteem a teen-ager could muster. Ethan Taylor, man-in-the-know, hotshot reporter.

Anyway, I was shoving my way through the VFW beer-breath forest when I heard this gravelly voice behind me. "Well, I'll be a son of a bitch." I froze. Literally froze. I couldn't move if you set my feet on fire. Finally, I was able to turn my head.

I hadn't seen Mack Taylor for eight years, but he hadn't changed much; a short, tight body, red curly hair over a prematurely wrinkled face scarred from too much surgery from too many brawls. He was standing at the bar. "Bar stools are for faggots and females, boy," he told me once, essential information for a twelve-year-old.

"That's you, ain't it boy?" the voice continued. God, he was doing his redneck thing. Mack had only a sixth-grade education, but his mind was about as sharp as they come and he read extensively and could put together a phrase better than most of my professors. But he had these personas that he would put on and take off like sweatshirts. Once, for no apparent reason, for about two years he talked like a Cajun. I swear. He had an accent thicker than Justin Wilson and kept at it, day and night for two solid years.

When a co-worker or an acquaintance (Mack never seemed to have real friends) would ask him what he was doing, he would say, "What for you make fun of my talk like dat?"

I asked Mom if he did it all the time and she just sighed and said "All the time." I tried not to think of the implications.

But today he was just a redneck and I was just another character in the traveling road show that was Mack John Wayne Taylor. In fact, I was named after Duke Wayne's character in *The Searchers*.

He bumped his way through the crowd and stood next to me. I was a good ten inches taller.

"Yeah, Mack," I said. "It's me."

"What's this Mack crud?" he asked. "Ain't I your daddy? Give me a hug!"

I stood there, my arms at my side.

"I thought you were dead," I said.

"Really?"

"No. I just wished it a lot." I don't know what made me say it. Normally I avoided any sort of conflict. That had a lot to do with my size and a lot of screwed up short guys that needed to fight my size.

He looked at me quizzically and then grinned.

"All the more reason to give me a hug. Let bygones be bygones." And he threw his arms around my waist and pressed his head against my chest like an eight-year-old saying goodbye to his mom. When I didn't respond he let go and stepped back.

"Well, damn, you got tall. Must have been the milkman after all."

"Must have been why I didn't turn out ugly either." Mack stared at me with that look again, like he was trying to decide whether he should laugh or kill me.

Finally he said, "My, my, my, listen to the mouth on him. He didn't get that from his momma. You old enough to drink a beer with your ugly old daddy?"

"Not now. I gotta see Mrs. Varnado."

"Son, we all gotta see Mrs. Varnado sooner or later, but you got time for a quick one with the old man."

I looked over at Mrs. V and she was leaning into Hargus and laughing, her hand now firmly attached to his forearm.

"I don't drink," I said. I did drink, actually. Now and then at a party or with my roommate after an exam, but I didn't want to drink now, not with him.

"Then it's time you started," Mack waggled two fingers at the bartender. The vet wearing a blue VFW hat drew two Michelobs out of the tap and set them in front of the Old Man. The bartender looked at me suspiciously, but kept his mouth shut when he saw the grim set of Mack's jaw. Pop had that kind of effect on people.

Once during one of Mom and Pop's many separations, when I was about six, Mack was living in a trailer just down the street from my grandparents where mom and I lived. He drove by the house. I was in the front yard playing home run derby with a squashed Coca Cola cup and a broomstick. Grandma and grandpa were out somewhere, probably shopping. Back then no one thought twice about leaving a five-year-old alone for a while in a small town like Port Gibson, Indiana. No one except Mack Taylor.

His battered pickup truck squealed to a stop and the driver's door opened. Mack yelled, "Where's your mama?"

"Working," I yelled back. I didn't have much respect for the old man even back then. I guess it was because he was always leaving. I learned to call everyone else "Sir," but never got the hang of it with Mack.

"Where's your grandad and grandmom?"

"At the store," I said.

"Come on boy, get in the truck." I still remember the sour smell of that truck, oil and gas and spilled whiskey. Cigarette butts piled up in the ashtray. He took me down to his trailer and set me up with my cup and broomstick in his fenced-in back yard. Within an hour there were about a dozen of his teamster buddies lounging around the place, drinking beer, laughing and waiting for something.

Long about four that afternoon something showed up: five city cop cars and two county cruisers. Sheriff Dolph Crites came to the door of the trailer and knocked. I had heard the sirens and I had come inside to see what was going on.

The sheriff was standing in the doorway towering over Mack. The Teamster buddies were all on their feet, most of them with their hands unconsciously clinched in fists. Sheriff Crites spoke calmly, but firmly.

"We don't want any trouble, Mack. Connie just wants the boy back home."

Through the door, behind the sheriff, I could see blue-shirted policemen and brown-shirted deputies posed behind their cars, aiming shotguns and pistols at the trailer.

"You tell Connie if she is going to keep the boy, she better keep him right. Don't leave him all alone."

"I'll tell her that."

Mack stared up at the sheriff for a couple of seconds and then without taking his eyes off of him said to me, "Go on, boy. Go on with this cop."

I just stood there. I don't remember being afraid. I just wasn't sure what I was supposed to do. I guess I was just overwhelmed.

Mack turned back to me. I remember it was then that I started to get scared because I expected him to be angry, but he wasn't. In fact, he gave me the most tender, loving look I would ever see on that beat-up face, and said softly, "Go on home to your Momma, Ethan. I'll come by and see you later."

I walked past the teamsters, past Mack, out the door and Sheriff Crites put my hand in his huge paw. I saw the dozen or so men behind the cars relax their aim and, even though I still wasn't exactly sure what had gone down, for the first time and not the last, I was impressed with my old man.

People just didn't screw around with Mack Taylor.

I took a sip of my beer. Warm and flat. Mack drank about half of his.

"So where's your Momma? I dropped by the house and pissed off a bunch of strangers."

"She is in Iowa."

"Iowa? What she doing in Iowa?"

"Living with her husband."

"I'm her damned husband."

"Not any more," I said. "She got married in August."

"She can't do that."

"She did."

"That's bigotry."

"Bigamy, Pop. And it isn't. Seems as if you and mom never really got formally hitched."

"We didn't?"

"Nope. Imagine my surprise."

"I thought for sure, way back when."

"Nope. Mom said you started out to make it legal several times but one or both of you would start drinking and next thing you know you were performing the marriage act without the marriage."

"She said that?"

"Words to that effect."

"I'll be damned. Well, don't our living together all that time, don't that make it, common-law or something?"

"Mack, between your trucking and running off with a cocktail waitress every eighteen months, you were never in town long enough to make it common anything. But even if you did stay all that time, in order to be legally common-law in the state of Indiana, you have to file with the government. You never got around to doing that, either."

"You sure?"

"Positive," I said. "I did the research."

"You did what?"

"I made sure everything was clear and legal for Mom's marriage."

"Why in the hell did you do that?"

"It made her happy. Besides, I wanted to find out if there were any loopholes. I didn't like the idea of being a bastard. But I suppose you get used to it, huh?"

"You little prick," he said looking up at me and then he smiled again. "You want another beer?"

"No, I've got work to do."

"Well, I want to talk to you when you have more time."

"Why?"

"I haven't seen you since you were fifteen."

"Twelve," I said.

"Time flies. I want to get to know you. Hell, you're the only bouncing baby boy I got, that I know of. A man should get to know his son."

"A man shouldn't abandon his family."

"I'm sorry. There. I've said it. Now let me try to make it up to you."

"I'll think about it. How long are you in town?"

"Until the primary," he said looking away from me.

"Of course you are. I bet there are teamsters coming back to Indiana from all over America. Jimmy Hoffa's revenge."

The bartender set another beer in front of Mack. Mack stared into it.

"The Brotherhood takes care of its own."

"Yeah. I remember."

"What is that supposed to mean?" And I saw that face that I hate. The narrowed eyes, the tight jaw, the lips pulled back in a death's head grin. The trouble face.

"I just mean that I remember how seriously you take your teamsters. How you guys always stick together."

"Oh." His eyes softened as though he remembered who I was, part of the family, on his side. There were two definite sides in Mack Taylor's world: his side and most everybody else. Either you were for him or against him and if you tried to stand in the middle of the road, you just got run over.

"Listen," I said. "I got to go. Here's my phone number." I scribbled it down on a bar napkin. "Call me."

"Sure."

"Really."

"I will."

I turned to walk away and I heard Mack say, "Don't stand too close to that asshole Bobby Kennedy."

I turned back.

"What?" I asked.

"You heard me."

"Why would I be anywhere near Bobby Kennedy?"

"You work for the newspaper, don't you?"

"How did you know that?"

Mack just shrugged. "Kennedy is coming to Port Gibson this week. Stay away from him."

"Bobby Kennedy wouldn't come within a hundred miles of Port Gibson," I said.

"Just stay away from him," my daddy said.

"Sure," I said and turned back to the wall bar where I had seen Mrs. Varnado. She was gone. So was Tony Hargus. It didn't take much imagination to figure out why. I turned back to dear old Dad, but he had pulled his own disappearing act.

When I went back out into the ballroom, everyone was gone. Everyone and everything. No bunting. No lights. No chicks in spangled bathing suits. No black-eyed girl thinking deep thoughts. Passing strange, I thought. Passing strange.

CHAPTER 3

Counting Kennedys

I went back to *The Free Press* office.

"That was quick." Mr. Varnado was still playing with photos and sipping bourbon out of his coffee cup.

"I couldn't find your wife," I lied.

"There wasn't a beauty pageant rehearsal?"

"There were a lot of kids running around decorating and then for some reason, undecorating."

Mr. Varnado grunted. "Real work. Charline wouldn't hang around for that. I'll call her at home. Get any pictures?"

"Nothing to shoot."

"No jailbait in bathing suits?"

"None," I lied again.

"Well, we gotta do something for Tuesday. Hey, I know, why don't you go check out that new whorehouse?"

"The what?" I asked knowing exactly what I had heard.

"Haven't you heard of the new whorehouse? They call it 'Tina's Massage City' or some other bullshit, but everyone knows what it really is."

Tina's Massage and Relaxation. Of course I knew about it. Every adolescent male in Port Gibson knew about the whorehouse. I had found out about it last month when we were counting Kennedys.

There was little to do in Port Gibson, only two movie theatres, one TV station, and the one newspaper. My two best friends, roommate Rick and a Kennedyophile named Sam Cooper, and I spent most of our time talking movies, arguing politics and counting Kennedys. Every Wednesday of every week, the new magazines would hit the racks and we would set off for the largest magazine rack in town at the local Greyhound bus station.

The object was to count as many Kennedys you could on the covers of the magazines and tabloids in a minute. It took three players. One of us would be the timer and the other two would stare at the magazine rack. It was illegal to actually touch the rack or the magazines. At the end of a minute the timer would yell "Halt" (not "Stop" or "Time" or some other sane thing, but "Halt"—who knows why) and the two players would announce their total of Kennedys counted and the person with the highest total won.

But the game was not over. If the highest total was disputed, and it always was, the tally had to be justified by the judge/timer. Sometimes this would produce heated arguments not unlike a close play at home plate. One argument as to whether or not Peter Lawford counted as a Kennedy went on for several months. It was a Hamilton-Cooper bout and I was the timer.

"He is a Kennedy by marriage just like Jackie," Sam Cooper insisted. Sam was the Kennedy freak who invented the game, but not its best player. "And we are not about to stop counting Jackie, are we?"

"But he doesn't have Kennedy in his name!" Hamilton maintained.

"Neither does Maria Shriver and we can't kick her off the list."

"We don't count Sargent Shriver."

"*You* don't count Sargent Shriver. If I see him, I am counting him."

"What do you think?" my roommate turned to me.

"I think if we start counting people who had sexual relations or allegedly had sexual relations with a member of the Kennedy family, we are going to have to expand the time limit," I said. "Papa Joe alone is said to have dated half of Hollywood."

"Dated," Rick snorted at my euphemism.

"And the record would inevitably fall," said Sam.

The record was seventy-two Kennedys on a snowy afternoon, November 22, 1964, the anniversary of the assassination. It was a most sacred record, like Ruth's 714 home runs, and no one had come within a dozen of it since we started the game that January.

And the record was mine.

"I rule," I said, "that we do not count Kennedy paramours but we do count their offspring."

"And Jackie?" asked Rick.

"Jackie is the exception," I ruled.

"And Joan?" asked Sam.

"Okay, Joan, too. I rule that we count only female paramours."

"Like Marilyn Monroe?" asked Rick.

"That hasn't been proved!" Sam screamed. He was really sensitive about the Marilyn-JFK rumors.

"Besides," I said in defense of my record, "even dead, Marilyn would add at least five covers every time, so what would be the point?"

And so the argument continued for months, springing up every time we had nothing better to do and, as I said, that was often in Port Gibson. Finally, we decided that we would only count Kennedys, their progeny and their spouses. Kennedy flings would not count unless a Kennedy was included in the headline or picture.

Lately we had added a new wrinkle to the game. The timekeeper could introduce a topic of conversation while the players counted. It increased the difficulty of concentration and it gave the timekeeper something to do. And that is how I found out about the house of ill repute.

"You know Port Gibson has acquired its very own whorehouse," Rick commented just before he started timing the minute. "Go," he added.

"What do you mean?" I asked, rapidly glancing over the magazines. Bobby seemed to be everywhere since he announced he was going to run.

"I mean Port Gibson has its own whorehouse. I overheard Dad talking with the chief of police about it."

There was an Ethel and a Joan and somebody decided to run that picture of John-John saluting his father's casket with the headline, "Is Bobby next?"

"Where?" I asked. Cooper wasn't saying a word.

"Near the warehouses down by the river," Rick said. "They are calling it a massage parlor, but Chief Randall says no one is fooled."

"How do they know it is a whorehouse?" I asked.

"They sent in an undercover cop and he said before he knew it, he was getting a knob job."

"Before he knew it?" Sixteen, seventeen, and there was Jackie up in the corner of McCall's.

"Yeah and once he got the knobber, he couldn't pull the plug. Entrapment, not to mention partaking in illegal activity. That is part of the problem. Bust the place and you are going to bust the cop. Time."

"Twenty-six," said Cooper.

"No way," I said.

"Way," said Sam. "Read 'em and weep." And we started counting Kennedys.

"The idea is that you pose as a college student," Mr. Varnado was saying, dragging my mind from the bus station to the newspaper room. "Which is convenient, because you are a college student. Just sort of stumble in there and ask for a massage and see what happens."

"It's Sunday," I protested. This assignment had me terrified. "It's probably not open. The blue laws."

"Son," Mr. Varnado said. "If they are selling what I think they're selling, they're breaking a lot bigger law than buying a loaf of bread on the Lord's Day. Just go down there and if it's open then see if you can get someone to make a grab for your crotch."

CHAPTER 4

The Massage Parlor

Port Gibson used to flood a lot. The archives at the *Free Press* are filled with pictures of people floating down Broadway, the main drag down by the Wabash River, with water topping the marquees at the old Rialto Theater. Every four years or less the river would become this raging torrent and would bloat up over the banks and wipe out the Port Gibson business district and every four years or less the merchants would courageously bail out their stores and start all over again until finally, and it wasn't until the late 1940s, some genius figured out that for the money they spent drying out the town two and three times a decade, they could build a wall.

So they built this floodwall all along Broadway to about four blocks west of downtown and then it stopped at a long natural bluff that cut in from the river and then rolled upwards into the green sward heading into the hills outside of Port Gibson.

But between the bluff and the river was "The Flats," an area of town that no one cared much about saving from high tide. It was here that the few Black families and a lot of what Mama called "White Trash" (best as I could figure, "White Trash" was anyone who was poorer than we were) lived in trailers or lopsided bungalows, or in one story, rambling shacks that got completely washed away when the Wabash burped.

Above The Flats, above the land and the people that the city of Port Gibson didn't care about, where the bluff ended and the hills began, was the warehouse district. It was too close to the flood plain for a decent neighborhood to grow, but far enough above it so that businesses could throw up cheap aluminum siding buildings and abandoned railroad cars to store whatever it was those kinds of companies stored.

And since warehousing, especially this kind of last ditch, who-cares warehousing, didn't take what you would call skilled labor, there was a ready workforce nearby. Lonely, desolate people working for companies that barely remembered that the warehouses and the people existed at all.

And evidently, in the midst of all this forgotten real estate, someone had planted Port Gibson's brand-new whorehouse. And now I got to go there, virginity and all.

I drove back down Main Street from the *Free Press* and then took a left on Broadway. About a half mile from downtown, I turned down Lindenwood Drive into the warehouse district. Lindenwood Drive was a dead end only about four blocks long. On the third block, on the left, was the only house in the Warehouse district. It was one of Port Gibson's ubiquitous bungalows built just after World War II. I grew up in one just like it. The large front windows had been spray-painted silver and a sign over the door read, "Tina's Massage and Relaxation."

"Relaxation," I thought. "Is that what they are calling it these days."

I did a U-turn in the parking lot and drove back down Lindenwood. OK. I had seen it. I suppose I could go inside, I thought. And do what? Find out what the deal is. I was a reporter. That is what reporters do. Find out stuff. Report.

"You always got to pay for sex," dear old Dad would tell his buddies when they came over to play poker, "one way or another." I guess I was finally about to find out.

But I passed it again and I was almost to the floodwall before I pulled another U-turn on the middle of Broadway. Why not? I asked myself, always a dangerous question. I was a reporter. Reporters investigated. That's what I was doing. I was investigating.

And maybe losing my cherry.

I pulled back into the parking lot. And did another u-turn. What was wrong with me? Why couldn't I just park the damn Corvair? Cautious, I thought. A good reporter is always cautious. I'll park down the street, behind one of the warehouses. Why? What was I afraid of? Who did I think would see me there? My mom? My dad? Who else was there?

There was no one on the street. The only people who would drive down here on a Sunday would be someone going to the same place I was going and what did I care if they saw me going into a massage parlor? Shouldn't they be more concerned about me seeing them? Wasn't I "The Press?" I started to drive back to the massage parlor parking lot and then abruptly turned the car into a side street behind a warehouse. No use announcing my presence to the world. I reached under the dash and pulled on the hand brake as if to solidify my determination.

When I got to Tina's front door, I almost knocked. I guess because it looked like someone's home—someone who happened to spray paint her windows silver. I had to remind myself that this was a place of business and you don't have to knock on the door of a place of business. I opened the door and stepped inside.

It was dark, especially compared to the bright spring day outside. My eyes adjusted like the fade-in of a movie. The place looked like someone's front room. There were two stuffed easy chairs, a coffee table covered with magazines, even a small portable black and white TV in the corner with the sound turned off. There was a musty smell, probably from the furniture and under that, the faint wisp of an orange scented perfume.

Off to the left, in the darkest part of the room, was a couch. Behind the couch was a standing reading lamp with what must have been an incredibly low wattage bulb. On the couch was a woman. A book lay open in her lap, but she was looking up at me. She wore a filmy green nightgown, short on both ends, her legs were pressed primly together and she wore glasses.

I don't know what I expected, but this was certainly not it. She took off her glasses. She seemed about a decade older than I was, though it was hard to tell in that light. Her hair was almost-white blonde, cut short in what they use to call a "Dutch boy."

I guess I was just standing there, staring. She asked, "Yes?" It was a nice voice. I could tell that even with just the one word. It had both timbre and lightness. She is a singer, I thought incongruously. I still stood there. My eyes adjusting. Everything, adjusting. I couldn't help it. Eighteen.

"Can I help you?" she asked. I felt like I was in a five and dime and had been caught contemplating shoplifting.

"I would like," I began and then stopped and looked around the room some more. There were pictures on the walls. Not erotic pictures not even interesting pictures. There were farm scenes and smalltown scenes like blown up Christmas cards without the snow.

"I would like," I began again, "some relaxation." There I was, all nerves and hormones and talking like a wise-ass. I think she half smiled, but again, it was hard to tell in the dim light.

"I don't think so," she said. She remained seated. The book remained open in her lap.

"Well, then a massage," I said.

"No," she said lightly, but firmly.

"Why not?" I asked.

"We don't do college boys," she said. "Do," the first real hint of sex, besides the long legs and mostly exposed pale breasts pushed together with the thin, oh so interesting, line between them.

"What makes you think I'm a college boy?" I hit the word "boy" a little too hard.

The girl just tilted her head and gave me one of those "who do you think you're kidding" looks that females must practice hours in front of a mirror, then she put on her glasses and looked back down at her book.

I crossed the room. I took out my billfold and fumbled out my press card. "I'll have you know I am a member of the press and I could write an article that would shut this place down in a New York minute."

I have no idea who I had become. Humphrey Bogart in *The Big Sleep*? Steve McQueen in *Bullett*? Whoever I was I wasn't me. I was hormones and confusion and frustration.

She looked up. She held out her hand. It was a nice hand. Decidedly feminine, but not delicate, a reassuring, kind hand. I gave her my press card. She glanced at it and gave it back.

"Give Mr. Varnado my regards and tell him I won't be able to make our usual Thursday. I have a doctor's appointment."

I just stood there holding my card.

"Friday will do. For Mr. Varnado. Not you, Mr. Taylor."

"I didn't know you could be choosy."

Bogart said that.

"For a whore?"

"I didn't say that."

That was McQueen.

"Whores can be 'choosy.' Whores have to be 'choosy.' It is how we survive."

"I didn't mean . . ."

"Leave." She took off her glasses and shut her book.

I couldn't leave. I wanted to explain something, but I wasn't sure what. I wanted to tell her that I liked her. That somehow I recognized something in her. Something of me. Something of my life. I wasn't sure what. I wanted to say all that, but I didn't know how to begin, but I didn't have to because that was when Bruno came in.

I didn't notice him at first. The other door to the front room must have opened quickly but silently. It led to the hall, which was darker than this room with a faint red glow, but even that glow was pretty much blocked out by Bruno. Bruno was big. Bruno was intense. Bruno's real name was Seb. I knew it was Seb because the girl stood up and said, "It's okay, Seb." But he still seemed like a Bruno to me.

"No it ain't, Jessi," Bruno said. It was a low growl. "The lady asked you to leave." His tone sounded familiar.

Anthony Quinn, I thought. *Requiem for a Heavyweight*.

"He's just a kid, Seb."

"I don't like kids," said Bruno and he took a step toward me.

I knew she was trying to help, but I still didn't like it. I could feel the color move up in my cheeks. Part of me was screaming that this was no time for me to lose my temper, but the rest of me was saying I just didn't care.

"Scram," said Bruno.

Scram? I thought. Scram? This buffalo actually said scram? I honestly believed I just thought this last part, but, evidently, I must have thought it out loud because the next thing I know Bruno had me by the throat and was squeezing me up against the wall.

"This buffalo is going to break your damn neck," Bruno was saying.

"No, Bruno, no!" I heard her say. Down, Bruno, down, I thought, this time, thank God, to myself.

"Are you going to leave?" Bruno asked me. His breath smelled like cheese and bell peppers.

"Yes," I croaked.

"Are you going to come back?"

You betcha, I thought.

"No," I said.

Bruno let go of my throat and grabbed a handful of shirt in his left fist while he opened the front door.

"Aren't you gonna tip the lady?" he asked.

"What?" I asked back.

"Tip the lady!" He flipped me around and shoved me back up against the wall. I was beginning to feel like Pinocchio before his "I got no strings" days. He took out my wallet. I had almost a week's pay in there. He took out three twenties and flipped them on to the coffee table.

"You always tip the lady," he said. Then he shoved me out the door. My wallet flew out over my head and landed about six feet in front of me.

Well, I thought, if that was a whorehouse, I certainly got screwed.

"Write it up," Varnado said.

"What?" I said. I was back at the newspaper pouring a cold Coke down a tender throat.

"Write the whole thing up. Well, you know, clean it up a little, the language and you know."

"Don't mention you."

"Yeah. But stick to the stuff about they don't do college boys. Twenty-one's the limit and as far as you could tell it was just a place to get a nice massage."

"But it isn't."

"How do you know?"

"A legitimate masseuse doesn't wear a green filmy negligee."

"How do you know? You ever get a "legitimate" massage?"

"Well, no."

"Then there you go. And leave out what she was wearing, too."

I was beginning to get it. I was set up. This whole thing was a whitewash of the massage parlor. Probably a deal Varnado made for services rendered. I got it and it was making me nauseated.

"I'm not sure I can do that."

"Do what?"

"Write the article the way you want me to."

"You damn well better write it and write it good!" he roared. Then he chewed on his cigar some and looked up at the ceiling. "Listen, I got certain community responsibilities, people I gotta answer to whether I like it or not. See? It's how things work, how you play ball, how you get along. Sometimes we gotta do things that stick in the craw." Then he drifted off and sort of winced as if he thought of something he didn't like to think about.

"But you gotta do 'em," he continued. "Look, I'll make you a deal. Write me this piece, clean it up nice and pretty, and when that goddamned Kennedy comes to town, I'll let you be the one to cover him."

"You know about Bobby?" I asked as if the Senator and I played bridge once a week.

"Of course I know about that rat-prick. I'm the goddamned editor of the goddamned news."

"Won't the other guys, the older guys be angry that you gave me the big story?"

"Yeah? So what? Screw 'em. They work for me. So you want the Kennedy thing?"

"Well, yes sir."

"Then write the damn whorehouse story the way I want. Deal?" He held out his cigar stained hand.

I was staring Satan straight in the eyes, but I didn't flinch.

"Deal," I said and I shook and I lost my cherry, but not the one I had intended.

CHAPTER 5

The Mansion

I lived in a three-story brick house with a wrap-around porch complete with Grecian Revival columns, an old-fashioned porch swing and, like I said, my best friend, Rick Hamilton. We called it The Playboy Mansion South because it was huge and half our fantasies were fueled by Hugh Hefner's publication. But soon we dropped the "Playboy" and "South" because it was just too juvenile even for a pair of horny eighteen-year-olds.

The Mansion was the last house on Main Street on the edge of town where the cornfields met the parking meters. It was a rental property owned by Sid Hamilton, the very Republican town mayor and Lincoln-Mercury dealer and Rick's father. Sid had bought the house from the estate of a dentist who committed suicide, which made the place both spooky and romantic for Rick's frequent female overnight guests.

Rick was a bright lad who had all but flunked his most important junior year of high school when Jane Lannigan, his steady since second grade, dumped him. His grades that spring were so bad that all the universities turned him down. However, Northern Indiana Teachers College would take any Hoosier who was breathing and had a high school diploma.

Rick got The Mansion on the conditions that he keep his grades up and work to re-elect Vietnam war hero Sam Ollestadt, the local Republican Congressman. I got in The Mansion because Rick and I became friends when we were in the senior play *The Taming of the Shrew* and I had enough money to split the utilities.

Since his lifelong girlfriend dumped him, Rick recovered by hitting more tail than a rocking chair in room full of kitty cats.

When I walked in The Mansion, he was having sex on the kitchen table.

The brunette was saying "Okay, okay, okay," like a nervous mantra. My roommate wasn't saying anything. He saw me walk in and gave me this goofy grin. The girl didn't see me. She had her eyes shut and kept saying, "Okay, okay, okay."

I got caught up in her monologue and added my own, "Okay." And backed out onto the porch. I saw the Sunday *Chicago Tribune* on the front steps, picked it up and sat on the swing to wait out Ethan's latest adventure. It didn't take long. In about fifteen minutes he walked out the front door and lighted a Marlboro.

"Okay, okay, okay?" I asked without looking up from the sports section. The Cubs were winning, the Viet Cong (according to LBJ) were losing, and the economy was breaking even. Nothing was as it seemed.

"First time I nailed her, all she said was, 'Not bad, not bad, not bad.' I claim progress not perfection."

He sat on the porch railing and took a short Budweiser bottle out of his sweatshirt pocket and took a swig.

"Do you even know this one's name?"

"Jennifer Something." He picked up the A section of the paper.

"Oh," I said, still pretending to read. "Related to that Charlene Something you were banging last week."

"Second cousin twice removed. Or was it three times?" He glanced at the front page and then threw it on the porch.

He stubbed out his cigarette half-smoked.

"God, I hate these things."

"Why don't you quit?" I asked half-heartedly.

"Good idea," he said and tossed me his pack of cigarettes. It had only three left.

"Now, whatever you do, whatever I say, no matter how much I beg or plead, do NOT give me back those cigarettes."

"Okay," I said and put them in my pocket. I would not throw them away. Later that day or tomorrow he would ask for them back and I would give them to him. It was a weekly ritual. The first time he gave me a carton and I took him seriously and hid it. He chased me up a tree swinging a tennis racket before I told him where it was. Now I just hang on to them until he needs another cigarette.

Friendship. Ain't it grand?

"You know there is no real news in that newspaper."

I tried to ignore him.

"All the real news happens behind the scenes."

I stared at my newspaper no longer able to concentrate, but I wasn't going to let him know that.

"The real nitty, the real gritty are left for people in the know. I happen to be in the know."

I had to respond to that.

"Rick, I am a newspaper reporter. I am more in the know than you will ever know."

"You don't know what I know now and you really wish you did."

I tried to go back to my paper. He snatched it out of my hands.

"I HAVE TO TELL YOU THE REAL NEWS!"

Never room with a drama major.

"Okay," I said. "Tell me."

"Guess who is coming to Port Gibson next Friday?"

"That's not telling. That's asking."

"No. Come on. Guess."

"Elvis," I said.

"Nope."

"Kris Kringle."

"No, really. Guess," Rick implored. He stuck out his lower lip for dramatic effect. He looked like a five-year-old on his first day of school, but not as tall.

"Benny Hill."

"Bobby Freakout Kennedy," screamed Rick and he did this little jig.

"Now we know what the F stands for."

He stopped dancing. "What 'F'?"

"RFK," I said. I went back to pretending to read. Rick snatched the newspaper out of my hands.

"Look at me! Aren't you excited? Bobby is coming to Port Gibson! Don't that just make your little Democrat heart sing?"

Now I was getting irritated. "I hate it when you do that."

"Do what?"

"Talk about the Kennedys as if they were your cousins or something." I did it too, but he put me in a pissy mood.

"What are you talking about?"

"Bobby did this. Ted said that. Jack used to cry at weddings."

"I never said Jack used to cry at weddings."

"You know what I mean."

"What am I supposed to call them? Mr. Kennedy, Mr. Kennedy and Mr. Kennedy? Wouldn't that be a bit confusing?"

"How about Robert Kennedy, John Kennedy, and Ted Kennedy?"

"Too respectful. I'm a Republican. Jesus, you can be a real killjoy sometimes."

He sat down hard on the porch floor. He pushed back his longish dark hair and looked up at me with those brown puppy-dog eyes. He looked like he was going to cry. I relented.

"I knew Senator Kennedy was coming to town."

"Did not!" Now he was twelve.

"Did."

"Did not."

"Varnado told me."

"Oh." He stood up and killed the rest of the beer.

"Can I have my paper back?"

He put it behind his back.

"You wanna know who told me about Bobby?"

"Okay. I'll bite. Who told you Robert Kennedy is coming to Port Gibson?"

"My Uncle Pete told me."

That got my interest.

"Uncle Pete, your *Newsweek* Uncle Pete?"

I had been hearing about Ethan's crazy journalist Uncle Pete ever since junior high. His ground-breaking civil rights coverage was one of the reasons I decided to become a journalist.

"He showed up yesterday and I spent the whole afternoon talking with him. He is here to cover Bobby coming to Port Gibson."

"You mean I may finally get to meet him? The legendary Pete Decker?"

"You better." He sat his butt down next to me on the swing. Rick was as unusually short as I was tall. Side by side we were Abbott and Costello. "Uncle Pete wants to talk to you." He casually scanned my newspaper. It was my turn to snatch it out of his hands.

"Me? Why, for god's sake?"

"I told him you worked for the paper and he said he needs a local news connection."

"Why doesn't he just talk to Varnado?"

"He says that Varnado is a Neanderthal, fascist son of a bitch and he would talk to him when George Wallace joins the N-double-ACP. Pete is a liberal. The black sheep of the family."

I jumped off the swing.

"Where are you going?"

"To your Dad's house to see your Uncle Pete."

"He's not there. He is at The Ramada."

"Okay," I said. I could hear the porch swing creaking and the newspaper rattling as I walked around the corner of the house.

CHAPTER 6

The Ramada

Pete Decker was a legend in the civil rights movement all through the sixties. He was standing in Montgomery defying Bull Connor and his fire hoses. He was there when they dug up those three Freedom Riders in Philadelphia, Mississippi. And when they rolled Martin Luther King's coffin through the streets of Atlanta, he was the only white man in a river of black sorrow.

But Hamilton had also told me that he was a son of a bitch.

He had been married four times before he reached thirty-five. He was the first man in a brawl and the last man to apologize. A man's man. Hamilton said he was courageous, brilliant, a champion of truth and justice and mean as a snake.

Of course, I wanted to meet him.

The Ramada Inn was on Henderson Hill overlooking Port Gibson not that far from The Mansion. At night you could see its neon red and white sign from my front yard. The Ramada bar was always rocking on Friday and Saturday nights. It was the only place in Port Gibson where you could drink a beer, listen to live music and not expect to get your head busted open. But on Sunday night, pretty much like the rest of Copiah County, it was as quiet as a tomb.

I parked the Corvair in the temporary parking space in front of the motel and walked into the lobby. Back in the sixties Ramada Inns always had a huge lobby with two staircases sweeping up to a balcony above the front desk. To the right was a dining room, empty except for a couple salesmen types lingering over coffee. To the left was the closed door to the lounge where the touring cover bands played their watered-down rock and roll Fridays and Saturdays.

I recognized the desk clerk. He was this English major I had shared a Shakespeare class with last semester. In Port Gibson there were only a few Negroes and no Mexicans or Asians, so the college students got a lot of the garbage jobs. I couldn't remember his name, but that was okay. I figured he hadn't noticed me. I don't think I was his type.

He was writing something when I approached the desk.

"Pete Decker's room, please."

He didn't look up.

"I'm sorry," he mumbled. "We don't give out room numbers. If you pick up the lobby phone, I will connect you."

I looked around. There was a red lobby phone over by a faded brown couch next to the restaurant door. I crossed to it. The phone had no dial. I picked up the receiver. I could hear a phone ringing behind the desk. I looked over at the desk clerk. He was still writing. The phone rang about six times. Finally, he took two steps to his right and picked up the phone.

"Hotel Operator, how may I help you?" I heard him simultaneously through the earpiece and across the lobby.

"Pete Decker, please."

"Do you want his room?"

I glared across the lobby at the chunky little blob. He still hadn't looked at me.

"Yes, please." No point in being rude. Yet.

"I will connect you." He seemed to be pushing some buttons. I heard the dial tone in my phone. It rang. It rang. It rang. There was no one there. I hung up. I walked back over to the desk.

"I would like to leave a message for Mr. Decker," I told the desk clerk. He looked up. I saw that he had a nametag attached to his maroon Ramada sport coat. Clark.

"Hi, Clark," I said with a tone of familiarity.

"Do I know you?" he asked.

"Dr. Davenport's Shakespeare Tragedies," I said.

"I took that class, but I don't remember you. Besides, my name is not Clark."

"But . . ." And I gestured toward his nametag.

"I left mine at home. I just borrowed Clark's."

"Okay." I took a deep breath. Stay calm. Desk clerks "lose" too many messages as it is. "I would still like to leave Mr. Decker a message."

"Phone message or desk message?"

"What's the difference?"

"A phone message, we turn on his message light on his room phone and he calls in for it. A desk message we give him when he walks by the desk if we happen to see him."

"Okay, then, a phone message."

"Then you will have to use the house phone and talk to the hotel operator."

"Do you hate me for any reason?" I asked "Clark."

"Why, no." He seemed genuinely surprised at the question.

"Have I done anything to offend you?"

"No."

I stared into his brown unblinking eyes. Why bother? I thought. I walked back to the house phone. I picked up the receiver. "Clark" went back to writing whatever it was he wrote. The phone rang and rang and rang. "Clark" finally picked it up.

"Hotel operator, how may I help you?"

"I would like to leave a message for Mr. Decker."

"One moment please."

I saw "Clark" move across the desk and pick up a pink pad of paper and move back to the phone.

"Go ahead," he told me.

"Tell him that Ethan Taylor . . ."

"Wait a minute. Are you Ethan Taylor?"

"Yes."

"Yes. Well, you see, I have this message for you from Mr. Decker."

"A message for me."

"Yes."

"Well, are you going to tell me the message?"

"I can't. It is in an envelope, a sealed envelope. I am not to open it. He was very explicit about that. I will have to give it to you unopened." He stared at me, still holding the phone to his ear.

"Okay," I said. "I will come to the desk and get it."
"That will be good." He still hung on to the phone.
"I am hanging up now."
"Oh, yes." We both hung up together.

I went back to the desk. He handed me an envelope. He seemed interested in the message so I walked out to my car to open it.

CHAPTER 7

The Marina

I pulled into the gravel parking lot of the Lake Masterson Marina. A tin shed with windows stood at the base of a long dock next to a lone gas pump. The message had said that I was to go to the marina and tell them my name. They would have a boat waiting for me. They did. A rowboat.

"This is it?" I asked this skinny, greasy guy when he showed me a gray dinghy with the long orange oars.

"This is what six bucks buys and that's all the guy gave me," he said. "And be sure and have it back by sunset or else I'm calling the cops."

I looked up at the horizon across the lake. It was after eight o'clock, but the red sun still hung well above the trees. We were in that part of the state that observed daylight savings time, so I had that on my side before my oil slicked friend called out the boat cops on me.

I gingerly stepped into the boat and sat down. It had been a few years since I had been in any kind of water vehicle. The lake was for the rich kids.

I knew what the oars were and how they worked, but I was still a little awkward pulling away from the dock. Much to Oilslick's amusement, I had to take one of the oars out of its lock and pushed off of one boat and then another until finally I had enough open water that I thought it safe enough to actually row. And I did. Slowly at first, tentatively, but after a dozen strokes or so, I started to get into it and fell into a rhythm that resembled competence.

Lake Masterson was beautiful that evening. The water was still and took on a deeper blue than in the afternoon. There weren't that many houses on the lake back then. Rich people still owned much of the lakefront and their greedy children hadn't grown up to subdivide it into cheaper houses and chain motels. Most of it was just trees and beaches and only about a dozen homes. There was a tourist court on the north edge and the girl's academy took up most of the east shore. The academy's flotilla of sailboats dotted the lake's surface like handkerchiefs on a clothesline.

In the middle of the lake was an island with a single house that people said was the summer home of some guy who lived in Chicago, that is, "Chicago" said with a hushed undertone that suggested, "You know what I mean." You could barely see it, but what you saw told you it was a two-story Swiss Chalet that showed white between the thick pine trees that insured privacy. There was a dock on the island's south end, but I don't remember ever seeing a boat there and buried in the trees was a single bright white light that never went out.

I had never been on the island and knew no one who had. There were indistinct and ominous rumors you heard about the place while growing up. Not ghost stories and the fireside spooky stuff that seemed to inspire investigation, just looks and whispers that kept away kids and the adults they became. Even my father had warned me, before he skedaddled, to keep my butt off that island in Lake Masterson. It was his one warning I heeded. So far.

And now I found myself rowing right toward it. Those were my instructions. Get in the boat. Head for the island. I had no idea what to do after that. I hoped it didn't involve actually getting out of the boat once I got there. Okay, I was a grown up, well almost, but it is the legends of childhood that die hardest.

I was working up a pretty good sweat when I stopped the boat about thirty yards from the island's dock and looked around. Off to my right, a large boat, the kind they use to pull two or three skiers, was bearing down on me.

It did not slow down a whit or alter its course a fraction. Whatever the reason, I thought, this is it. I have been set up. The old man warns me about Kennedy and now someone wants to kill me.

I didn't even touch the oars. The Incredible Hulk couldn't row that dinghy far enough and fast enough to get away from that boat. When it got close enough, I could see that the driver or skipper or whatever you call him was wearing sunglasses and a Cubs cap. I had seen photographs of Uncle Pete and this could be him, but I wasn't sure.

Here it came, twenty yards, ten . . .

Screw it, I thought, and jumped into the water. I'm not sure what my reasoning was. I think it had something with just not wanting to sit there and get smashed up like JFK's PT 109. And perhaps I figured that if I was far enough under water, the boat or its propellers couldn't get me. Or maybe I wasn't thinking at all and just panicked. Regardless, I jumped, kind of an up and over the side jump, so that I was under the water when the motorboat turned abruptly not ten feet from my dinghy and cut its engines.

I stayed down for as long as I could. The water was April-freezing. I had opened my eyes and could clearly see the bottom of my rowboat and decided it would be best if I swam underneath it and came up on the other side.

When my head popped above the surface, I inhaled desperately and grabbed the side of the rowboat, almost turning it over on top of me. My ears were ringing, but even above that inner noise, I could hear someone screaming, "What the hell do you think you were doing?"

CHAPTER 8

Uncle Matt

"I thought you were going to ram me."

I was sitting shivering in my wet clothes on the cushioned seat next to Pete Decker. We were putt-putting out to the middle of the lake in his huge powerboat, slowly towing my rowboat behind us.

"Now why would I want to do that?" he asked.

"I heard you were a son of a bitch." He laughed. He had the whitest, straightest teeth I had ever seen on a human being. They glistened when he smiled, a tight, tense facial reaction that really didn't convey happiness, just an ironic, terse physical response to grim amusement.

"I am a son of a bitch," Uncle Pete said. "But I wasn't trying to ram you."

"What were you trying to do?"

"I was making a dramatic entrance. I'm in show business, boy. I gotta keep up the image."

"Show business? I thought you were a journalist."

"Journalism is show business. Don't you know that? All the world is a stage, and we are just the barkers that beckon the suckers to take a look see."

Great. A son of a bitch and a cynic. He was a big guy. Not as big as me, but a lot stronger. He had hauled me out with just one arm. And did I mention his hair? Pumice stone white. Premature, the guy didn't seem much more than forty, but his hair was solid white and combed straight back like Elvis or that detective on the cover of Shell Scott novels.

"Got a towel?" I asked.

"Nope," he said. "I didn't expect anyone to go swimming."

"Neither did I," I said.

The corners of his mouth pulled back in that toothy grin again. I pulled Ethan's soggy Marlboros out of my pocket and flipped them overboard.

"What was that?" he asked.

"My roommate's cigarettes."

"Nope." He jerked the boat around in a tight circle throwing me against the side.

"Pick 'em up,"

"What?" I asked.

"Pick up your damn cigarettes."

I looked down at the pack floating in the water. The boat was at least four feet above it.

"I can't reach them."

"It's pollution. Nicotine kills the fish."

"Do you have a net or something?"

"Swim for them."

I looked into his mirrored sunglasses and saw Cool Hand Luke.

"I'm not going back in that water."

He shoved the throttle all the way down, reached away from me, below his seat, and pulled out one of the biggest handguns I had ever seen in my life. He pointed the sucker right at me.

"Fish out the damn cigarettes."

"You're not going to shoot me."

He fired a shot just past my left ear. I screamed. I jumped back in the water.

"Fish out the cigarettes!"

I did.

This time I had to haul myself back into the boat. I put the soggy cigarettes on the deck. Pete looked down at them.

"Is that all right?" I asked.

He pointed to the bottom of the boat. "No fish down there," he said.

We languidly moved across the face of the lake. The sun was touching the top of the trees on the shoreline. For some reason I stopped shivering.

"What kind of gun was that?" I asked Pete.
"Forty-four magnum," he said.
"Kind of big, isn't it?"
"Dramatic. I told you. It's all show biz."
"Well, the show is over. I want to go home."
"No, you don't. You want to find out why I got you out here."
"I'm not interested. In you, in show business, all the crap."
"What crap is that?" He looked highly amused.
"The whole thing. The gun, the boat, the sunglasses." He laughed and took off the glasses.

"Better?" He had these incredible blue eyes, almost white in their pure paleness.

"I still want to go home."
"I got something important to tell you."
"I don't care."
"Journalist to journalist."

Now he was patronizing me. Then my original idea popped back in my head. Dear old dad. The teamsters. I fired my own cannon.

"Like what? Like someone is going to assassinate Bobby Kennedy?"

Pete shut off the boat engines.

"How do you know about that?"
"Journalist to journalist?"
"What exactly do you know?"

I didn't. I guessed. "I know that you are down here from Chicago because you think there is going to be a mob hit on RFK."

"Where did that come from?"
"Privileged sources."

Pete snorted. "Privileged sources! You talked to your daddy."

My turn to be surprised.

"How did you know that?"
"I make it my business to know the whereabouts of John Wayne Taylor."

"Why?"
"Ask him."
"I'd rather not."

The famous Pete Decker snorted again.

"There's more to it than just your Daddy being in town."

Pete reached back down from where the gun went and this time came up with what looked like a gold plated Zippo. He thumbed it open and ignited it.

"Nice lighter for a guy who doesn't like cigarettes," I said.

"Not tobacco," he said. Down went his hand and up came a joint.

"Jesus," I said.

"Jesus, indeed," he said.

"Is that why we are meeting in the middle of a lake? So you can smoke dope?"

"No that is just a perquisite."

"Perquisite. Cute word."

"The main reason we are out here is that it is safe. No prying ears."

"Unless I am wired."

"If you were, it is shorted out by now." The smile. "I need you because I need someone in this town. Someone who has a connection to the local news pipeline. Someone I can trust."

"What makes you think you can trust me?"

"I've checked you out. You're a bright boy with a decent writing style. Good grades, no arrests, an all-American Boy Scout set of principles. No girlfriends, no complications."

Just one small visit to a whorehouse, I thought, but kept it to myself.

"And you don't share Varnado's antebellum viewpoint," Pete continued.

"Great. You like me. Now will you take me back to the marina?"

"Not yet."

"It's close to sundown. The grease monkey on the dock said he was calling the cops if I didn't bring the boat back by sundown."

"The grease monkey on the dock has gone home by now. I gave him three hundred bucks. He left as soon as you paddled out here."

"The jerk."

"The world is full of them."

"I still want to go back."

"Tough. First of all, it is not a mob hit."

"It's not," I said. Humor the druggie, I thought. The rule is always humor the druggie, especially if he is armed.

"I found out about it through my connections with organized crime, but it's not them." He said "organized crime" like he was singing an aria. He squeezed out the burning tip of the joint and stuck the roach in his mouth and swallowed.

"Does *Newsweek* know you smoke grass?"

"*Newsweek* knows what I tell them. Nothing more, nothing less, nothing else."

"If it is not the mob, who else would want Bobby Kennedy dead?"

"Who doesn't? Johnson hates him more than Ho Chi Minh. Do you think Lyndon would have stepped down from re-election if Bobby hadn't forced him out? He hates him. Always has. He and his dead brother."

I wasn't buying LBJ as Lee Harvey Oswald.

"Who else?"

"Ever hear of Project Mongoose?"

"Project who?"

"After the Bay of Pigs, the CIA made several attempts on the life of Fidel Castro."

"Wait a minute. Isn't there something in the Constitution that says we can't go around knocking off heads of state?"

"Not in the Constitution, but it's a law."

"So?"

Uncle Pete lit up another joint.

"Who the hell obeys the law?"

"Okay, so the CIA tried to kill Castro. So what?"

"So the President knew about it."

"So?"

"But the President didn't want to be directly involved. That law thing you mentioned."

"So?"

"So he put the Attorney General in charge of it. That way the man most responsible for enforcing federal law is not going to be investigating the guy in charge of breaking federal law when that guy is . . ."

"The same guy. Attorney General Robert F. Kennedy."

"See? I told you were bright. And Cuba found out all about it. Revenge, mi compadre."

"So Castro wants to kill Bobby."

"Right. And don't forget the CIA."

"The CIA?"

"Bobby was the one who convinced JFK to cancel the air support for The Bay of Pigs. Bobby is the one guy alive outside of the administration who can nail the CIA for illegal covert activities."

"But wouldn't that sink Bobby, too?"

"Not if he handled it right. Completely discredit the CIA and then disband it when he becomes President, then anything the CIA says looks like pay back."

"You think Bobby would do that?"

"He has already promised it. It is in his campaign fliers in California. Stop the war. Eliminate the CIA."

"Jesus."

"And I've already seen a couple of CIA operatives lurking around town."

"In Port Gibson?"

"One of them is a native."

"Who?"

"Now that would be telling."

"How do you know this?"

"I wasn't always just a journalist. I did some work in international affairs."

"CIA. Port Gibson," I muttered. "Sheriff Crites?" I guessed.

"Don't think so."

"Who!"

"Back when I was working with the White House . . ."

"You worked in the . . ."

"Bobby had this Green Beret on his desk when he was Attorney General. Special Forces."

"I know what a Green Beret is. I heard the song."

"I gave it to him."

"So?"

"I got it from a guy in the CIA."

"So?"

"That guy is in town. Cherchez le Green Beret."

"The Green Berets are the army, not CIA," I said.

Pete shrugged. "Suit yourself."

"Is this guy still in the Green Berets?" I asked.

"Retired," said Pete and then he added, "But once CIA, always CIA." And then he lit up the new doobie.

"Then there is the FBI," Pete said with his lungs full of smoke.

"The FBI?" I followed the yellow brick road.

"Hoover loves Johnson." The smoke rushed out his mouth. "Johnson hates Bobby. Hoover hates Bobby. And Hoover has all this stuff on JFK."

"What kind of stuff?"

"Sex stuff."

"Sex stuff? On President John F. Kennedy?"

"The Encyclopedia Britannica should have so much information."

"Why?"

"Hoover likes to keep files. His own private files."

"Isn't that illegal?" It was becoming a tired question.

"Uh-huh. But who is going to stop him? Lyndon won't. Lyndon loves J. Edgar. Everyone else is scared of him. Except Bobby. And the head of the FBI is a presidential appointment. He who appoints, fires."

"Bobby is going to dump Hoover?"

"It is a known fact. If he lives to be president. And then there is the Ku Klux Klan. Pretty active, I hear, in this part of Indiana. Bobby integrated Ole Miss. That really stirred up a hornet's nest of sheets and hoods. And to top it off, Hoover and the FBI infiltrated the Klan so thoroughly in 1962 it is rumored that the grand dragon at that time was a Special Agent."

"Where do you get this stuff?"

"Just solid journalism."

"How come none of this gets published?"

"If the country knew what was really going on, there would be a riot that would make Detroit and Watts combined look like a fire drill."

"What happened to the freedom of the press and the right to know?"

"Come into the circus, step inside, step inside," he sang. "Then you got your Civil Rights movement."

"They want Bobby dead? But I thought it was Bobby who stopped the riots after Martin Luther King's death."

"That is so much political bullshit. He barely slowed them down. If anyone thinks that some nasal twanged Yankee from Boston is going to make one bit of difference to the Black Power movement, they have been smoking too much of this ganja."

Pete leaned against the boat's steering wheel and stared off at the setting sun. The lake was dead silent except for an occasional splashing of a fish jumping.

"No, sir," he said after a while. "Most of the real hotheads in the movement, the Panthers, others, they are real pissed off at the Kennedy boys. They think Bobby and Jack moved too slowly when they were in the White House. Hell, if it were left up to the Kennedys, the 1964 civil rights act would have never passed."

"You're kidding."

He did that Uncle Pete shrug again.

"It took Lyndon to get it passed. It wasn't even on the boards when JFK was President."

This was a whole lot for an eighteen-year-old to absorb. Even a bright Boy Scout like me.

"And then, of course, there are your daddy's people."

"Who?"

"Mack Taylor and the Teamsters."

"Look, I just made that up. I really don't think Mack is in town to kill Bobby. The teamsters are just here to vote in the primary."

"Vote! That is not what your Daddy does." Pete shook his head and chuckled. "Vote."

"How do you even know Mack?"

"Boy, everybody in Chicago knows your Daddy. He is what the union calls an enforcer."

"A what?"

"When somebody steps out of line, the union sends in a few thugs to break some legs, threaten the children, maybe burn down a house."

"Are you saying that is what my father does?"

"Nope. It's when they step way out of line that's when they give your Daddy a call. He wires automobiles. You see Mack Taylor hanging around your Cadillac, you best not turn on the ignition."

"Car bombs?"

"Boom," said Uncle Pete.

Dear old dad? An "enforcer" for the union? Boy, that explained a lot. I remember hot summer nights with my windows open and the sound of hushed voices in the back yard. I remember thinking, "It's a strange time for a barbecue." The respect he got from the local cops. That's why mom didn't want me to tell him where she moved. Everybody was scared of the old man. Everyone but me. I didn't think he would wire up my Corvair. But how did I know? Really know? I didn't.

"So you see, when my sources tell me that someone is going to knock off Bobby Kennedy, my only questions are where and when. I got a good line on the who and the why. A bunch of 'em."

"Too many."

He looked at me with a curious expression.

"Yeah, I guess. So will you do it?"

"Do what? I still don't know why you are telling me all this stuff. Or if I believe it."

"I am telling you all this 'stuff' because we are sitting on the story of the century. I am telling you all this 'stuff' because for some stupid reason I like you. I am telling you all this 'stuff' because I need a local, someone who knows the back streets and the underside of Port Gibson and will keep his ears and eyes open."

"So I can save the life of the next President of the United States and you can get the credit?"

Pete stared off at the horizon again. The sky and the lake had turned that deep purple that happens right before all the red disappears. Still no ripple. Not a sound.

"I didn't say anything about saving anybody's life, kid."

"What?"

"The first thing a journalist has to learn is never get in the way of the story."

"You mean if you knew where and when Bobby Kennedy was going to get killed, you wouldn't do anything to stop it?"

He turned and looked at me, straight in the eyes, as if he were looking for something specific. I tried to outstare him, but something made me look away.

"Sure, kid. If we find out anything for certain, we won't let anything happen to the senator."

"Okay," I said, even though it wasn't.

"There you go. We're a team." He held out his hand. It was large, with long narrow fingers. I took it. He flipped it around into one of those soul shakes. I followed awkwardly. I had as much soul as Richard Nixon or Dr. Pepper.

He started up the engine. I stood up and begin to crawl over the seat.

"Where are you going?" he asked.

"Back to my boat."

"I'll give you a ride."

"It's a nice night. I'd rather row."

"No, let me give you a ride."

"No, thanks."

He looked off again, this time at the island. He seemed to be weighing something.

"Suit yourself."

I grabbed the bow of my rowboat and untied the rope that attached it to Pete's stern. I got in. Without a word, without a wave, Pete jammed the throttle forward and his boat took off like a shot.

After I tied the dinghy up to the marina dock I looked back out at the lake. Pete was running his boat back and forth just off shore. When he saw me looking at him, he took off around the backside of the island.

I had an idea.

I got in my Corvair, turned on the lights and started it up and turned it so I was facing the lake so Pete could see my tail lights. I waited until Pete's boat cleared the island before I drove around the Marina parking lot and out onto the road that bordered the lake. I drove about a hundred yards to where the road turned sharply away from the marina and back toward town. I shut my headlights off. I turned off the ignition. I got out of the car and walked the fifteen or twenty yards back to the trees just above a narrow beach.

In the fading twilight I saw Pete tying up his boat to the island's dock.

CHAPTER 9

The Big Sleep

When I got back to The Mansion, it was lit up like the Chicago Fire. No, forget it. The Chicago Fire was a two-year-old's birthday cake compared to my house. There were poles all over the front yard with strings of white lights going from tree to pole to pole to trees. Floodlights were being placed on the roof of the porch. And a bunch of county jail inmates were putting up a circus tent in the front yard. The Mansion's insides were lit up, too. It looked like every light in every room was blazing.

I drove my car up the long driveway that joined with Main Street and swung around to the back of the house. Strange cars and pickup trucks filled the graveled oval that served as a parking area. I dashed up the stairs to the back porch and into the kitchen, letting the screen door slam behind me.

Rick was leaning against the counter blowing on a pinwheel with pictures of Bobby Kennedy on its propellers.

"What whacko turned this place into Disneyland?" I asked. Rick raised his eyebrows and pointed off to my left into the pantry doorway that separated the kitchen from the dining room. There stood his father, the mayor and our landlord, Sid Hamilton.

"Oh, hi, Mr. Hamilton. Sorry about the whacko crack," I told the skinny, smiling mayor.

"That's all right, son. I've been called worse."

"But what is going on?"

"We are having a party," said the mayor.

"For Bobby," said Rick between twirling the campaign pinwheel with short breaths.

"Here?" I asked.

"It was my brainstorm," said Mayor Hamilton. "Port Gibson should have a reception for Senator Kennedy. He may be a Democrat, but he is the former President's brother and all and he is a United States Senator, but we couldn't really have it in my home, a Republican mayor and all."

"Besides, Mom threw a fit. She hates the Kennedys."

"Well, not hate. She, uh, thinks Jackie destroyed fashion. Something about pink hats and Italian clothes designers. And well, uh, then I thought of your place. Neutral ground, so to speak, and, after all, I own it. But it wouldn't be the same as the homestead of the leading county . . . You understand."

Remarkably, I did. Mr. Hamilton was prone to incoherent rambling sentences that, if left to themselves, would never get him elected dogcatcher. That is why Mrs. Hamilton wrote his speeches and made him stick to the text.

"So I have taken the liberty, well not the liberty, exactly, because it is my house damn it, to, well, liven up the place a little bit."

"When is this reception going to take place?" I asked.

"Tuesday," said Hamilton.

"Tuesday?" I echoed.

"They have stepped up the visit. Bobby is speaking Wednesday evening."

"No beauty pageant?" I thought of a pissed off Mrs. Varnado.

"No," said Mayor Hamilton. "*The Free Press* will have its beauty Pageant. The girls will just have to work a little harder and a little faster to be ready."

"They have to redecorate the VFW?"

"No," said Mr. Hamilton. "They figure Bobby K, a large crowd. It's going to be out at McNeil Auditorium, out at the girl's academy."

"Why not at the college?"

"Something about the AC being shut down for the summer. Takes too long to get it cranked up."

I went to the refrigerator and opened it and took out a Pepsi. "What happened to the beer?" I asked innocently. Rick did a very satisfying freak out.

"What beer?" asked Mr. Hamilton.

"You know we don't keep beer in the house," said Hamilton, Jr. "He's kidding, Dad."

"Yeah," I said. I popped the Pepsi bottle cap on an opener nailed to the wall. "Just kidding. Well, goodnight, guys. I am bushed."

"It's not even nine," Rick said.

"Long day," I said and walked into the hallway.

My room was at the top of the back stairs. It was the smallest bedroom in the house, but it was on the corner and had four windows, so I got a bit of a cross breeze in the summer. That was important. In 1968 the only air conditioning in Copiah County was at the college and in the movie theaters. Even the churches just had hand fans supplied by the local funeral home.

Rick had furnished my room with pieces "borrowed" from the prop loft at the college. I had a chest of drawers from and a vanity from *Cat on a Hot Tin Roof* and the wicker trunk from *Fiddler on the Roof.* Even the bed was a canopied four-poster without the canopy that was from an ancient production of *Camille.*

And of course like everyone else in college at that time, I had posters on my wall. Behind the door, I had that shot of Jane Fonda, cross-legged and nude on the beach. You could only see it when the door was closed. I know, pathetic for a virgin, but I still had all my hormones and they needed an outlet. Above my headboard I had the required blow-up of James Dean, but I considered myself more of a Richard Burton man, so I had Liz and Dick from *Taming of the Shrew* at the foot of my bed. Besides, Liz had that cleavage going for her.

I threw myself on the four-poster and contemplated Petruchio's grinning, bearded face. Bobby is coming to my house, I thought. Jesus, life was moving fast.

I remembered going to sleep in my grandparents' house. I had the one upstairs upstairs in the bungalow on Washington Street. I would stare at the slatted wood ceiling. It had a water stain shaped like the head of a dog, like a Lab or a cocker spaniel.

I would lie there and watch the lights of the passing cars flow up one wall, across the dog and disappear. I never figured out how that worked. The lights of the car passed parallel to and a floor down from my bedroom and yet it tracked across my wall and ceiling as if it were coming straight out of the floor.

Even in this house on some warm Sunday nights, like that one, with the windows wide open and the slightest whisper of a breeze stirring the filmy white curtains, I would always hear something, sometimes the music from an Assembly of God church behind the cornfield across Main Street. I would listen to those people shout and sing and somehow I would fall asleep. I didn't hear it that Sunday night. I wonder why.

Maybe that is what I need, music. I thought about getting up and turning on the stereo or the radio, but I didn't. It seemed terribly important that I just lay there, all alone in the quiet and find that one slippery moment between consciousness and sleep, between reality and dreams—that I have an awareness of that moment—that somehow God would speak to me in the quiet and tell me who I am.

Strange, I remember that night clearly, the last night that nothing happened. I remember that somewhere in that nothingness, there was an epiphany. I remember a siren far off that didn't seem to come any closer, just drift away and I remember wondering why there would be a siren on a Sunday night in a Port Gibson.

I remember a sense of clouds behind my eyelids and the soft patter of something in the breeze, leaves or wings or voices, then the voices grew louder and more distinct and told me something, something I knew I should remember but I didn't. And somehow, I fell asleep.

Two hours later I was wide-awake.

CHAPTER 10

The Bus Station

Monday, April 29, 1968

I lay in my bed, knowing that I needed sleep, but I had a lot of nervous energy built up and all the stuff that Pete Decker told me kept bouncing around in my head like a pinball.

That's what I needed. Pinball. The virgin's ultimate relaxer.

I went down the backstairs and out through the kitchen. Not a creature was stirring. I got into the Corvair and drove until I saw the neon glow of the Copiah County bus station.

Port Gibson did have an airport, but it was mostly for private plane traffic and one Ozark Airline's DC-3 that dropped off passengers two or three times a week. There was no train station and since the demise of the paddle wheeler, no boats unloaded travelers on the shores of the Wabash. The inter-city form of travel for most of the Midwest in those days was the bus and Port Gibson had a bus station. Boy, did it have a bus station.

As long as I can remember parents were telling their children that they did not want to hear of them hanging out at the bus station and so, of course, as soon as they could walk, most kids wanted to hang out at the bus station. It was the only public building that never closed. So if you were fourteen and out with a bunch of your buds "camping" in someone's backyard and you had a sudden hankering for a cup of root beer at three o'clock in the morning, the only place to go was the soda machine at the bus station.

It was the hub of sin in my little town. Often you could find an all-night poker game there or checkers being played for money. For a while there was a teenager named Sarah Brown who lived behind the bus station and was said to "do it" for a dollar. And there were always the pay phones for those late-night calls you didn't want your parents to overhear and sometimes there was the little gray man and his stump.

I pulled into the empty parking lot under the sign of the racing dog. Greyhound Bus Lines. It has been so long, I don't know if they still exist. Used to be they were everywhere, in every town on every highway, but I haven't noticed one of their buses in years.

I kept a jar full of change on my back floorboard under the MacDonald's wrappers and Pepsi bottles. I dug out the jar and walked toward the station.

Quasimodo sat outside in the glare of the floodlights that lit up the bus parking area. He was wearing his usual faded grey cotton suit and an almost matching fedora. Under the jacket he always wore a stained white shirt. Never a tie. He looked nervously around the parking lot until he saw me. Then his mouth cracked open in a wide, almost toothless grin.

Rick had dubbed him Quasimodo or just "Quasi" in seventh grade when we had to read *The Hunchback of Notre Dame*. This ancient guy had been around town forever and he always seemed the same age. When we were kids, we would follow him down the street and yell things at him. "Hey gramps! Hey gimp!" One leg seemed to be shorter than the other.

Once, Rick hit him in the butt with a tin can and he turned around and started screaming at us. We laughed until he pulled out a wicked little automatic and fired three shots into the ground near our feet. We ran all the way back to Hamilton's house and told his father who told us to "Leave that old fool alone. He's more trouble than any of you can handle."

When we got older, Rick found out what the deal was. This little gray man sold moonshine. Rick first tried to buy some from him when he was fourteen, but Quasi shooed him away. But when he saw Rick driving me around in a car, he waggled his crooked fingers at us and we pulled over and made our first buy.

He had gotten in the back seat and told us to drive to the bus station. We parked in the lot and walked to a clearing just past a row of trees on the other side of the station. From the hollow of the only stump in the field, he took out a Mason jar of clear liquid. I leaned over and looked in the stump. It was empty. There had been just the one jar, as if he had been expecting us.

"How much?" Rick asked. He just shook his head.

"Taste first," he said. He took off the jar's lid and filled it full of liquid and for some reason handed it to me instead of Rick. With more than just a few misgivings, I raised it to my lips and he shook his head again.

"Test first," he said. "Slosh it around and then throw it out." I did. "Now set the lid on the stump." I did.

He took out a lighter with a United States Marines seal on it and ignited it. Then he held the lighter over the lid until the residue from the whiskey caught fire.

"See that flame?" he asked me. "See how it is pure blue? If'n you see any yeller in that flame, you don't buy no whiskey, not from me, not from nobody. Yeller means it's got lead impurities and that'll leave you blind, crazy or dead."

He blew out the flame and pointed to the jar.

"Now, taste. Just a little."

I considered taking a gulp because I was sixteen and a wiseass, but I thought about what he said about "blind, crazy or dead," and a just took a sip. I let the liquid stay on my tongue for a second. The whole inside of my mouth went numb. Then I swallowed it.

Lord, God almighty.

That stuff seared down my throat as if it were still on fire and hit my stomach like a shot of lemon juice on acid indigestion. Then it started. A soothing warmth simultaneously moving up my chest and down toward my feet, filling me instantly with a feeling that was at the same time melancholy and comforting. Then I started throwing up.

Rick grabbed the bottle out of my hand before I dropped it and threw down a long deep swallow. He coughed and I looked up to see his eyes watering, but he didn't puke.

"Five dollars," Quasi told us with a grin. Rick couldn't give him the money fast enough. I never touched the stuff again. Well, not for two years.

As I walked past Quasi into the bus station, his mumbling became coherent and I heard, "You shopping, newspaper boy?"

"No, sir," I said and wondered how he knew what I did. I didn't stop to find out because I could hear the bells and flippers going crazy inside. Someone was playing a pinball machine. Someone was playing the hell out of a pinball machine.

I walked inside the long narrow waiting room and there in the corner someone was playing the Williams' Viking pinball machine, MY pinball machine with my unbeatable top score of 145,622.

Only it wasn't just someone. I only had a three-quarter view from the back and she was dressed differently in jeans cutoffs, a blue t-shirt and a matching blue baseball hat, still barefoot, but I knew without thinking, that this was the same girl.

The girl sitting on the floor of the VFW. My lady in black.

I walked up to her right. The cap had LA on it and the T-shirt read Dodgers in script. I couldn't help it. I leaned in to look at her face.

"You're crowding my space, Ploughboy," she said.

"Ploughboy?" I thought, but stepped back.

"You're beating my score," I said.

"Oh, yeah?" She shook her head as if her hair were in her eyes. The dark eyes, still lined with black only this time not in repose, this time focused and smoldering. "How long has it been up there?"

"Six months," I said.

"Well, say goodbye, corn picker, because it is on its way to . . ." She did a provocative shake of her hips and shook the machine just enough to guide the silver ball on the back flipper and flipped the ball up past the well-endowed Vikingette to the row of shields. The lights and bells did their magic dance and the score jumped past 148,000.

"History!" She said and turned to look at me. She let the silver ball roll past the flippers. She still had three balls lined up behind the plunger. Without looking at the machine, she shoved each ball into the launch-row and snapped the plunger. The balls zipped around the curve of the track then bounced off the toadstool bumpers, careened off the spears and swords and settled into the sea monster's mouth at the bottom without her flicking a single flipper. Final score, 152,468.

"Why did you do that?" I asked without thinking. "You might have topped two hundred thousand."

"Might have?" she said and tossed her head again. I liked it when she tossed her head. "I have topped two hundred thousand so many times it's like a *Gunsmoke* rerun. My top score on the Viking is 274, 502.

"My god," I said.

"Four hundred and ninety-eight damn points short of two seventy-five. I almost kicked the damn machine over. My mother took away my dessert for a week."

"Your mother took away your dessert?"

"I was only twelve, Ploughboy. I wasn't allowed out by myself. In fact, I am still not. Buy me a Coke."

I looked at her. Who was this girl? She's not allowed out by herself? We just met and she demands that I buy her a Coke?

Then she smiled.

I walked over to the machine, took fifteen cents out of my jar, put it into the machine, pushed a button and a plastic cup dropped into the slot and filled with coke syrup and soda. I brought it back. She hadn't moved from the machine. I handed it to her.

"Thanks, Ploughboy."

"Why do you call me that?"

"What do you want me to call you? Hoosier? What the hell is a Hoosier, anyway?"

"My name is Ethan."

"Funny, you don't look Jewish."

"I'm not."

"I know. It's a punch line to a joke."

"What's the joke?"

"I'll tell you later. I am Jewish."

"Really?"

"No, I'm lying about my religion. It's what I do. Of course I am. Don't I look Jewish?"

"I don't know. I've never met anyone Jewish before."

"Of course you haven't."

"What's your name?"
"LJ."
"What does LJ stand for?"
"Big letter L. Big letter J."
"Your parents named you LJ?"
"Right on the birth certificate."
"Why?"
"It's a Jewish thing. You wouldn't understand. Listen, I imagine you came down here for the same reason I did. So where is this dude?"
"What dude?"
"The old dude who is supposed to sell grass at the bus station."
"Quasimodo sells grass?"
"Quasimodo? The guy's name is Quasimodo?"
"It's a Hoosier thing, you wouldn't understand."
And I got the smile again.
"Touché. So you know Quasimodo."
"We have done business in the past."
"Cool. So if he's not in the bus station, where does he hang out?"
"He's on the bench just outside."
"No."
"Yes."
"Then what are we waiting for?"
"But I . . ."

She shoved her coke cup into the swinging-top trashcan and ran out the front door.

"Didn't come here to buy grass," I said to an empty waiting room.

By the time I got outside Quasi and LJ were heading out of the parking lot toward Quasi's stump. I ran to catch up with them.

"Young lady says you call me Yamamoto. I ain't no Jap," Quasi said as I fell into step next to him.

"Quasimodo," I said. "It's a character in a novel." Quasi looked up at me without breaking stride. "A noble character," I added.

"I ain't that neither."

"No," I said.

LJ didn't say anything, just stared straight down as we walked. I don't think she was used to walking through a pasture. Probably afraid she might step in something.

"What is your real name?" I asked.

"None of your beeswax," he said.

I had to agree with him.

He stopped when we came to the stump. He reached down inside and pulled out a baggie filled with what had to be marijuana. He handed it to LJ who opened it and inhaled.

"Don't you trust me?" the old man formerly known as Quasimodo asked.

"No," LJ said. "I've been burned before."

Quasi cackled. "Ain't we all, little girl, ain't we all. How about you, newspaper boy?"

"No," I said. "I, uh, don't smoke." LJ turned to me with a curious look on her face as if I had just announced that I breathe underwater.

"I knew that!" He cackled again. "I knew that! How about a jar of the usual?"

"No, thanks. I don't have much money on me."

"On the house." He lifted a small jar out of the stump. He put his USMC lighter on top of it and handed it to me.

"No thanks." I said and LJ subtly kicked me. Hard. I winced. "Don't piss off the connection," she whispered and turned her glowing smile on Quasi. He showed her his gapped mouth.

"On second thought, maybe I will. Thanks."

I unscrewed the lid and went through the purities test. Quasi looked at me smiling like a chem lab teacher testing a prize student. When I was finished, I screwed the lid back on.

"Taste it," Quasi said.

"Now?" I asked.

"Now," he said.

I stared down at the jar stupidly. I was afraid I was going to puke all over LJ's bare feet and we would never conceive children together.

She grabbed the jar out of my hand, twisted off the cap and took a healthy swallow.

"Crap almighty!" she said, but she didn't throw up and handed the jar back to me. Quasi stared up at me like a puppy dog begging for a Milk Bone.

I tentatively raised the jar to my lips and took a sip. A volcano erupted on my tongue.

"Come on, Ploughboy. Take a real drink," LJ said.

And I did.

Maybe because of the initial sip, maybe because I had some before or maybe because Quasi had taken pity on me and gave me a milder batch, but this time when I took a full swallow, the liquid went down a lot smoother and gave me that warm glow without the pain and convulsions.

"There," I said.

"Now," said Quasi. "Now that I got you all relaxed and listening, I want to tell you something for that newspaper of your'n."

I had no idea what was coming, so I took another pull off the jar. LJ had sat down on the stump and was busily rolling a joint about the size of a Tampa.

"We killed that son of a bitch John and that nigger Martin Luther King and we're gonna kill that smartass Bobby, too, if'n he don't get in line."

"What?" I asked. I really couldn't believe what I just heard.

"We're gonna kill that smart-ass prick Bobby Kennedy, you wait and see."

"Who are we?"

"The poor people. That's what done it before. Lee Harvey Oswald, he was a poor man. Same with that white trash what shot King. They say some rich fellers hired them to gun down those sons of bitches, but it wasn't. It was just us poor people that had enough.

"That Kennedy is a rich bastard and rich bastards suck the blood out of us poor folks 'til we can't stand it and then we rise up. We rise up like the wheat in the fields, too many of us to stop. They train us with guns in their wars and put us out in the world and expect us to just sit there and take it. Only it don't happen. Not no more. You wait and see. John first and now Bobby, maybe Teddy, if he don't watch it."

Counting Kennedys, I thought.

Then he looked at me suspiciously. "You ain't working for that Kennedy boy are you?"

"No," I said, suddenly scared and not sure why. "Just the newspaper. You know that."

"I guess," he said grudgingly. "But there's some from around here that need killing just as bad and you just watch. You just watch. The next couple of days is gonna be a reckoning, you mark my words."

"What do you mean 'a reckoning'?"

"That's all I'm saying. The next couple of days there is gonna be a reckoning. You put that in your paper and you'll be famous before it's over. Now go home and don't drink that whiskey while you're driving."

And he turned and shambled off toward Sarah Brown's house.

"What was that all about?" LJ asked and licked her homemade cigar.

"I don't know. A lot of weird things are going on since Senator Kennedy is coming to town."

"Tell me about it." She stuck the joint in her mouth and started to light it. I blew out the match.

"What are you doing?" I demanded.

"Flaring up a doobie. What do you think I am doing?"

"In public?"

"We are in the middle of a field in the middle of the night in the middle of nowhere USA. I've gotten stoned in a Sears parking lot at noon."

"Not in Indiana you haven't. Cops can smell that stuff a mile away and they are always sniffing around the bus station late at night."

"You got a better idea?"

"My place is not far from here."

"I bet it isn't."

"That's not what I . . . I just meant it's safer. You have a car?"

"No."

"I'll take you. You can get safely stoned and then I'll take you back to wherever."

"Okay."

We started walking back to the bus station.

"You really don't smoke dope?" she asked.

"No."
"Weird."
"Maybe."
"You gonna drink that stuff?"
"Maybe."
"Good. Because I don't like to get trashed alone."
And that's the last thing I remembered about that night.

CHAPTER 11

The Draft

I knew it was morning because the phone was ringing. That was what my head was telling me, "It must be morning because the phone is ringing" and through the layers of sleep another voice was telling me to answer it. It rang and rang and I lay there barely waking up, barely conscious of a decision to ignore the voices and just let the damn thing ring and I did and it still rang so I finally picked it up.

My mouth was dry. My throat was dry. I suspected my blood was dust in my veins. Someone was poking an ice pick in my brain just behind my eyeballs.

"Yeah," I said not bothering to hide the sleep in my voice. The room was white with daylight and I looked at my Baby Ben alarm clock. It said 8:15. My brain said, "I want to just die." A stern female voice said, "Mr. Taylor, please."

"That's me," I said. I didn't give an inch on the sleep-in-my-voice thing trying to elicit some sort of apology from my first-thing-in-the-morning-don't-you-know-I-have-a-hangover caller. None came.

"This is Mr. Ollestadt's office calling. Mr. Ollestadt would like to see you this morning."

"Who is Mr. Ollestadt?" I asked. There was a pause. It seemed that the woman on the other end of the line was not used to being asked this question.

"Why, he is Mr. Sam Ollestadt of Ollestadt, Waggoner and Smith. He is also your new Congressman." Ah, Rick's boss. The mind awakes.

"Then why didn't you say it was Congressman Ollestadt's office?" Not half there and already giving the world a hard time.

"Because it is not Congressman Ollestadt's office. This is the office of Ollestadt, Waggoner and Smith. Congressman Ollestadt's office is in Washington."

"Okay," I said. "I got it."

And I did get it. Sam Ollestadt, Rick's boss, was the recent appointment to the United States House of Representatives when the venerable Gus McDowell collapsed, it was said, mid coital eruptus in a Maryland hideaway. Ollestadt was also a prominent attorney in Copiah County and most significantly to me, the head of the local draft board.

"Why does Mr. Ollestadt want to see me?" I asked.

"I am sure I don't know," sniffed the voice on the phone. "I have just been instructed to inform you that he has some time between the hours of nine and ten A.M. and he would like to see you in his office at 1426 Broadway if that is convenient."

"Well, it isn't convenient, but it may be possible," I said.

"Does that mean that I may tell him that you will be here at the appointed time?"

I swung my legs off the bed and sat up, still wrapped in the sheet. I was naked. I wasn't used to that. And there was that pounding in my head and a desert in my mouth. I wasn't used to that, either.

"I suppose. Yes. I will be there. When is that again?"

"Between nine and ten."

"Fine."

"When shall I tell him you will be here?"

"Between nine and ten," I said. This lady was getting on my nerves.

"Can you give me a more specific time?" she asked.

"If between nine and ten is good enough for Congressman Ollestadt, then it is good enough for me," I said.

"But . . ." the voice began.

"Goodbye," I said. And then I hung up. That wasn't nice, I thought. I will probably pay for it down the road, but Jesus, it is only eight fifteen in the morning. She probably wanted to call me at eight. She probably thought she was doing me a favor by waiting fifteen minutes.

Man, the draft board. And I had to get drunk last night. My body ached from sleeping in every wrong position trying to get comfortable without my pajamas and there was this cotton-like feeling in my thinking channels and that dry-mouth, headachy, dizzy and nauseous, weak feeling which Rick felt every day. And now I get to see my congressman.

I pretty much knew what was going on. Like most eighteen-year-olds, I had dutifully registered for the draft on my birthday this past October. But unlike most eighteen-year-olds, I had checked that little box indicating that I was a conscientious objector.

It seemed like a good idea at the time. LBJ had just cancelled graduate school draft exemptions and I could see that undergraduates would soon follow. I really wasn't that conscientious and didn't really have any major objections to the current conflict overseas. It wasn't that I was against their war, I was just against them sending me over there to fight their war and probably getting me killed. I had thought that all I had to do was to check that little box and the whole thing was over.

I was wrong.

About a month later the government sent me a large packet with all sorts of information and forms that dealt with my conscientious objection. It seems I had to prove to LBJ that I was indeed a sincere conscientious objector and not only that I just did not want to go to Southeast Asia and blow away people I had nothing against, but I did not want to go to Southeast Asia and blow away people I had nothing against on religious grounds.

My problem was that I had no religious grounds. My mother was a Methodist and my father was a kind-of Catholic. I remember that he wouldn't eat meat on Friday, but that was about the extent of it. To my knowledge he never set foot in a Catholic Church from the day I was born. But he insisted that I be raised a Catholic and my mother insisted that I would be a good Methodist and the upshot was that I was neither.

Not that either one would have helped me. As I found out through my draft board paperwork and some independent research in the college library, neither of these religions afforded sanctuary for the conscientiously objected because neither Methodist nor Catholic had any particular qualms about taking up arms for the mother country and murdering enemies of the state.

Only the Quakers, the Amish and a few of those fringe sects that didn't cut their hair and went to church on Saturdays had legitimate grounds, according to the United States Draft Board, to claim conscientious objection.

However, I did discover in my research that there was a national draft dodgers organization that had recently successfully pushed through the legal concept that one could indeed be a conscientious objector on philosophical grounds, independent of any organized religion, if the draft dodger could convince his local draft board through written and oral arguments that his objections to the war were not based upon his own self-preservation, but a sincere and personal belief in a divine entity that frowned on the wholesale slaughter of human beings. That to me smacked of pure academic BS and if there was anything that I was good at back in the spring of 1968, it was pure academic BS.

So I started my research. I looked up famous conscientious objectors. I read Kierkegaard and Vonnegut. I read about Reinhold Niebuhr and Samuel V. Debs. I went through the newspaper archives and found everything I could about what was happening to Mohammed Ali, David Harris, and the Berrigan brothers. I read *Soul on Ice* and *The Making of a Counter Culture* and listened to Bob Dylan and Joan Baez. By the time I sat down to write my essay I knew two things for sure. Bob Dylan was a poetic genius who could not sing worth beans and I was a genuine conscientious objector.

This was why I was being summoned to the offices of Ollestadt, Waggoner and Smith between the hours of nine and ten in the morning. I lay back down to clear my head.

That was when I saw the note. It was under a Los Angeles Dodgers baseball cap next to me in a dent in my bed.

LJ. Part of the evening came back to me in a rush.

LJ. What happened after the stump?

We came back here, obviously, but then what? I picked up the note and put it in front of my face and tried to focus.

"You were wonderful last night! I feel like a new woman! I borrowed your car. I'll return it this afternoon after classes. XXXOOO, LJ."

I was wonderful? She feels like a new woman? I am naked? What happened? Did I finally get laid and I DON'T EVEN REMEMBER IT?

Lord God Almighty!

And now I had to see the congressman in half an hour.

So I walked down the hall wrapped in my sheet, grabbed a shower, dressed in something a little more presentable than my usual jeans and t-shirt and went to the kitchen in search of breakfast. The roommate wasn't up yet, so anything I found in the fridge was fair game.

The beer that had disappeared the night before had miraculously been replenished with two quarts of Budweiser. I found an apple and half a large can of peanuts. I reluctantly skipped the beer, no Bud breath for the congressman, and took the apple and the can of nuts.

One of the many advantages of living with a rich kid is that Rick had two vehicles, a souped-up army surplus Jeep and a '65 2+2 Mustang fastback. I took the keys to the Jeep off of the hook by the kitchen door and stepped outside to brave the sunlight and the offices of Ollestadt, Waggoner and Smith.

LJ. A new woman.

I did not feel like a new man.

OW&S was in a large Victorian house that had been restored and painted a lively sky blue with off white trim giving the place a Disney effect. I could practically see Windy and Peter and Nana peering out of one of the many gabled windows

The foyer was a small room with a tall ceiling. There was a mirrored hat stand flanked by a couple of uncomfortable looking captain's chairs and a deep brown stairway that went straight up and back to a landing and then turned forward to continue on up to the second floor. To my left was what appeared to have once been a dining room, but now was a conference room with a large oval table and three walls lined with bookshelves between two bay windows.

To my right was a smaller room with more bookshelves and a large oak desk behind which sat the stern visage of, according to the nameplate, a Mrs. Frieda Bellamy. Mrs. B was a bone-thin woman. You could tell she was tall even when she was sitting down. She had slightly graying hair pulled neatly back in a schoolmarm's bun. Her dress was an unaccountably drab purple, buttoned up past her neck where silver-sequined horn-rimmed glasses hung from a chain. She put the glasses on her nose with a military-like snap when I approached her desk. Here, I was certain, was the owner of the voice that had roused me a little more than an hour before.

"May I help you?" It was indeed the clipped, New England Yankee accent of the phone call and I knew immediately that she had no intention of helping me or anyone else other than her boss. Ever.

"I am here to see Congressman Ollestadt," I said.

"And your name is . . ." she asked like a third-grade teacher trying to elicit the capital of South Dakota.

"My name is Ethan Taylor," I said as if I was on "To Tell the Truth." She didn't get it.

"Mr. Taylor, between nine and ten," she colored her words with sarcasm.

"That's me," I said brightly.

"I will let him know that you are here." She said "him" as though he were the only "him" in the world, or at least the only "him" she would ever bother to mention.

I stood there waiting for her to let "him" know and she just sat there staring at me, not moving. Somehow, we were stuck in some sort of stalemate and I wasn't sure as to what I was supposed to do to break it. Finally, I took a step back and she picked up the phone. I paused and she paused. I took another step back and she dialed one number. Another step, another number, until I turned and went back into the front hall and sat in one of the captain's chairs.

"Mr. Taylor is here to see you, Mr. Ollestadt," I heard.

No, Congressman Ollestadt here. No, sir. That was for those Washington nabobs. Down here he was Mister before his appointment to Congress and will remain Mister until Mrs. Bellamy felt the first frostbite in hell.

After a few minutes I heard footsteps on the upper flight of stairs, quick, light footsteps, and then I saw him on the landing. He was not a tall man. He had thinning sandy hair and he was much younger than I had imagined, probably in his early thirties. He wore a dignified brown suit and his posture was pure and erect, though not like a soldier. It was lighter, like his step, as if a string were gently pulling his head up toward the ceiling.

His face was smiling and he seemed genuinely cheerful as he thrust out his hand. I stood up. I took his hand. His grip, too, was light. I guess that was the word for him. Everything about him seemed light. As if his whole presence seemed to say, "There, there, nothing to be worried about. Let's not take this thing seriously." I could sense how this would work wonders on a panicked client or on a worried constituent.

"Mr. Taylor, so good of you to come. Let us go into the conference room, here." And he led me into the large room across from Mrs. Bellamy. He indicated a chair at the far end of the table and while I sat, he turned and closed the large pocket doors that slid into the walls.

"We have doors like that in our house," I said for lack of anything better to say.

"I bet you do," he replied. "You live in Mayor Hamilton's house, don't you? On the edge of town?"

"Yes," I said. I wondered how he knew or why he bothered to find out.

"Where the reception for Senator Kennedy is to take place tomorrow?"

Ah, that.

"Yes, sir," I said.

He took off his suit coat and held it over a hook on a hat tree.

"You don't mind?" he asked.

"Of course not," I said. I suppose it was the polite thing to ask, but I wondered if anyone told him, "No, by God, I won't have you parading around in shirtsleeves in front of me!" He dropped the coat on the hook.

"Congratulations on your appointment, Congressman," I told him, trying to match his manners with some of my own. He waved his hand as if brushing away flies as he sat down across from me.

"I suppose you know why we are having this little chat?" He opened up a file folder in front of him on the table.

"My conscientious objector application?"

"Right on," he said. He looked up at me and smiled. I couldn't tell if he was trying to be cool or just putting me on. "I have read your essay over and over. A very nice piece of writing. Especially for an eighteen-year-old. Someone touch it up for you?"

"No, sir. I write professionally for *The Free Press*."

"Oh, The North Indiana Klansman. Does Mr. Varnado know that you have filed as a conscientious objector?"

"No, sir. Is there any reason he should find out?"

"Nope. Not unless he looks it up. The draft board rulings are a matter of public record. But I don't think you have a worry in the world because I don't think you will be given conscientious objector status because I don't happen to believe a single word of this pile of crap." The congressman tapped the manila folder on the tabletop.

"Sir?"

"Crap, bullroar, donkey doo-doo. You are familiar with the terms?"

"Yes, but . . ." I tried, but he held up his right hand like a traffic cop and leafed through my essay with his left.

"As Jean Paul-Sartre stated in *Being and Nothingness*," he read then leafed some more.

"I can only agree with George Santayana when he said . . ."

"Dietrich Bonhoeffer, a personal hero of mine, said . . ."

He looked back up at me. The only thing I could think of was, the man has gray eyes. I don't think I have ever seen genuine gray eyes.

"Dietrich Bonhoeffer?" he asked. "Dietrich by God Bonhoeffer? 'A personal hero of mine?"

"Well, yes," I said. "I think his stance against Hitler in Nazi Germany was one of the most courageous . . ."

"Right, but what did you think of *Das gute im Mann*?"

"I'm sorry. I don't speak German."

"Of course you don't. What do you think of his famous work, *The Good in Man*?"

"I think he raises some interesting points, especially concerning the presence of God in a world dominated by evil, such as was Germany in 1939 . . ."

"There is no '*Good in Man*."

"That may be your interpretation, but I've always felt . . ."

"No, Mr. Taylor, I mean that, to my knowledge there is no published work called *The Good in Man*, by Dietrich Bonhoeffer. I would think that you would know that about your personal hero."

"Well, maybe personal hero was a bit of an exaggeration. My enthusiasm sometimes . . ."

"Don't you understand?" The good congressman was getting a little excited. The lightness was leaving and there was this strange fire behind his eyes. "*The Good in Man* does not exist! I made it up. Like you made it up this hogwash. This is a textbook fill-in-the-blank report on pacifism, cleverly written, adroitly researched, but it has nothing to do with your actual beliefs and your convictions."

"Maybe not at first, but after I got into it . . ."

"Do you have any beliefs and convictions, Mr. Taylor? I mean beyond drinking beer, getting laid and keeping your worthless ass out of Southeast Asia?"

This was starting to get weird. I opened my mouth but no words were forthcoming.

"Well?" The Congressman asked.

"Of course I have beliefs and convictions," I finally managed to say.

"Let's hear one."

"What?"

"One single belief or conviction."

"I believe in my fellow man," I offered without looking the Congressman in the eye.

"You believe in your fellow man to do what?"

"To do what?"

"Yes, what is it you believe in your fellow man to do?"

"I believe in my fellow man to behave in a . . ." I almost said manly. ". . . in a humane manner."

"And what does that mean?"

"You don't know what humane means?" I asked. Oops.

"I know what humane means." He was now fully pissed off. I mentally bought my plane ticket to Saigon. "I want to know what you know humane to mean."

"Decent, civilized, rational."

"Do you believe that the Vietnam War is decent, civilized or rational?"

"No."

"Then it is not humane?"

"No."

"Then who do you think exactly is fighting this war in Vietnam?"

"Sir?"

"Who is fighting the goddamned war?" The fire in his eyes roared to a crescendo.

"The United States, the Viet Cong, uh, North Vietnam . . ."

"Your fellow human beings, Mr. Taylor. Your fellow goddamned human beings! Those humane guys you believe in, the decent, civilized and rational. They are over there sticking punji stakes up the asses of babies and napalming villages into being and nothingness. So if that is who you believe in then why the hell don't you want to go over there and join them?"

I sat there stunned. I started to say something, I am not sure what, and then I stopped. Congressman Ollestadt was staring at me. Somehow in his diatribe his vest had come unbuttoned revealing a faded ink stain on his blue Oxford shirt.

Finally I said, "I don't know."

He held my attention with those gray eyes for another long breath and then he said, "That is the first honest thing I have gotten from you. Thank you." He leaned back in his chair.

"I would like to think that if that was the subject of . . ." He lifted my essay and let it fall back to the table "I would be more inclined to support your claim."

"What?"

"A simple, 'I am a conscientious objector, but I don't know why'."

I tried trotting out the simple truth again.

"I didn't know until I began my research, but by the time I finished, I sincerely . . ."

He waved at flies again.

"I don't want to hear it."

"So does that mean that I am not going to achieve conscientious objector status?"

"Achieve?" Congressman Ollestadt shook his head. "Do you think this is something you earn? That you study for and become? Like achieving dentistry?"

Achieving dentistry?

"Either you are or you are not a C.O., Mr. Taylor, and I am convinced that you are not."

I stood up.

"Then are we done here?" I asked.

"No, no," he said. He waved his hand again. "Sit down."

I sat down.

"First thing Thursday morning, after the Senator's speech, I will hold the quarterly meeting of the draft board. We will consider issues such as," and he pointed disdainfully to the filing folder, "this. I will present your essay to the board with no comment on my part either pro or con."

"But why? If you think it is insincere . . ."

"I don't 'think.' I know it. But I am going to give your petition a chance because. . . Tell me, in your research, did you happen to come across the number of conscientious objectors that the Copiah County draft board has approved? In its entire history? We are talking the whole thing: Vietnam, Korea and the two world wars."

"No," I said.

"Then I will tell you," he said. "None. And there have been several applications. More than you would imagine. Do you know why the Copiah County Draft Board has not approved one single conscientious objector application in its entire illustrious history?"

"Because it is Copiah County?"

"One would think, wouldn't one? But no. The reason why the Copiah County Draft Board has never approved a single conscientious objector application in the entire illustrious history of the Copiah County draft board is that in its entire illustrious history no one on the Copiah County Draft Board has given a good goddamn. For over half a century the Copiah County Draft Board has rubber stamped every single C.O. application 'Refused' because not one single human being on any of those boards wanted to actually review the merits of any of those cases."

"Why that is incredibly irresponsible!"

"Not unlike someone trying to get out of the draft by writing a bullshit essay?"

I kept my mouth shut. It seemed wise.

"Actually, it really isn't as bad as it sounds," the Congressman continued. "Did you know that when you are rejected by your local draft board you get an automatic appeal to your state draft board?"

"No."

"I didn't think so, and neither do most of the other applicants. You see the Copiah County Draft Board wasn't as much denying C.O. status as passing the buck. Pretty much a 'we don't want to bother with this, so let the state of Indiana handle it' kind of thing. And I bet that this draft board is no different than all the rest, so that is why I am going to demand that they consider your application. I suspect that many of the other members are not as well-read as yours truly and certainly do not have my keen bullshit detector, so, you see, you may still have a shot."

"Why are you doing this for me?"

"I am not doing this for you. I am doing this for all the poor suckers that went before you and the ones that will come after you, the guys that have a genuine moral, philosophical or religious objection to war."

He sat staring at me. I stared back. What was supposed to happen now?

Once again, I stood up to go.

"Why don't I feel like saying thank you?"

He stayed seated, his hands clasped behind his head.

"I don't know. I may not be acting with your best interests in mind, but you are certainly the beneficiary."

I walked around the table and held out my hand.

"You're right. Thank you." I was a little surprised that he took it. He didn't stand up, but he took it.

"You are a bright boy, Ethan Taylor. And, whether you know it or not, you have many gifts. Don't let those gifts get the better of you."

"Sir?"

"You will figure it out."

I had no idea what he meant. Not yet.

As I opened the sliding doors I noticed something on the top of the bookshelf to the right of the doors. It was a green beret.

CHAPTER 12

Jessi

I went from Ollestadt, Waggoner and Smith to the newspaper; from the three-ring circus to the sideshow. I had this almost neurotic need to check out Uncle Pete's rap as soon as possible. Anything to get Ollestadt's quirky lecture and his green beret out of my head. And didn't Decker say something about "look out for a green beret?" So I went straight to Mr. Varnado and presented Pete's "Everybody but the Boy Scouts is out to kill Kennedy" conspiracy theories leaving out the essential "Assassination in Port Gibson" subtext.

"Pete Decker is out of his tree," said Mr. Varnado.

"*Newsweek* doesn't seem to think so," I countered.

"*Newsweek*," Varnado grunted. "Pete Decker hasn't been on the staff for years."

"What about the Martin Luther King funeral? His picture and byline were in the magazine."

"That was an exception. Hell, he was the only white man those niggers would talk to. Other than that, Decker has been persona non-grata in the respectable journalism world for quite some time."

"Why is that?" I asked, but I knew the answer.

"Rumor has it he has a drug problem." Mr. Varnado grinned, took his cigar out of his mouth, and sipped some bourbon-laced coffee. *The Free Press* was buzzing with activity for the next day's edition and the anticipation of Bobby's imminent arrival.

"So you don't think Bobby is in danger?"

"Nah, one dead Kennedy a decade seems like more than enough. Besides he's not gonna be President. Hell, he won't even get nominated.

Hubert has the knee-jerk, nigger-loving liberals and the war hawks behind him. Hawks and bleeding hearts. No one can beat that combo—except of course for my man Dick."

Varnado had been a Nixon man since the beginning. He liked to say he would have voted for the gleam in Daddy Nixon's eye.

"You just cover the party at your house, get some candid photos of the candidate in the john or something, and let Pete Decker run around looking for CIA spooks and organized crime on his own time."

"What do you want me to do today?"

"I don't know. Get some man on the street bullshit. Ask people how pissed off they are that some jungle bunny loving, long-haired, pinko, Massachusetts fag is coming to our fair city."

"In other words, keep it objective."

"What? Oh, yeah, right. And don't go spreading around any of this assassination bullshit, okay?"

"Yes, sir," I said. "Do you mind which street?"

Mr. Varnado just grunted.

Now that I had the ammunition to write off Pete Decker, I had to see her again. Not LJ. Well, yes, LJ, but I had no idea where LJ or my car was. But I needed a female presence, a feminine, something. I wasn't sure exactly what, but I knew Jessi had it in spades.

She was the most feminine woman I had ever seen off of a movie screen. Her job was sex. Her clothes, the very little of them I saw, were sex: her smell, her touch, her essence, sex. And I was an eighteen-year-old virgin and I had no idea how to find LJ and talk about last night. So Jessi seemed like the most illogical and compelling choice.

It was easier to park inconspicuously across from the massage parlor on Monday morning than it was on a Sunday night. I blended in with a hundred other cars. The warehouses and the welding shops were fully staffed and Tina's Massage and Relaxation was doing a booming coffee break business. It seemed that every fifteen minutes, some guy was entering or leaving the tan and grey bungalow.

I had no idea if she was even working that morning. If I had thought about it at all, I probably would have guessed that she wouldn't be, figuring if she closed the place down last night, she wouldn't be on the "A" shift. But I was young and stupid and I had had a hunch, so there I was crunching on Planter's peanuts and staring at Tina's front door.

I guess my best thought was that she would have to leave for lunch, but that didn't necessarily follow either. It was a house. It more than likely had a kitchen. There was no reason why there wouldn't be food inside. But still I waited. All I knew was I had to see her.

Shortly before noon a kid in a Volkswagen pulled up to the front door and carried in three white flat boxes. Pizzas. Great, that should just about cinch it, I thought. No one is coming out now, but I was wrong. Evidently Jessi does not like pizza because minutes after the pizza guy pulled away, she came walking around the far side of the house. She was wearing jeans and a man's white shirt with the sleeves rolled up, like she just slipped out of some stranger's bed and borrowed his shirt. Always sexy. She got into a black and gold Firebird and did this speedy swivel maneuver in reverse and then peeled out of the parking lot.

Now Ethan's Jeep may have been surplus, but with his dad's three fifty-seven Chevy engine in it, the sucker could move. Miss Jessi whipped her Burt Reynolds car right out of The Flats and out toward the highway and I followed right along with her. About a mile and a half outside of town, she pulled into The Sands Motel, a little Mom and Pop place with one of those neon signs of a woman in a one piece and a bathing cap stretched out as if she were diving into a pool. Jessi parked in front of the little square "Pancake House" attached to the lobby.

I drove on past so as not to look as if I was following her. I don't know why that seemed important. I mean, I was, after all, following her, but somehow it seemed cooler if I could make it look like I accidentally walked into the same place where she was having lunch.qqq

I drove about three miles down the road, turned around in a picnic rest stop, drove back and parked on the opposite side of the restaurant from the Firebird. I walked in the place and saw her in the booth farthest from the door. I sauntered over and sat across from her.

"Hi," I said brightly. "Fancy meeting you here."

"Go away," she said, not even looking up from her cardboard menu.

"Do you remember me?" I asked.

"Go away."

"I saw you last night at . . ."

"Don't say it." She looked up at me with fierce green eyes.

"Work," I finished the sentence. "If you remember correctly, I am with the *North Indiana Free Press*. Today I am assigned by our fearless leader, I think you said you know him, to ask the man in the street, or in this case, woman who works the street . . ."

"I'm warning you!"

"What they think about the impending visit to our fair city of the celebrated Senator from New York, one Robert Francis Kennedy."

"Bobby Kennedy is coming to Port Gibson?"

"Ah, something to capture the attention of the lovely miss."

"Missus."

"What?"

"I am the lovely Missus and answer my question."

A waitress in a banana yellow uniform with white lacy trim came up to our booth.

"Hi, honey, and what will we be having today?" the waitress asked in that grandmotherly tone adopted by waitresses all across the Midwest.

"Is there any chili left?"

"He made some fresh just five minutes ago."

"Give me that and a glass of buttermilk."

"I sure do wish I could drink buttermilk like you and keep my figure."

The waitress was thin as a breadstick, but she was right. There was no figure.

"What will you be having, young man?"

"The young man will have nothing. He is on his way out," Jessi said.

"Aw, Jessi. After all we meant to each other?"

The waitress glared at me.

"I think she is asking you to leave."

"Your name wouldn't be Bruno, would it?" I asked.

"My name is Harriet and your name is Mudd if you don't pack yourself on out of here."

"Just give me a minute." I told the waitress. She looked at Jessi.

"Just a minute," Jessi said.

"And a Pepsi," I said.

"I don't think so," said Harriet and she spun around and moved back toward the swinging door at the rear of the restaurant.

"I think I prefer Bruno," I told Jessi.

"Okay, you can stay long enough to tell me about Bobby. When is he coming to town?"

"Well, he was supposed to come to town this Friday, but now he isn't."

"Mind if I smoke?" Jessi asked and without waiting for a reply pulled out a pack of Kents.

I grabbed an art school pack of matches out of a lime green ashtray and lighted her cigarette. She reflexively touched my hand with hers, but quickly snatched it away when the tip was lit.

"So if he is not coming Friday, when is he coming?"

"Well, there was some talk about Thursday, but that didn't last long."

"When?" she asked. She glared at me like a cat about to spit.

"He is going to give a speech Wednesday at the beauty pageant, but I happen to know that he is arriving Tuesday night."

"Great. Thanks. Now get out of here."

"Don't you want to know where he is going to be Tuesday night?"

"Why would I want to know that?"

"I don't know. You seem interested. You seem like a fan."

"I am not a fan. There is nothing to do in this burg. I just thought that a Kennedy might bring a little excitement."

"Uh-huh. So I guess you wouldn't be interested in being invited to his welcoming reception."

"Right. Like that is going to happen."

"Hi honey, here is your buttermilk." Harriet was back. "Are you singing tonight?" she asked Jessi. Jessi gave her a "Dear God I wish you hadn't said that" look.

"Singing?" I asked. "You sing? Where?"

"In the shower like everyone else, I imagine," said Harriet. She was trying to recover the fumble, but I had the ball and I was seeing daylight.

"Oh, come on, tell me," I told Jessi. "I'm a journalist and you know what they say, there is no such thing as bad publicity."

"Now you just leave her alone!" Harriet was still trying to cover. "I'm sorry I said that about singing. But Charlie and I sure did enjoy you last Wednesday."

"Where?" I asked again.

"None of your beeswax!" said Harriet. "Honey, do you want me to call one of my truck driver friends to get him out of here?"

"It's all right, I can handle mister . . ."

"Bond," I smiled. "James Bond."

"Mr. Taylor."

"All right. But he starts being a nuisance, you just give me the high sign," Harriet said and moved off to the counter to deal with a couple of her beefy truck driver buddies in flannel shirts with rolled-up sleeves.

"Seriously," I said trying to look as serious as possible. "I can get you an invitation to Bobby's party."

"What? A press pass?"

"Better than that. I know the host. You might say he and I grew up together."

"Somehow I don't have you pegged for high society."

"I am wounded."

She ignored my hand on my heart. "So? What?" She asked. "Someone from high school who hasn't gotten around to disowning you?"

Well, yeah, I thought, but I said, "Better than that."

"What?"

"Tell me where you sing."

"In the shower. What's your connection?"

"Where else?"

"In my car." She gave me the stare.

"Where do you sing in front of people?"

"In my car in traffic. I roll the windows down."

"Where did you sing last Wednesday night?"

"Are you going to get me to the Kennedy thing?"

"Yes."

"How?"

"It's going to be at my house."

"Bullshit."

"Scout's Honor," I raised my right hand, three fingers extended.

"Why?"

"My roommate is the mayor's son."

Jessi put out her cigarette thoughtfully and then leaned back in her booth, crossed her arms and looked me in the eyes.

"Really," she said.

"Really," I said.

"And you can get me in."

"It's my house."

"Cisco's."

"What?"

"I sing at Cisco's. It's a place . . ."

"I know Cisco's. The whole college knows Cisco's. They don't card."

"No, but if they catch you under age, they break legs."

"I've never been caught." Because I had never been there.

"Maybe you should be. Teach you humility."

"I know humility," I said. "I'm just out of practice."

"Where is your place?"

"West Main Street. The big brick house with the Corinthian pillars at the edge of town."

"I've seen it. And they are Doric pillars."

"Everyone in Port Gibson calls them Corinthian."

"Then everyone in Port Gibson is wrong. What a surprise." She stubbed out her cigarette. "Look it up." She took out another Kent. "Now you may go."

"Where do you live?"

She just kind of snorted.

"How am I going to take you to the party?"

I lighted her second cigarette. This time she didn't touch my hand. She exhaled.

"I'll meet you there."

"How will you know what time to be there?"

"What time should I be there?"

"Right after I pick you up."

She sighed a stream of cigarette smoke. "I'll be there at ten. Every party is going at ten."

"What if the Senator has been there and gone?"

"Then I will be there at eight."

"But what if I'm not there to introduce you? If I don't pick you up . . ."

"If you want me at your little party, you will have to meet me at your door at eight PM sharp. That's the deal."

"Okay," I said.

"Homemade chili, fresh from the pot," Harriet said and set down a bowl and a plate of cellophane wrapped crackers in front of Jessi. "Careful it is hot." Then she turned to me. "If you're not going to order some food, I am going to have to ask you to leave."

"Then I'll have some chili," I said.

"Fresh out," said Harriet.

"Then a hamburger," I said.

"No buns," said Harriet.

I got the drift. I slid out of the booth.

"I'll see you tomorrow night," I told Jessi.

"Probably," said Jessi.

I smiled and gave a two-finger salute. Harriet stood there and glared like a sentry on duty.

"Oh," I said. "Be sure and change from your work clothes." Jessi looked at Harriet significantly and then looked back at me. Still grinning, I turned and walked out of the Pancake House.

"Jerk, jerk, jerk," I said to myself as I got behind the wheel. No wonder I was a virgin.

CHAPTER 13

Turk's One Stop

I still hadn't gotten my "Man on the Street" interviews, so I decided to head over to Turk's One Stop, the Negro grocery store in The Flats. Few people in Port Gibson had adjusted to the terms "Black" or "African American." Us local "liberals" called them "Negroes." Most everybody else called them "Colored" or worse.

Besides, it was my turn to buy the house beer and I knew that between my hangover and Rick 's dates, those quarts wouldn't last long. Turk never carded because the cops just didn't care what the town Negroes did as long as they didn't bother white people. And I was still in asshole mode and I knew an interview with a black man would piss off Varnado no end. Especially if I didn't tell him until after it was printed.

Turk's was a square, one story brick building set on top of a tall concrete base that kept the store dry except during the very worst floods. It looked like all the other family-owned little grocery stores in Port Gibson except that it still had a potbellied wood stove in the center and its meat cooler contained whole pigs' heads and souse and fatback instead of leg of lamb, veal or ground sirloin.

"Anything else, young man?" Turk Mitchell, the white-haired proprietor of the store looked at me over black thick-rimmed glasses. His richly veined, smoky grey hands rested on my six-pack of Bud and a copy of *The Indianapolis Star*. A couple of middle-aged black men were playing a checker game by the cold stove. They had been actively engaged in some sort of debate when I had entered the store, but they had gone quickly silent at the appearance of Mr. Varnado's intrepid reporter.

"Yeah, Turk," I said. "I am supposed to ask people about what they think about Bobby Kennedy coming to Port Gibson."

"This for school?"

"No. This is for the newspaper."

"Mr. Varnado's newspaper?"

"Yes."

"You sure Mr. Varnado is going to be wanting my opinion on the matter?"

"Well, no. As a matter of fact, I am fairly certain that Mr. Varnado will NOT want your opinion on the matter, but there is no reason why I have to tell Mr. Varnado exactly whose opinion I am putting in the paper."

Turk chuckled. I liked Turk and I always assumed that he liked me. His store was close to my mom's house and I had been coming in there since I was twelve. Occasionally, when no one else was in the store, we would have more than just a casual exchange of greetings. And I knew his twin grandsons. They had constituted two-fifths of the only decent basketball team in the history of Port Gibson High and had since gone off to become legends as the "Twin Oaks" at the University of Illinois.

"That sure would be something to see what I say in that Mr. Varnado's newspaper, yes sir."

"It will be in there," I said. "I guarantee it."

Turk looked at me then looked down and then looked up at the ceiling. I glanced to my left. The two checker players had stopped their game and they were looking intently at Turk.

"Well, sir, this is what I think. I think that Mr. Bobby Kennedy is a good man. Yes, sir, a good man, and he means well and all. That speech he give in Indianapolis when Dr. King was murdered was something else. I was there along with a few thousand others. It was the first most of us had heard of Dr. King's death. It took real courage for a white man to stand up in front of thousands of black people and tell them that another white man had murdered Dr. King. But he told us that he understood what had happened because he had lost a member of his family, that a white man had shot his brother. There wasn't another politician in the country that could have stood there and told us that. No, sir. And he don't like that war, neither, and that is a good thing. Mr. Lyndon, he has been awful good on civil rights. I got nothing to say against him on that, but it seems like this war has become mostly black people fighting for the white politicians and that is no good. I think Mr. Lyndon knows that now and that is why he quit."

I pulled one of the Buds out of the cardboard carton and popped the top, dropping the tab inside the can. I took a long swallow. My hangover breathed a sigh of relief.

Turk stopped talking while I took my drink.

"Aren't you going to take any of this down?"

"It's all up here, Turk." I pointed to my head.

"Yeah, but I'm afraid it's going to end up all down there." He pointed to my beer. "Get out your pencil and paper and get some of this down so an old man don't feel like he is blowin' hard and useless. Hear?"

"Yes, sir," I said and took my note pad out of my back pocket. I patted my pockets and Turk handed me the Bic pen that he kept by the cash register.

"Now put down that part about black men fighting a white man's war."

"Turk, you know Mr. Varnado is not going to print anything like that."

"I know, but it's something that I don't want you to forget. Just because it don't get into the newspaper, don't mean it isn't true."

I heard a chorus of "Yes, sir" and "Tha's right" from the checkers players, but when I looked over in their direction they were studying their game again.

"All right," I said and I scribbled "Black men, white man's war" on my pad.

Turk read my writing. "That's not what I said."

"It's just a note. I'll remember what you said. Now tell me more about Bobby and try not to make it sound too colored." Okay, I was a little pissed at being told what to do.

Turk looked at me and shook his head.

"Sorry," I said. "I'm in a crappy mood."

"Mr. Robert Kennedy," he began rather formally, "is his own man. Back in the beginning, back when he was Attorney General, he didn't seem to be on nobody's side. Folks were getting lynched in Mississippi, hosed down in Alabama, and they even put Dr. King in jail and the Attorney General seemed hard put to get him out."

"What about the integration of the University of Mississippi?"

"Oh, that was just a pissing contest between him and that governor. Same thing with George Wallace standing in that doorway of the University of Alabama. Just a show for the TVs. But after his brother got killed, that is when Mr. Robert Kennedy changed. You could see it in his eyes; in the way he held his head. He became sad. He became serious. He became like one of us, sad and determined. You can put this in your paper. You can say that this citizen thinks it is an honor to have Mr. Robert Kennedy in Port Gibson, Indiana. But you can also say that I worry for him running for President like he is doing. No black man is gonna stick his head out like Mr. Robert Kennedy is doing without getting it blowed off like they done to Dr. King, like they done to Medgar Evers. I know you can't print this neither, but write it down just the same. Since his brother was killed, Mr. Robert Kennedy has known the sorrow that every black man in America lives with every day and because he knows that sorrow and understands, they got to stop him before he does something about it. And this little peckerwood town is as good as any place to stop him dead. That's what I think about Mr. Robert Kennedy coming to my hometown. You got all that?"

"Yes, sir, I do. And I'll try to fix it up so I can get some of it in the paper."

"I understand you got to do that, but I would appreciate it if you wouldn't fix it up so much that it don't look like nothing I would recognize."

"I'll do my best."

"That's all I can ask a man can do."

"How did you find out that Kennedy was coming to Port Gibson?"

"If a man listens, a man hears things. He still going to be talking at that girl's academy?"

"Wednesday evening, McNeil Auditorium. Do you know where that is?"

"At that girls' school where they hold the high school graduation a while back?"

I remembered now that one of the floods had dumped a load of mud on the high school gym floor about three years ago and they had to have graduation at McNeil.

"That's it."

"That's where my grandsons graduated."

"How are the Twin Oaks?"

"Wilson, he is fine, but Franklin, he didn't do so well with his grades this last year and they had to let him go. The army got him."

"I am sorry."

"The Lord will take care of him. He come a long way to get himself killed now."

"I guess."

"Listen, do you know where Mr. Bobby gonna be, come Tuesday evening?"

"Yes," I said cautiously. I didn't want Turk to know that Bobby was going to be at my house. I didn't want to disinvite him to the party, but I knew that with Mr. Varnado and the other Dixiecrats and Republicans in attendance, an entourage of Negroes was going to be a little more than I could handle.

"You gonna be where he is gonna be?"

"Probably," I hedged.

"Could you do something for me?"

"Maybe," I said.

"Come Tuesday night the Reverend Randolph is going to have a prayer service for the lives of the boys fighting in that war and for the life of Mr. Bobby himself at the Assembly of God church. You think you could tell Mr. Bobby about that service and invite him to come over for just a spell? He don't have to speak or nothing, just kind of drop in and maybe shake a few hands."

"I'm not sure I'm going to be able to talk directly to the Senator," I said.

"Just if you get the chance," Turk said. Somehow without my noticing, a second six-pack had appeared next to the first one.

"I'll do what I can," I said. "Where is this church?"

"Oh, you know where it is," Turk said. "It's just beyond the cornfield across the street from that big house you live in."

"I am not sure when I will be seeing the Senator. It might be kind of late."

"We are starting the service at ten o'clock. We figure Mr. Bobby should be at that party they are throwing for him about then. You know. That party they having down at your place? Right across Main Street from our church?" Turk smiled a big open-mouthed smile.

CHAPTER 14

Dear Old Dad

I still hadn't gotten my man in the street material, not enough to constitute the kind of space Mr. Varnado wanted me to fill up. Most of what Turk had given me was unusable for what Ollestadt had called "The Klansman." And Jessi was pretty much a bust. And I still had to do the laundered whorehouse story. But I had these two six packs minus one beer, so I could always resort to what I sometimes had to do when Varnado gave me ridiculous assignments: go home, pop open a beer or two and make something up. Then I would have plenty of time to go to The Cisco Kid and check out what night they had a blonde chanteuse with cat-green eyes.

The circus tent obstructed my view, so I didn't see the dented gray pickup truck parked on the lawn until I got nearly to the gravel oval behind the house. At first I figured it had to be one of Sid's workmen putting on some finishing touches for the party, but then I saw that the driver's door was open and the left turn signal was flashing.

I gathered up my six packs and went over to the truck to check it out. The keys were in the ignition and turned on to the accessory notch. The floor was covered with twelve different brands of beer cans. The ashtray was spilling dead Camels onto the splitting, green vinyl seat cover. I turned off the indicator and pulled the keys out of the ignition. I looked for any sign of ownership, but there wasn't a scrap of paper in the cab. I tried to open the glove compartment, but it was locked. "Who locks their glove compartment?" I asked myself, and then it hit me. Out of the blue, with no real reasoning behind it, somehow I knew beyond a shadow of a doubt that this beat-up hunk of junk belonged to my dear old daddy. I walked around to the front of the house just to make sure that he wasn't lying passed out on the grounds somewhere and then went in the front door.

He could easily be inside the house. It wasn't locked. People didn't lock up their houses in Port Gibson back then. I sometimes wonder if that is still true. I started to yell, "Is anyone here?" and then I saw him passed out on the couch. Asleep, he looked shriveled and hairy and harmless, he had lost his shirt and smelled like a pile of Schlitz. He was breathing through a wide-open mouth. His Peterbilt "Gimme hat" was still on his head. Our two quarts of Budweiser lay empty on the floor.

I thought about waking him up, but then I thought again. Wake him up and he is either going to be drunk or hungover and either one usually meant that he was meaner than a constipated rattlesnake. I went back to the kitchen and put the beer in the fridge. That was no good. If dear old dad woke up before I was aware of it, the house beer would last about fifteen minutes. I went into the pantry and got Rick's ice chest that he took on his coed "picnics."

I emptied three ice trays into the cooler, topped it off with tap water and the beers and put it in the large room off the downstairs hall. This was once the master bedroom with a walk-in closet under the front stairs and its own bathroom. Mr. Taylor, bless him, had put in a slate pool table and added his family's old stereo and TV console. A ceiling fan and a door leading to the back porch made this the coolest room in the house in more ways than one. Rick had requisitioned a large "L" shaped bar from *The Iceman Cometh* and we called it "Party Central."

Down the hall, the foyer could easily hold twenty or thirty people. It had a huge crystal chandelier and an upright piano that was built right into the wall of the stairwell.

The stairs themselves went up three flights, making a kind of a corkscrewed "U" shape. At the first landing was a stained-glass window.

At the top of the stairs was a kind of balcony that led to Rick's bedroom. The balcony had a rail and you could lean over it and look straight down into the back part of the foyer at the house telephone.

A long hall connected that front balcony to the back of the house and my room. Another bedroom and a bathroom branched off the hall. The bedroom was used to store a lot of the Hamilton family junk and boxes of financial records.

Across from my bedroom and next to the back stairs was the door leading to the attic. Up there it was large and dirty and irregularly shaped with four dormer windows and deep, dark eaves that were alive with sounds of pigeons and mice. There were boxes of the dead dentist's records and even some of those hanging plastic bags that looked like brightly colored telephone booths filled with the doc's clothes that no one had bothered to claim or remove.

Rick said that the attic helped him get laid. He said he would tell girls that it was in the attic that the dentist had pulled the plug and then he would take them up there and let the rustling birds and their tipsy imaginations take over. He said there was nothing like fear to get a woman's libido jump-started.

I wouldn't know.

The first floor was similar to the second floor. At the bottom of the back stairs, two hallways made a "T." The longer hallway ran the length of the house from the front foyer to the back stairs and the smaller hallway connected the kitchen and the West back porch with the doors leading to the East back porch and the door leading down to a nasty smelling fruit cellar that flooded at least once year.

The East side of the long hall was the room that was now Party Central. On the West side of the hall was the kitchen that led to a long pantry that led to a huge dining room that Mr. Hamilton had just the day before filled with a large ornately carved oak table and ten matching chairs for the Kennedy reception. The front living room where Mack was crashed on our very masculine, very hetero black leather couch had huge openings with the sliding pocket doors, like in the congressman's office, that could isolate it from the dining room and the foyer.

Almost every room downstairs had its own fireplace. Mr. Hamilton told us that none of them worked, but I am pretty sure that he just said that to keep us from accidentally burning the place down. It was kind of a miracle that with all the drinking and drugs and sex going on in that place, no one tested one.

I did almost all of my writing on my electric portable Smith-Corona. I usually kept it up in my bedroom on the *Cat* vanity next to the extension phone. During the day, however, especially during the summer, when my room was particularly hot, I would put the typewriter on the bar in Party Central and sit on a stool and write there. This was a doubly good idea this afternoon because it allowed me to listen for the first stirrings of Dear Old Dad.

I finished the Tina story and I was about halfway through my third imaginary interview, the one with a wealthy society matron that approved of Bobby because his family "had all that money, and money, no matter how one acquired it, was a sure sign of God's approval," when Mack made his entrance, leaning on Party Central's door frame.

"What the hell is that ungodly racket?" he complained.

"It's called work, Mack," I said. "I know you union types are not familiar with the term."

"You know you are out of beer?"

"No, but if you hum a few bars, I might be able to fake the melody."

He ignored me.

"What kind of college boys are you with no goddamned beer in the house?"

"The religious kind," I said. "I've been meaning to ask you. Have you been saved? Catch." I reached into the cooler and threw him a Bud. He caught it one handed. I was impressed. He ripped off the tab and threw it on the floor. I looked down at the tab.

"Nice," I said.

He tilted the can over his mouth and poured. The yellow stream fell three inches through the gap between the can and his lips.

"Would you mind putting on your shirt?" I asked.

He emptied the beer can without losing a drop. Practice makes perfect.

"Don't know where it is." He threw the empty beer can back to me. I dropped it in the cooler.

"Got another one?" Mack asked.

"Let's go up to my room. Someone might see you down here."

"What? You ashamed of your old daddy?"

"Yes." I closed up the ice chest and picked it up. I walked past Mack and headed down the hall. I turned back toward him. He was still leaning against the doorway. His head was hanging down to his chest. I shook the cooler so the ice and cans rattled.

"Come on," I said. Mack lifted his eyes more than his head and pushed himself away from the doorframe. He negotiated the stairs easier than I thought he would and only bumped against the walls three times moving down the hall.

I set the cooler on my vanity. Mack stood in the room and took in the vanity and the canopy bed.

"What kind of faggot lives here?" he asked.

"The kind of faggot that wants you to put on a goddamned shirt." I threw him a sleeveless sweatshirt. Mack laughed as he put it on.

I got a Bud out of the cooler and sat backward on the vanity chair. Mack fished out another beer and flopped on the floor, resting his back against my bed.

"How did you find me?" I asked.

"Old Army trick," said Mack. "I looked you up in the phone book."

"You were never in the army."

"Don't mean I don't know their tricks."

He was drinking his beer more slowly now. The color was returning to his face.

"So what are you doing in Port Gibson?" I asked.

"I just want to see my bouncing baby boy. Anything wrong with that?"

"Uh, huh," I said. "After six years, why the sudden parental solicitude?"

Mack whistled loudly. "Parental solicitude, you did go to a couple of them college classes. Can't a man just want to be near his son?"

"Are you sure there isn't another reason?"

"What do you mean?"

"Some sort of work?"

"Well, trucking is kinda slow and I picked up a fill-in job bartending."

"Bartending? What do you know about *mixing* drinks?"

"I know a lot, wise ass, but where I work, all you got to know is the difference between a shot and a beer."

"You seem to have that down."

"I don't see you sucking on a cream soda."

I chugged down my beer for effect and stifled back a gag-reflex. I opened another one. "You ready?" I asked.

"Not quite yet." He cocked his head and gave me this curious look. "Why don't you like me?"

"You mean other than the fact that you abandoned me and mom?"
"Yeah, other than that."
"You use to yell at me a lot. I hated it when you yelled at me."
"Hell, I yell at everybody."
"Everybody is not your kid."
"I never hit you. Lots of guys hit their kids."
"Lots of guys are around long enough to hit their kids."
"You're really stuck on that leaving thing."
"You cheated on mom."
"Not in the same town."
"What about Connie the dog shampooer?" I asked.
"Your mom told you about that?"
"Damn near every night."
"Connie lived in a trailer."
"So?"
"The trailer moved around a lot. She wasn't always in town."
"And that makes it okay?"
"That makes it out of town. Jesus, Ethan, I tried not to throw it in your mom's face, okay? That was the best I could do. I really loved you guys, but she made it so hard to stay around. She always wanted me to be somebody better, somebody nicer, somebody different. I tried. I really did. It just didn't happen. And it made me feel like crap. But she was right. You guys deserved better."

"Yeah," I said. "We did."

"So can't we just let it go? Start over?"

"I don't know," I said. And I didn't. "How long are you going to be around?"

"A month or two. Maybe the summer. Depends on how long they need me to work the bar and if trucking picks up."

"Do you really drive a truck?"

Mack looked genuinely surprised. "Of course I drive a truck. I'm a Teamster, aren't I?"

"I have never seen you in a truck."

"I drive one out of a yard. I don't park an eighteen-wheeler in the driveway."

"I've seen other guys do that."

"Yeah, well, I didn't like bringing my work home. You don't crap where you eat."

"Whatever that means."

"It means I didn't want to bring any trouble to my house, to my family."

"What kind of trouble?"

"Union trouble. There were some pretty tough times back when you were a kid. Hey, don't you remember going on long rides when you were a tyke?"

"No. What are you talking about?"

"I use to take you and your mom all the time. I remember we once went all the way out to California. You couldn't have been much more than two."

"And I'm supposed to remember that?"

"People remember strange things. I remember my Dad taking me once to see the Brooklyn Dodgers when I could barely walk. I remember holding on to his hand the whole time and being scared to death of the giants swinging the clubs. I remember the uniforms and the "B" on their hats. He swore it never happened, but l remember it."

"Why did you quit taking us on runs?"

"It got kind of dangerous and your mom got spooked."

"Dangerous? How?"

"Give me another beer and I'll tell you." I flipped him a can. "Got any cigarettes?" I saw some of Rick's Marlboros on the pool table. I grabbed them and tossed them to him. "A light?" I pitched him some matches.

"You want me to smoke it for you, too?"

He smiled. "I think I can handle it." He ripped the filter off the Marlboro and put it in an empty can. "It was back in the Faber and Green wars." He paused to light the amputated cigarette.

"The what?"

"There is this big construction company, Faber and Green. Ever heard of them?"

"Oh, yeah, they are on the wire all the time. Don't they get a lot of the government contracts for army bases and power plants and stuff in Vietnam?"

"Yeah, which gives you an idea of what kind of clout they got. Lyndon Johnson's buddies. They refused to organize. They thought they were tougher than everyone else and didn't have to treat their people like human beings. Overtime just meant that you didn't go home much. Guys were getting killed and crippled almost every day on their construction sites because they were either too tired to pay attention or Faber and Green just didn't want to shell out the bucks for safety equipment. So since the other unions couldn't get a foothold, a couple of organizers came to us."

"Just a couple? If the employees didn't want to go union . . ."

"They wanted to. They wanted to in the worst way, but they were too scared. Faber and Green had an army of thugs and every time someone got a little too active with talking about a union, that someone disappeared. Not fired, you understand, disappeared. Or maybe his house would burn down. Or he would have this terrible accident after hours when nobody was around. The employees got the message. But the Teamsters, we weren't afraid of nobody. Hell, back then we owned the highways. We'd go on strike and this country would be on its knees in forty-eight hours. That's why Johnson and the Kennedy boys had to bust us. We were getting too big. We had too much say in how their pals could push around the little guy."

I didn't want to get into that with the old man. I didn't want an argument. I wanted to find out about him. Who he was. What he did. I wanted to know that Pete Decker was full of crap.

"So the Faber and Green employees came to the Teamsters," I steered him.

"Yeah, they came to us and we said, 'No problem.' From now on, when Faber and Green needs construction supplies, they are gonna get lost or stolen or maybe shipped to the wrong state. Things happen." Mack smiled again. Something about that smile. It made me feel warm inside, calm, safe. No wonder women liked him. He got up and went to the beer cooler. "Hey, you're running kind of low."

"I wonder why?" But that didn't stop him from popping another top. Now he started pacing while he talked. "So F&G started using scab trucking companies. Guys out of Texas and Mississippi where they don't got enough sense to organize. So naturally we had to dissuade those truckers from taking to the road."

"How did you do that?"

"You know, a few picket lines. Some friendly phone calls in the middle of the night."

"Car bombs."

"What?"

"I heard that sometimes the union used to blow people up in their cars when they thought employers got a little out of hand."

"And where did you hear that?"

"Over the newspaper wires. People talking."

"Well, don't listen to that trash." Mack threw his cigarette butt in a beer can, scooped up the Marlboros, took out another cigarette, ripped off a filter and lighted it. He stopped pacing and jabbed his forefinger at me. "I never killed nobody. No one has ever been able to stick that on me."

"I never said . . ."

"All right, I was arrested once. Back in '62. You're probably gonna find that out sooner or later. But it didn't stick. No one was supposed to get hurt."

"What happened?"

"A truck got blown up. It was late. A couple of kids had crawled into the sleeper to pretend they were camping or something. No one knew they were there."

"Did you set the bomb?"

"The court cleared me of everything."

"Yeah, but did you do it?"

He stopped his pacing and stared me right in the eye.

"What do you think?"

"I don't know," I said.

"That's right. You don't know. You weren't there. You don't know what was going on. We just wanted what was right, what was fair."

"Pete Decker says you are an enforcer for the union."

"Pete Decker is out of his tree." The same phrase that Mr. Varnado had used. I wondered if Pete was a member of the Audubon Society.

"You know Pete?" I asked.

"Yeah, I run into him once or twice. He covered my trial. He wrote all sorts of nasty crap about me and when they let me go, he took me out and bought me a beer."

"You drank it?"

"Why not? I figured he was just a working stiff like me, but then he kept trying to pump me, trying to get me to confess anyway. But I didn't. You know that fruitcake smokes dope?"

"Yeah."

"He's been almost busted himself a couple of times. Spent the night in a Georgia slammer. *Newsweek* had to spring him. Did he tell you they canned him?"

"No, but Mr. Varnado did."

"Jeez, Varnado, he's another piece of work. You hang out with some pretty pathetic people, buddy boy."

'You ever smoke marijuana?" I asked.

"Once. It made me puke up a whole pint of Jim Beam. Haven't touched it since. You?"

"It just makes me sleepy. I know this girl who smokes it all the time. She likes it, but it flattens me out."

"Can't get it up?"

"No! Dammit! Dad!"

"Hey! You called me Dad!"

"Don't get used to it. Listen, I've got to finish an article before five . . ."

"Yeah, I gotta get cleaned up, too. I'm behind the till tonight."

"Where are you staying?"

"The fish camp. You remember, out on Panther Creek."

"You still have that?"

"No reason to let it go. Sometimes I'm at the Sands Motel. It's out on . . ."

"I know where it is. I live here, remember?'

"Yeah. Well, thanks for the beer and the cigarettes." He put his second cigarette in the beer can ashtray. "Next time get some without filters."

"I'll try to remember that."

"And stay away from that Pete Decker. He is trouble."

"You would know."

"No, I'm serious. He's a crazy son of a bitch and if he ain't careful he is going to get himself killed and you don't want to be around when that happens."

"Okay." Mack looked pretty intense. I figured it was best just to agree with him and go on.

"Now come here and give your old man a hug before he leaves." Mack smiled and spread his arms.

"What?" Not this again.

"Give your old man a hug for the road!" He kept his arms spread like some sort of demented crucifix. I stood up and took a couple of steps. He swooped down on me and wrapped his arms around my back and pressed his cheek into my chest. His voiced vibrated against my sternum.

"You're just not very good at this, are you?" Mack mumbled against my chest.

"I guess not."

He let go of me and grinned up at my face.

"We got time to practice." He turned and walked out the door. Then I heard him say "Oh!" in the hall. He appeared back in the doorway.

"Come on down to the club tonight and I'll pay you back those beers. They got this hot brunette that sings on Mondays and Wednesdays."

"Where do you work?" I asked, but I had a feeling that I knew.

"A place out on the highway called The Cisco Kid."

"You say she is a brunette?"

"Yeah, but she wears a wig. Makes her look French or something."

Ah hah.

CHAPTER 15

The Cisco Kid

The Cisco Kid was a fight bar. Not the fights on the tube, but the fights on the dance floor. Couples would come in ostensibly to hoof through the Texas two-step or a countrified version of the jitterbug or even a polka, but when the males got good and boozed up, the females would either goad them into taking a swing at some guy or outlandishly flirt with some poor sucker so that their bruiser escort would feel compelled to drop a roadblock on his ass.

In 1968 north Indiana this was called entertainment.

I finished my "on the street interviews" and it was almost eight o'clock before I drove the five miles northeast of town to Cisco's.

Cisco's, of course, was named after the black and white western in the fifties. It was the only TV show with a Mexican hero, who, of course was played by a Romanian and his not so bright Mexican sidekick who was, of course, played by a California native of Italian descent.

And the Cisco Kid Bar and Grill was just about as Mexican as the TV show. The walls were covered with license tags, various arrangements of rope and barbed wire, and rodeo posters. There was a Winchester carbine above the cash register. Above the Winchester was a highly disregarded sign that reminded patrons that it was illegal to carry firearms in an establishment that sold liquor.

There were two coin operated pool tables, a small bandstand and, for the size of the place, a fairly large dance floor.

The only other reference to south of the border in the place was a picture of The Cisco Kid himself on the men's john door and a picture of Carmen Miranda on the "Ladies." The rest of Cisco's was like its primary clientele: dirty, mean, angry, All-American redneck.

The boys in Cisco's loved America, Raquel Welch, John Wayne and blowing holes through things with shotguns. They supported the war, college football, segregation, NASCAR and haircuts. They hated commies, hippies, faggots, foreigners, niggers, and traffic cops. Real Americana circa 1968.

Monday night and the place was jammed. Jessi must be quite a singer, but I figured that. Even with the wig, at least some of the guys must know what she did at the massage parlor and word had to get around. Come hear the hooker sing.

The old man was behind the bar along with a tall redhead whose prominent bust line hit him about at the nose. Willie Nelson was singing on the jukebox about being crazy. Three couples were leaning against each other and shuffling around on the dance floor. Mack saw me as soon as I walked in. He waved and leaned over and said something to this bearded guy wearing a GMC hat sitting next to the three unmarked beer taps.

The beard looked at me and grinned while Daddy freshened his shot and brew. When I got to the bar, the guy took his drinks, stood up and regally bowed and gestured to his barstool. I smiled nervously and sat down. The beard laughed and moved off toward a shuffleboard table on the far wall.

"How did you do that?"

"He's a brother," Mack said. I assumed he meant Teamster and not soul. He stuck a mug of whatever came out of the tap in front of me and called to the redhead, "Hey, Lacy, come over here and meet the kid."

"I'm busy, Mack," she said. And she was. She had a tequila bottle in each hand and was pouring into a double row of about a dozen shot glasses. Two guys in straw cowboy hats and a chubby platinum blonde were drinking them down almost as fast as Lacy was pouring.

I looked around the room. Tonight there would be no table service because there were no tables. Jessi was an SRO kind of girl. There was a square of a running counter that outlined the dance floor so that people could have something to set their drinks on. The only chairs were the barstools. I felt privileged and conspicuous and more than a little nervous. I figured the trick to survival in a place like Cisco's was to keep a low profile.

"You'll like Lacy," my Dear Old Dad told me. He yelled at Lacy, "She gives great tit jobs!" She flipped him off.

Then Mack got really busy and I sipped on my very cold, very bitter beer. Every five minutes or so, he would come back and top off my mug. Once Lacy came by. Up close she was gigantic in all proportions. Big red hair, big red lips, big blue eyes and of course that big top shelf ballooning out of a low-cut red St. Louis Cardinals t-shirt. She liked to lean over and inhale, giving a man the illusion that the whole world was nothing but mom's lunch box. By then I had about four beers, so I couldn't help but burst out in Bob Hope's theme song.

"Thanks for the mammaries," I warbled.

She smiled and batted those ungodly long artificial lashes at me and said, "Yeah, you're Mack's boy, all right."

"I try not to think about it," I mumbled into my beer.

"Your daddy's all right," Lacy admonished me. "He may get a little wild at times, but he always does what he says he's gonna do, and that's hard to find."

"Lacy!" One of the cowboy hats screamed from the other end of the bar.

"Keep your pecker in your pocket!" she screamed back at him. "You coulda done much worse," she told me. "Believe me, I know."

Long about 8:30, the house band drifted on to the bandstand. It was already set up with drums and amps and speakers. The drummer was the oldest, a grinning, gum-chewer in his early forties with shoe-polish black hair slicked back like those motorcycle gangs in Roger Corman movies. He wore a white t-shirt with the sleeves chopped out and black jeans and engineer boots.

The guy plugging in his lead guitar was shaped like a golf club, long neck, no chest, but a real beer gut. He had a crew cut and wore a purple and green, yoked shirt with white fringe. A huge rodeo belt buckle topped skin-tight blue jeans that bottomed out over black, impossibly pointed boots with a red, white and blue eagle emblazoned on each front.

The bass player was the real trouble. He was short and stocky with a square Waylon Jennings dark brown beard. He had a low, flat black cowboy hat with a band of silver dollars around the crown. His face was almost as beat up as my dad's with a particularly ugly scar running from his left ear down to his chin. I was pretty sure that his left eye was false. But what really gave his game away was his brown curly hair. It flowed out from under his hat and rambled on down past his butt. You just didn't sport hair like that in a place like Cisco's unless you could whip everyone in the place.

In most nightclubs when you see the band come out, you can expect to be subjected to a good half hour of tapping on the drums, stroking guitar strings, the odd chord and other irritating noises, but not The Cisco Kid. These guys walked on, plugged in, and calmly waited. I noticed they were looking up above me in the corner and I looked over my shoulder and I could see a skinny guy on a pre-fab deer stand jutting out of the wall about ten feet above the ground leaning over a sound mixer.

The boys just stood there and looked and waited. The crowd got quiet too. The talk faded out. The glasses stopped clinking. A few people said "shush" to a couple of guys in the corner that hadn't figured it out yet. Even Dear Old Dad and Lacy stood silently behind the bar, almost perfectly still.

Then the lights went out.

Not a slow fade, no dimming of the houselights like in a theater. It was a blackout. Suddenly. With no warning.

Then, bam! A spotlight hit the stage and there she was. Sitting in a pool of gold. She was wearing an elegant and modest plain black cocktail dress and a single strand of pearls. The black wig was one of those pageboy things that you imagined on a French chanteuse in a World War II movie. And flat black sunglasses that made you wonder if she could see anything at all. And vampire red lipstick that somehow lightened her already cloud-white skin. She held a silver microphone that barely touched those red, red lips and her head tilted down so that the straight black hair fell over her cheeks. I knew it was Jessi because I was looking for her, but I wasn't sure that even if these boys had spent a lunch hour or two at the Tina's, they would recognize the singer as their afternoon delight.

Her lips barely moved, so you were hardly aware of where the sound was coming from. It was a deep, throaty whiskey voice, hoarse but with incredible alto tones that seemed to come out of the head itself. Warm inviting tones, unaccompanied by the still immobile band behind her.

"Wellllll, I wish I was in the land of cotton."

It was sad and slow and familiar, but at first I couldn't place it. She paused. Took another breath without raising her head.

"Old times there are long forgotten."

God, it couldn't be. And it wasn't. Not really. Not the same song. Not the battle song of a forgotten south. Hers was the ultimate soft cry of pure anguish and loneliness. Another deep breath.

"Look away," she whispered. "Look away," she whispered. "Look away, Dixieland."

Then the band came in. Lightly, reverently, softly for all their amplifiers and raw testosterone.

"In Dixieland where I was born in, early on one frosty mornin', look away, look away, look away, look away, Dixieland."

It was strange. This wild crowd, these yee-hah, finger-whistling boys and cigarette-throated women were struck silent as if by a witch's curse in a fairy tale. And when she finished her last familiar syllable, I expected applause or shouts or something, but as long as she kept her head down, as long as she didn't move, no one dared to breathe.

Then she jumped off her stool, lifted her microphone above her head and shouted to the ceiling.

"Wellllllllllllllllllllllllllllllllllll!"

"I wish I was in Dixie!"

And the place burst into screams and applause and whistles.

"Away! Away!"

The lead guitar player had picked up a fiddle and the band joined in on:

"I wish I was in Dixieland! Away down south in Dixie!"

I was mesmerized. The crowd was mesmerized. She played us like a finely tuned baby grand. We responded precisely to her every stroke, her every mood. My chest seemed full and open. I was standing up beside my precious bar stool and didn't even notice when Pete slipped in behind me and sat down.

"She gives great head, too," he leaned over my shoulder and yelled in my ear.

"What the hell are you doing here?" I screamed back.

"Looking for you!"

"Well, you found me. Now give me back my seat!"

"Away! Away! Away down south in Dixie!" Jessi sang.

"Finders keepers!" And he gave me his toothy grin.

"Away! Away! Away down south in Dixie!" She waved her hand at the audience to join her. They did. "Away! Away! Away down south in Dixie!" While the audience went bananas, Mack came around the bar and sidled up to Uncle Pete.

"Give the kid his seat!" Mack screamed over whistles and cheering.

"Screw you!" Pete screamed back. Mack turned away as if he were going back behind the bar. Then he pushed a couple of applauders to the side and spun quickly around, catching the rungs of the wooden bar stool with his right boot. The barstool went down with Pete on top of it. Pete's butt had barely touched the floor when Mack was kicking him rapidly in the head. People cleared away from the bar area forming a circle so they could watch the fight.

"Oh, come on, guys!" Jessi called into the microphone. "I just got started!"

"We're done here," said Mack. And he was. And so was Pete. He lay motionless on the floor, a slight trickle of blood coming out of his left ear.

"Jesus! Look at those boots!" Mack said pointing at Pete. I looked. They looked like some sort of snakeskin with an embossed rattlesnake on the ankle.

"They look like he stole them off of some faggot cowboy." He had a point.

"Brad!" Mack called to the big, bearded Teamster who had given up his seat. Brad and another mountain-sized man with a Peterbilt hat grabbed Pete under the shoulders and dragged him to the back of the bar.

Jessi said from the bandstand. "I don't know about you folks, but I need a drink. Back in ten." The audience booed, more Mack than Jessi, while she put the microphone back in the stand. The band gave her some traveling music as she disappeared behind a black curtain to the right of the lead guitarist.

"Where are they taking him?" I asked Mack as Brad and his friend disappeared through a door.

"Out back," Mack said. He set up the barstool and patted it for me to sit back down.

"They're not going to kill him, are they?"

"I don't think so," said Mack. "But you never know. Teamsters."

Mack moved back behind the bar. Some were patting him on the back, some were still booing, a lot of them were screaming drink orders. He ignored them all. He came over to me and filled a fresh mug with beer.

"I didn't need the seat that badly," I said.

Mack shrugged. "It's the damn principle. Besides, I have been wanting to kick that bastard's ass ever since my trial."

"You missed his ass."

"Yeah, I must be getting old."

"I'm going to see if he's all right."

"Aw, he's fine." Mack was pouring beers like a waterfall.

"I'm still going to check."

"I'll hold your seat."

"Try not to break anyone's leg."

"No guarantees." Mack gave me that fatherly smile again. I couldn't help it. I grinned back. I was afraid I was beginning to like the bastard.

CHAPTER 16

Out Back

"The son of a bitch got me with a sucker punch," Pete was sitting on a rusty barrel. I had brought him a bar towel filled with ice. He pressed it to his head. Dried blood matted a sideburn and stained his camel hair Jacket.

"No punch to it, Pete," I said. "Mack kicked you in the head."

"Kicked me when I was down."

"How was he going to kick you in the head while you were up? He's too short."

"Give me a fair fight and I will kill that little peckerwood."

"Sorry, Pete, Mack doesn't fight fair. Never did. Never will."

"Then I will shoot the bastard."

"Then you better plan on massacring a whole union. Those Teamsters don't particularly like having their herd thinned."

"Crap."

"Yeah, that's about it. Now what was it you wanted to talk to me about?"

"What?" Pete asked. He took the ice away from his head and gingerly touched his ear. "God dammit!"

"Okay." I stood up. "I can see that this is not a good time to have a conversation."

"No, stay," Pete said. I stayed. He reached his right hand into his Jacket and came out with a folded piece of paper, "I want you to look at this."

I opened up the paper and looked at a photocopy of a newspaper article and a picture of four guys wearing KKK robes with their hoods off.

"What's this?"

"Recognize anyone?"

I looked at the photo again. They were four unremarkable doofusses, looked to be in their teens. The caption read: "Get them while they are young. The Klan goes to high school."

"Nobody I know."

"Look again. This is out of *The Birmingham Times-Telegraph* in 1928."

I stared at the picture for some sort of clue. Then something about the guy on the far right with the goofy grin seemed familiar. Suddenly I saw him with less hair and a big cigar stuck between his fat lips.

"You guys sure know how to screw up a set." The voice came out of the darkness. The tip of her cigarette glowed brighter as she inhaled, revealing those cat-green eyes that seemed to glow by themselves and then go dark as she pulled the cigarette away from her mouth.

"I had nothing to do with it," I said.

"There wouldn't have been a problem if you hadn't wanted your seat back," said Pete.

"That wasn't me. That was Dad."

"Mack is your father?" asked Jessi.

I literally scuffed the ground with my shoes and looked down.

"Yeah," I said.

"If you would have said that earlier, I might have taken you a little more seriously. Hey, Pete, what are you doing all the way down here besides getting your butt stomped?"

"It was a sucker . . ." And he looked at me. "Kick."

"Ain't they all?" she asked and threw down her cigarette and crushed it out with her black pumps. She reached in her purse and pulled out a pack of Kents. "Seriously, Pete, what brings a news hack like you out of the Windy City?" He had his gold Zippo out and lighted her Kent. She did her hand trick.

"I'm just doing what every journalist has been doing for the last decade. Find a Kennedy and follow him."

"That so?" Jessi asked. "Which one?"

"Bobby," he said.

"In Port Gibson?" Jessi asked.

I had told her all this in the Pancake House. Why was she pretending not to know about it?

"Yeah, he's supposed to give a speech Wednesday. In fact, he is going to be at the kid's house Tuesday night."

This whole conversation was getting on my nerves. Not only did I not understand what Jessi game was playing, but also there seemed to be a sexual tension between those two that I didn't like at all. So I lobbed a grenade in Uncle Pete's direction.

"Pete thinks someone is going to blow Bobby away in Port Gibson," I said with forced casualness.

"Really?" Jessi exclaimed. "Cute little Port Gibson?"

"Goddammit, why don't you just tell everybody?"

"I didn't know it was a secret." I turned to Jessi to change the subject before Pete built up too much steam.

"What's with the wig?" I asked.

"You like it? I got it in Amsterdam."

"What's with the wig is what's with the sunglasses," Pete sneered. "She doesn't want the cowboys to know she's a whore."

She walked up to Pete with the saddest expression on her face.

"Aw, Pete, is that blood on your ear?" She pointed to his left ear.

"Where?" Pete reached up to touch his ear, but before his hand got there she slapped him hard right where the blood trail began.

"Damn!" Pete screamed.

"I don't much like that term, 'whore,' Pete. I prefer massage specialist, or, to be more precise, physical psychotherapist. And I don't give a crap who knows what I do at the parlor."

"So the wig?" I asked

"It helps me get into character," Jessi said. "My stage persona, Jeannette Baudelaire. Like it?"

"Jeanette Baudelaire, the singing slut?" asked Pete. Jessi drew back to hit him again, but Pete grabbed her arm with his left hand and backhanded her with his right. Jessi dropped to the ground.

He was so quick, I had barely realized what happened.

"One shot is all you get, Missy," he said. I moved between Pete and Jessi. I turned my back to Pete to see if Jessi was all right and offered her my hand. Jessi gasped and put her hand to her mouth and I turned back around and saw Mack behind Pete with his nickel-plated, snub-nosed .38 revolver pressed up against Pete's head.

"How many shots do I get, Pete, baby?" Mack asked. "Give me half a reason, you son of a bitch, just half a reason." He was pulling on the double action trigger so hard that I could see the hammer lifting off the firing pin.

"Easy, Mack, easy. She hit me. I was just defending myself."

"I don't really care, asshole." Mack pushed Pete's head to the side with the point of the gun. The hammer pulled back further.

"You don't want to shoot me," Pete said.

"Mister, in a lifetime of being wrong, you have never been more wrong than just now."

Jessi tapped me on the leg, I turned around and she grabbed my hand and hauled herself to her feet.

"Don't shoot the prick, Mack. I think you would be doing the miserable son of a bitch a favor." She beat Cisco dirt off her black skirt.

"Whatever you say, babe." Mack gave Pete's head one more shove with the gun and then took a step back, but he still kept it pointing at Pete's head.

Babe? I thought.

"I got to get back inside, Pete, but I want you to leave before I do," Mack said.

"All right. I'm tired of playing cowboy and dancehall madam, anyway."

Mack cocked the pistol.

"I'm going. I'm going." He pointed to me. "Call me in the morning."

"I don't think so," I said.

"You're going to want to hear what I have to say about that picture."

"I doubt it," I said.

"Suit yourself," Pete said. "Gentlemen," he said to Mack and me. He faked tipping an imaginary hat. "Lady," he sneered. Then he turned and lumbered back around the building toward the parking lot. Big man. That backhand must have hurt.

Jessi must have been thinking along the same lines because she moved over to Mack and turned her right cheek toward him.

"How does it look?" she asked.

"It's starting to swell up and turn purple," Mack said.

"I was afraid of that. Hell. I can't go back in there like this."

"They are going to riot if you don't."

"Handle it, will you Mack? I just can't do it."

"All right. I'll take care of it, then I'll run you home."

"You can't leave. They will eat Lacy alive."

He dropped to his knee, rolled up his pants leg and put his pistol in his boot and rolled down his jeans.

"Yeah, you're right. You want my keys?"

His keys, I thought. Where was her car?

"No, thanks. I'll see if I can get Junior here to give me a ride."

Mack cocked his head to one side and closed one eye as he studied me.

"I'm not sure I trust you with him."

"What, Mack? You think we're pinned or something?" Jessi asked.

"Not hardly. Just make sure he wears a rubber."

So much for starting to like the old man.

CHAPTER 17

The Jeep

"So," I said as we pulled out of Cisco's parking lot, spinning gravel into the night. "You and the old man."

"Not hardly," said Jessi in an imitation of Mack's growl.

"What about all that 'make sure he wears a rubber' bullshit."

"He was kidding." She took off her wig so it wouldn't blow off in the Jeep. "Does that bother you?"

"What?"

"If I were seeing your father."

"'My father!' My god, I don't think I have ever thought of him as 'my father'."

"What do you think of him as?"

"Mack, The Old Man, sometimes, or Dear Old Dad or That Prick."

"You didn't answer my question."

"I was hoping you would forget it."

"I didn't," Jessi said.

"I noticed," I said. Monday night in the Indiana countryside. Not another car in sight. "Yeah, I guess it would bother me."

"Why?"

"I don't know."

"You and I barely know each other."

"I know."

"Does the massage parlor bother you?"

"No."

"Why not?"

"I don't know."

"I'm sorry. You have used up your 'I don't knows'. I need something with a little more depth."

"I don't know. Sorry. I guess it's because what you do is what you do. I mean it's really none of my business. You have a lot of sex. I don't. What's the real difference?"

"You don't what?"

"Have sex."

"Ever?"

I had never confessed this to anyone before. Well, Rick, one night while drunk. But certainly never to a girl, a woman. But somehow this felt all right.

"Yeah."

There was a silence. I was afraid she was going to use the "V" word, but she didn't.

"Ever come close?"

"A couple of times, I think. But we ended up talking all night."

"You know, that is why I get half my business."

"Why?"

"Sometimes the johns like to talk more than screw."

There was another silence.

"I don't," I said.

She giggled.

"How would you know?"

"I know."

"Do you want it to be perfect? The first time. Do you want it to be with someone you love?"

"Sometimes I think of it like that. Most of the time I just want to get it over with."

"Spoken like a real man." She fished out a cigarette, expertly lighted it in the fifty mile an hour wind and exhaled. "Some of them want it to be special. Some of them like to pretend I am their girlfriend."

"But you are not."

"No."

"Never?"

"Never."

There was a long silence. We were coming into Port Gibson. I could see the glow of the large yellow sign with red lettering that said, "Welcome to Port Gibson—City of beautiful homes, schools and churches."

"Where are you staying?" I asked her.

"The Sands. But I don't want to go there."

"Where do you want to go?"

"I don't know. I just don't want to go home now."

"Monday night in Port Gibson, not a whole lot of choices."

"No. Take me to your place."

My heart stopped. I found it difficult to breathe.

"You sure?" What an idiot!

"Yeah. I want to see what kind of place merits the presence of a United States Presidential Candidate."

CHAPTER 18

The Roof

When we pulled up to the house Jessi pointed to the dormer window on the third floor and said, "Let's go up there."

"You sure?" I repeated. "It's just a dirty old attic."

"Positive," and she was out of the Jeep and into the house before I could raise further objections.

I followed her. My Corvair was parked next to Hamilton's Mustang in the old barn behind the house that now served as a two-car garage. I was so distracted by Jessi that the only thought that occurred to me was "Good, LJ brought my car back."

When I was inside, Jessi was racing up the back stairs as if she were born in the place. I ran after her. I was just at the attic door when I heard her shriek. My first irrational thought was "My God, there *is* a dead dentist up there." I ran up the attic stairs.

"What's wrong?" I asked as I reached the top. But nothing appeared to be wrong. Jessi was spinning around in the middle of the boxes and clothes bags, her arms outstretched, each hand carrying a black shoe.

"Nothing." She was still spinning. Then she stopped and looked at me, her eyes positively lit up. "This is wonderful!"

"This attic?" I asked.

"Yes! Oh, and look at the dormer windows! Good god! What is wrong with you? Don't you know they are supposed to be open?"

I walked over to her. "Well, no."

"That's what they are there for. To let the heat out to help keep your house cool. Here." She handed me her shoes and then turned her back to me.

"Unzip me."

"What?"

"Unzip me! Surely even you have unzipped a girl's dress before."

I didn't want to get back into that so I said, "Okay," and unzipped her black dress. She pulled it quickly over her head and handed that to me. She was wearing matching black lace panties and bra and a garter belt. The effect was more erotic than if she had been completely nude. Of course, that was the point. I found breathing difficult.

"Put this someplace where it won't get dirty," she said and walked off to a window. I carefully hung the dress in a banana-yellow clothing bag

"Come help me with this," she called. I went over to where she was pulling on the little handle at the bottom of the window.

"Here," I leaned over. My nose was virtually in her cleavage. She didn't move so I tried not to notice. It didn't work. I pulled half-heartedly on the lip of the window. I was distracted.

"You call that trying? You push on the top and I will pull on the bottom." Even in my virginity I knew not to argue with a beautiful woman once she takes her dress off. I pushed. She pulled. The window didn't budge.

"It's no use," I said. "It's painted shut."

"God, do you give up this easily on everything?"

"Well, yeah," I said brilliantly.

"No wonder," she said. She turned and moved around the attic looking for something.

"You see, my Aunt Gladys had an attic just like this, only cleaner," she said in a breakneck patter. "I lived up in that attic for four years, from twelve to sixteen. It was great. I could be by myself all I wanted, and believe me with her four sons, I wanted to be alone a lot. And with a ladder and the dormer windows and some good climbing sneakers I could come and go as I please. Ah-ha."

She was bent over into one eave. When she turned around and straightened up, a truly wonderful move, she was holding something long, black and straight in one hand and what looked like a bent stick in the other.

"The very thing," she said and literally skipped back to me. When she set the long straight thing on the window sill I could see that it was part of a tire jack. In her other hand was a tire iron.

"Here hold this," she said. I held the jack upright and she placed the tire iron in the Mack's sleeve and pumped until it was just under the top of the window frame. Then she hooked the edge of the jack under the frame and started pumping again. And what a pump it was. Her breasts bounced up and down just under my chin. I thought my heart would beat itself right out of my chest.

At first the window frame creaked and made a slight cracking sound as if the window would come apart. She slowed down her pumping and then the whole window moved slightly and then it was open.

"Voila!" Jessi exclaimed.

There she stood, flushed and breathing heavily from all the pumping, her legs white in the moonlight, matching her platinum hair, her green eyes dancing, taking a decade off her face. She was an exultant teenager, full of spirit and life.

"Come on," she said. "Let's go out there!"

"On the roof?"

"You've never been on your roof?"

"No, not up here," I said stupidly. Did I mean that I had somehow been up on my roof down there? Down where?

"Let's go" and she took my hand and placed one incredible leg over the windowsill. I reflexively held back.

"But you are not dressed."

"You're complaining?"

"The neighbors . . ."

"And exactly when was the last time they looked up on your roof for a semi-nude woman?"

"Never," I said and let her pull me out of the attic. "But I think I am going to start."

When we got out on the roof she let go of my hand. After the dusty heat of the attic, the late May night seemed positively balmy. She stood there like a Maxfield Parrish print, a slight breeze ruffling her hair.

"God, I can't believe you don't just live out here."

It was pretty spectacular. The window faced Main Street. I could see the church on the other side of the cornfield where Turk wanted me to bring Bobby. I looked past Jessi off to my right and I saw the blinking lights of Port Gibson, the old-fashioned concrete streetlights that still used filament lamps that gave off a thousand variations of yellow and white light.

I could see Hubble Creek, the stream that ran past the house where I grew up. And although I couldn't see it, I could picture the creaky footbridge that I crossed every day on my way to elementary school.

And I could see off to the left the Ramada on what used to be called Henderson Hill, the highest point in the county. There, before his kids sold it to the motel chain, Old Man Henderson would have his annual Fourth of July hayride and fireworks for what I now understood were the "underprivileged kids." I never felt underprivileged as I ate more watermelon than my little stomach could possibly hold and played tag and hide-and-go-seek until dark with a hundred other kids, mostly from The Flats, and then watched the most spectacular fireworks that have ever arched above terra firma.

This all ended when I was eight and dear old dad happened to be in town and threw a fit because "No family of mine is gonna take charity from some rich bastard that lives on a hill." That Fourth of July I watched the fireworks on Henderson hill from on top of the fence in my back yard and I cried so hard I fell off and fractured my wrist. I have hated the Fourth of July ever since.

Now Henderson Hill was a Ramada Inn. You can't beat progress.

"I can't believe you have never been up here," Jessi said.

"I can't either," I said. "It is like I am looking at a postcard of my life."

I looked at her and she was staring at me with a strange, speculative look. Her hands perched on her white hips.

She sat and patted the slanted space next to her. I carefully walked over there. Roof walking was not my forte. I sat down awkwardly and she put her hand on my shoulder to steady me. I grabbed her in mild panic and I think she must have misunderstood my intentions because she hit me with a firm stiff arm to the chest, and I started sliding toward the edge of the roof and a three-story fall. I managed to hook my left foot in the rain gutter and stop the skid. I lay there spread-eagled with every inch of my body grabbing on to that roof as if I were made of suction cups.

"You all right?" Jessi asked above me.

"Oh, just dandy," I said not daring to move.

"You want a hand?"

"Nope. I'll get up myself." And I did, slowly, carefully. I crawled back up next to Jessi and sat up again. My mind was a whirl of confusion.

"Sorry about that, but I didn't want you to get the wrong idea."

"I wasn't trying anything. I just . . ." I couldn't explain without looking like a total idiot. She looked at me speculatively.

"Good God," she concluded. "You really weren't! I just wanted you to know that just because a girl takes her dress off, doesn't mean she wants to have sex."

"I know." But I didn't.

"I just didn't want to get it dirty."

"Sure."

"Not that I would never want to have sex with you."

"No?"

"Yes."

"When?"

"I don't know. Maybe tonight. Maybe years from now."

"Are you just saying that to make sure I let you in to the party?"

"The Russian Army couldn't keep me out of that party."

"Then I will cancel their invitation."

"I am serious."

"So am I."

"Too serious," she said. Then she stood up.

"Where are you going?" I asked.

"Home."

"Please don't. Sit a while longer. I'll lighten up."

"Promise?"

"See?" I put on a ridiculous grin. "Smiling."

She sat back down.

We stared out at the night and I wracked my brain for something un-serious to say.

"Tell me something. Why is it so important that you come to the party?"

"Where were you when John F. Kennedy was shot?"

That threw me into left field.

"I don't know."

"Come on. Everybody knows where they were, if not at the moment, at least when they heard about it."

"Let's see, 1963, I was thirteen, that's junior high school. I don't know. I guess I was in class. I just wasn't paying attention."

"I was there," she said.

"Where?"

"Dallas. Dealey Plaza. I was watching the President and Jackie in the convertible when he got shot."

"Whoa!"

"And let me tell you one thing, he was shot from that grassy knoll. I was just behind it. I saw a gun fired right in front of me. I saw the guy who did it. I took his picture."

"You took his picture? What happened to it?"

"I still got it. I ran home and got the kid and dropped her off at my sister's house and caught the next bus to Austin and I have not looked back since."

"You have a kid?"

"I had two. One didn't make it." I guess there was something in my face because she went on to say, "What? Don't you think whores can have babies?"

"You just look so good for a mother."

"Nice try. Do you have any cigarettes?"

I thought about lying to make myself seem older, more sophisticated, but it wasn't a moment for lying.

"No," I said. "I don't smoke."

"Figured."

"Did you tell anyone about all this? About Dallas and all?"

"At first, yes. But people would just look at me strange, unless, of course they wanted to, uh, date me and even some of them, afterwards, would tell me I was crazy. A few times though, when someone would believe me, I would get scared, like they knew that I knew because they knew, too, and they knew that someone would have to shut us up or maybe they were that someone. When that happened, I usually left town. And changed my name. In Dallas I was Katrina. Now I am Jessi and I just keep my trap shut."

"Why did you tell me?"

"Because it is important that I come to that party and it's important that you know why so you can do your best to introduce me to Bobby."

"I'm not sure I can do that."

"I just said do your best. I want to get rid of that picture. I figure he's the only one I can trust with it. The President's brother. I've tried to get it to him before, but every time, something or someone got in the way. You may be my last chance."

We stared off again.

"What happened to the first kid?" I asked.

"I don't really know. They call it crib death. I came home from work. I was a waitress back then—I was only seventeen—and my husband was there and some emergency medics and some cops. He said he didn't do anything. He was watching the tube and listening for problems from the kid and he looked over once and the kid wasn't moving. He left me shortly after that. I got some papers once in the mail, but I'm not even sure we are divorced."

"How about the second one, the little girl?"

"She's fine. She still lives with her aunt in Dallas. Her dad is a musician. He's always on the road somewhere. I read about him in the papers."

"Who is he?"

"God, you're nosey."

"Newspaperman."

"Yeah, right. More like a newsboy."

"Ouch."

"Get over it. You're younger. I'm older. I'm the one who is supposed to be sensitive about age."

"So who is the musician?" I asked again.

She just shook her head and crushed out her cigarette and flicked it off the roof.

"Come on," she stood up. "Take me home."

"Don't you want to hear the story of my life?"

"What story? You were born here, you grew up here, you are still here."

"How did you know that?"

"Mack and I talk between sets."

"I thought you didn't know he was my father."

"I knew he had a kid. I just didn't expect it to be you. I like your father. He's a good man. Like I said, you ought to give him a break." She walked back toward the window. I stood up. My legs were stiff, almost asleep. I followed her through the window. She was standing in the middle of the attic again.

"In the yellow bag," I said. She went to the bag and got out her dress and put it back on.

"You know you are welcome to crash here," I offered.

"Yeah, I know. But I'm not going to."

"I won't try anything."

She turned her back to me and I took the hint and crossed to her and zipped up her dress.

"I know that, too. And that would probably piss me off almost as much as if you did try something." And I thought I was confused before.

I didn't know where my keys were, so we took the Jeep again. We didn't talk at all. She spent the whole ride smoking and staring out the side. That was fine. I had no idea what to say anyway and it actually felt kind of nice just riding with her in silence. I was too young to know then that it is the woman that you can just be quiet around that is the one worth keeping, but even then, I suspected that ride was something rare and wonderful.

When I parked in the Sands lot, I opened her door like a gentleman and she slid her legs out of the Jeep primly together like a lady. She stood up and arched her back and looked at me as though she were trying to make up her mind about something. Then she placed her hand gently on my cheek and kissed me lightly on the lips.

"Good night, Ethan," she whispered. I knew enough this time not to grab her and she walked off and disappeared around the side of the motel.

I knew I wasn't in love, but it was the next best thing.

When I opened the door to my bedroom, I saw LJ sitting on my bed wearing the Dodgers hat and my blue Oxford shirt and as far as I could tell, nothing else.

"LJ!"

"Who's the bimbo?"

"What bimbo?" I asked even though I knew.

"The blonde."

"She's not a bimbo."

"She's a blonde; she's a bimbo," said the brunette sitting near naked on my bed.

"What are you doing here?" I still hadn't moved from the doorway.

"Well, I was walking along Main Street and this sudden gust of wind came and blew all my clothes off, so I jumped into your Corvair and drove over here so I could borrow your shirt."

I just stared at her.

"We had a date. Tonight. I was to return your Corvair and we were going to work on your problem."

"What problem?"

She kind of shook her head and crossed her eyes.

"Your virginity problem. But it looks like you already solved it."

"What? No. Jessi? No. We didn't. I didn't. But we were? You and me? We were going to?"

She swung her legs, and what legs, off of the bed and stood up. Yep. Just the shirt.

"You don't remember? Last night? Anything?"

"Well, yeah, now that you mention it . . ."

"You haven't a clue." She scooped up a pair of jeans and off the floor and put them on without flashing me an inch. "You got drunk, passed out and forgot everything!"

"Well, yeah."

"Jesus H!" she said. She pushed past me and slammed my bedroom door behind her.

I opened the door and shouted after her as she ran down the stairs. "Do you need a ride?"

"Nah," I heard from below. "I still have your car keys."

"What the hell was that?" Rick was standing at the end of the hall in just his boxers.

"I just spent the night with two almost naked women and I still haven't been laid."

"Huh," Rick said. "I think you may have just set some sort of a record." He turned back toward his bedroom and then he called over his shoulder. "Uncle Pete wants to see you again. There's a note on the kitchen table."

CHAPTER 19

The Hotel Room

Tuesday April 30, 1968

The next morning I put my romantic difficulties somewhere in the back of my head and I parked Rick's Jeep next to a huge ancient white Chrysler Imperial and then knocked on the door to room 146 of the Ramada Inn.

The first words out of his mouth when he opened the door were "What are you drinking?" I was amazed by his cheerfulness after last night's run-in with Dear Old Dad. Then I saw the reason why.

His motel room was hangover heaven. He had the floor unit air conditioner going full blast. His dresser was covered with all the major booze groups and mixers. A Coors ice chest was filled with Coors beer, rare in Indiana in 1968. A cornucopia of pills was spilled across his nightstand.

He had cleaned the blood off of his face and head, but he hadn't shaved and I suspect he hadn't bathed either. Not that he smelled bad, unless you dislike the stench of the boozer's best friends, Aqua Velva and Listerine.

He was wearing jeans and a white, sleeveless t-shirt that for some reason is called "a wife-beater." Once again I was amazed at what good shape he was in. He was a muscled guy in his upper arms and shoulders. Mack was lucky to take him by surprise, although luck had little to do with it. When you are Mack's size and you are constantly taking on guys Pete's size, surprise is a favorite strategy.

I smelled no marijuana under the after-shave and booze odors so I asked Pete if he had run out of dope. "I smoke marijuana," he replied (he pronounced it Mare-hee-hwanna, giving it a supposed Mexican lilt), "when I want to see the beauty in life. I get drunk when I want to dodge life's crap."

After he fixed us a pair of screwdrivers, the usual proportions of vodka and orange juice cheerfully reversed, he sat in a chair next to the pharmaceutical nightstand, popped a couple speckled pills and propped his feet up on the bed. I found a chair and dragged it over to the pseudo-bar. I nursed my drink and he guzzled his and we looked everywhere but at each other until Pete threw out the opening gambit.

"You probably don't like me very much," he said.

He waited for me to say something and when I didn't, he asked, "Do you?"

"Do I what?" I asked.

"Like me."

I gave in. When in doubt, tell the truth. "No, Pete, I guess I don't."

"Don't blame you," he said graciously, waving his drink and slopping it on the ugly purple carpet. "I took your barstool. I beat up your father." He paused as if waiting for me to correct him. I didn't bother. "But like me or not, you gotta respect me."

I sipped my screwdriver and thought, "Why do I have to respect a tired old drunk?" And then he answered my thought.

"Ten years ago when Civil Rights was just a folk song, who do you think went down to Alabama and covered it when no major news service would even acknowledge there was a problem? Me. Me and a guy named Gene Shales from Oregon. Ever hear of him?"

"No," I said. And I hadn't.

"Yazoo City, Greenville, Greenwood, Green Hell, Mississippi, we were there. And then there was that bombing of the *Delta Democrat-Times* in 1962. Do you remember that?"

"I think so," I said trying to humor him.

"No you don't!" He shouted. "You know why you don't?"

Because I was too young? I thought. Because when I was twelve, I was too interested in comic books and baseball cards and not what was happening three states away? Or because the Indiana press didn't care then and six years later they still didn't? But I managed to keep my mouth shut. I just shook my head and hoped that would do. It did.

"Because it didn't happen!" Pete leaned forward and whispered intently. "It never goddamned happened! Because Gene and I stopped it. We stopped it dead. *The Democrat Times* was the only liberal newspaper in the south. The only goddamned liberal, nigger-loving, lynching-hating newspaper in the south and it was right in the middle of the Mississippi goddamned Delta. Of course they wanted to blow it up. They wanted to blow it up, burn it down and bury the ashes. Gene and I found out about the plan when we were sitting in this jail up in Clarksdale. They put us in with this old redneck drunk."

He took a drink.

"As usual in those towns, Gene would keep his Yankee mouth shut and I would do all the talking in my thickest drawl. And this guy thought we were somebody important because we were in our coats and ties and he figured if somebody important was in jail with him it had to be because someone had found out about the bombing."

Pete paused and looked around blankly as though he had not only forgotten what he was talking about, but where he was and what I was doing there. Then he picked out a few more pills, swallowed them with his last slug of Smirnoff and OJ and continued.

"And that was all I needed to know. I didn't ask him what bombing, or something stupid like that. No, sir, I am a seasoned journalist." He stood up and walked over to the dresser. "Want another?" he asked me.

"No thanks," I said holding up my half-filled glass.

"Here, give that to me," Pete said. He tried to take my glass but instead he knocked it out of my hand and it crashed against the dresser. The broken pieces fell into an empty drawer.

"Oops," he said. "Don't worry. Plenty more where that came from." He picked up another hotel water glass and began splashing vodka and orange juice into it. He handed it back to me with no ice.

"Where was I?"

"You were being a seasoned journalist," I said. I sat back down. I didn't bother to add ice. I didn't bother to take a drink. Pete didn't notice. He dropped some Coors ice cubes in his drink and returned to his chair.

"Yeah, a seasoned journalist knows when to keep his mouth shut and not ask questions. I knew this was one of those times. I just nodded and grunted like the redneck rat prick knew exactly what my business was and he just laid the whole thing out for us. You see, it was right around the time James Meredith decided he wanted to go to school with the white kids at Ole Miss, right around the end of June, first of July. I remember cause this guy was talking about giving Hodding Carter a fourth of July he wouldn't forget."

I had to ask.

"Who is Hodding Carter?"

"Jesus, boy, you don't know who Hodding Carter is?"

I shook my head.

"He is just the greatest civil rights newspaperman in the twentieth century! He had been giving racists a hotfoot with his Delta newspaper since 1947 when he won the Pulitzer Prize. So by '62, the rednecks were really fed up and ready to do something about him and his paper. You see, Hodding had this rival, a segregationist newspaper up in the northwest part of the state, run by a cigar-chomping racist named. . ."

"Raymond Varnado."

"Our boy in the photo. And it just so happened that a bombing specialist had showed up in Raymond's little town of Sardis, Mississippi, a fellow who showed up because it seems he was running away from a bad marriage and some union troubles up in Indiana. Raymond decided to hire this fella to blow up the *Delta Democrat-Times*."

"You're talking about my father, again, aren't you?"

"The one and the same."

"You know I don't believe any of the crap you say about him. You're just pissed off because he kicked you in the head and stopped you from beating on a woman last night."

At this Pete looked directly at me. His eyes seemed to clear up and his hands quit shaking as he pointed his forefinger at the bridge of my nose. "I hate your father, but that's not why."

"What? You hate him because you think he planned to blow up some newspaper five years ago?"

"No," Pete said quietly and it was the soft tone in his voice that made me want to listen.

"Then what?"

"First, let me tell you what Gene and I found out."

"You mean what this drunk guy told you in a jail cell?" I dipped the words in sarcasm.

"Yeah. And what Gene and I tracked down through some contacts we had in the Klan and the FBI, which were pretty much the same thing in those days."

"The Klan and the FBI?"

"They were both so infiltrated that you didn't know where one began and the other ended. Agents kept arresting other agents. Damn embarrassing." He chuckled, took a drink and stared up at the ceiling again. The silence grew until I interrupted it.

"So you spoke to someone in the FBI."

He kept looking at the ceiling, but he started talking again.

"Right, and when we contacted the Feds, we got a direct order through the magazine to keep our nose out of J. Edgar's business, that we were interfering with a major covert operation. Major covert bullshit! The FBI knew that the Klan had hired your daddy to blow up Hodding. They <u>wanted</u> your Daddy to blow up Hodding. Hodding was a pain in the ass for everybody. He didn't care who he attacked as long as he was right and they were wrong—a very dangerous position for any journalist. You're gonna find out that in this business there are all kinds of devils out there and if you are gonna lock horns with one of them, you better have two or three of the others backing you up, or else you gonna find yourself frying in four kinds of hell. You gotta pick your enemies as carefully as you pick your friends, if you're gonna survive in this game."

He stopped again as if he were giving his mouth a chance to catch up with his brain. He got up a little unsteadily and walked over to his sporacket hanging on the closet door handle. He rummaged around the inside pockets and then looked over at me.

"You got any smokes, boy?"

"No," I said. He nodded and walked around the room looking through pockets and in drawers as he spoke.

"You see what the Feds were aiming for was a grand slam. Blow up the paper, no more Hodding. Catch your daddy, no more Teamster bomber. Connect Varnado, knock off a Klan Grand Dragon."

"I take it that didn't happen."

"Nope."

"Why not?"

"Me and Gene. First we went to Hodding. Told him what was up. Then Hodding got on the phone and called Washington, DC. You know who he talked to?"

He stopped searching for a cigarette and towered over me.

"Who?" I asked.

"The Attorney General of the United States of America, Robert Francis Kennedy. I don't know what happened next, but the *Democrat-Times* did not go boom and Hodding is still in Greenville blasting holes in every demon he sees."

"So what do you have against my father? Even if he is who you say he is, he didn't do anything."

"He killed Gene."

"What?"

"The son of a bitch killed one of the finest newspapermen who ever lived and my best friend."

"Oh, come on."

Pete just stood there over me and stared. There was something in his stare. I had to ask the next question.

"How?"

"Car bomb. You see just because Hodding and his newspaper were safe and sound, Gene and I were not satisfied. We were onto a story, a great story that would bring every news agency in the world down on that little redneck corner of the world. But we needed more proof. So we backtracked to the source. We drove our Ford Fairlane into Varnado's backyard, into Sardis, itself. Gene's plan, as he put it, was to shake all the banana trees and wait for the tarantula to fall out. The first thing we did was go around to all the speakeasies and ask about Klan activity."

"Speakeasies?"

"Oh, yeah, Mississippi was dry until 1966. If you wanted to do your drinking in public, it had to be in private 'clubs.' These could be found in the back of gas stations, above general stores. We even found one in the basement of a church. Jesus saves, but moonshine pays the bills. It was in the basement of that Baptist church that I first met Mack Taylor. He was sitting at the far corner of this makeshift bar they had thrown up over some shuffleboard courts. Gene was going on in his loud Yankee accent, pretending he was drunk. The fact is, he never drank. He'd order a beer and hold on to it and get louder and louder as if it were his third or fourth. I saw many a cracker bartender look perplexed like maybe he had been serving more beers than he could remember. Of course, I drank some, but not much. Not in those days. And hell, I don't think I had even smelled marijuana. So we sat there with Gene screaming about nigger this and nigger that, hoping to attract some Klan attention when your daddy kind of ambled over from his corner. I remember every word the son of a bitch said to Gene."

"'You ain't no Klan,' he told Gene. "You a newspaperman or a cop. You' too soft to be a cop, so you must be a newspaperman. A Yankee newspaperman. You best get on home, Yankee newspaperman, or else someone gonna send you back dere in a coffee can.' And the strange thing was he said all this in the thickest Cajun accent. I remember because I thought, 'This Irish bastard doesn't look like any Cajun I have ever seen.' And I have seen plenty. Anyway, so then Gene looks him in the eye and says, 'Coffee can? How are you gonna send me home in a coffee can?' And your daddy says, 'Cause dat's gonna be all dat's left a you dat fit in nothin' but a coffee can, you stay round here.'

"The next morning Gene turned on the ignition and he and that Ford Fairlane were blown into the next county. The Feds said someone had put dynamite under the seat just to make sure that there would be nothing left of the corpse. Not even enough to fit in a coffee can. Their exact words."

Pete paused to take a sip.

"I had stayed late in that church after Gene had left and was sleeping it off in the motel room. I spent a week looking for Mack Taylor, but he had flown the coop. And so had Raymond Varnado. And funny thing, here they are together again the day Bobby Kennedy is coming to town."

Then he sang, "You better not pout, you better not shout."

Pete sat back down and smiled as if he had won some grand debate. I wanted to blow it off. The whole story. My boss, my father, the bombings, but one thing just stuck in my head. Pete said Mack was speaking in a thick Cajun accent, just like he did when I was a kid.

"So what has all this got to do with me?" I asked.

"Hell, I just wanted you to know it wasn't anything personal against you when I see that your Daddy and your boss spend the rest of their lives in prison."

"What? For an unsolved murder six years ago? That was another time, another state, and as far as I know, some other people."

"I'm not talking about then. I'm talking about now. Here. Port Gibson. When your daddy tries to kill Bobby Kennedy, I am going to be ready for him."

"Thanks." I stood up.

"Just wanted you to know."

"I thought you had something important to tell me, not this hypothetical fairy tale."

"Oh, I do. Tonight at your party? Don't stand too close to Bobby."

The same thing Mack told me at the VFW. The same thing Quasi said.

And then there was a knock at the door. Well, actually, it was more of a pounding. And then a voice.

"Decker! Open up!" It was a loud growl, like Anthony Quinn in *Requiem for a Heavyweight*.

"Oh, hell," said Pete.

"Friend of yours?" I asked.

"Business associate."

The pounding started again. "Decker!"

"He doesn't sound friendly. You want to try jumping out the window?"

"Just open the door before I have to buy Mr. Ramada a new one."

I opened the door. I was right. Bruno. And beside him was his twin brother, Elmer. They were not here to play Password.

"What the hell are you doing here?" Bruno asked me.

"Tending bar," I said. "What can I get you?"

"Nothing," Bruno said and he pushed me behind the door.

"Hello, fellas," I heard a voice say. "What's up?" It sounded like Pete's voice, only it was ten times more drunk than Pete had been just a few moments ago. I looked around Elmer and I saw Pete slumped in his chair, his chin resting on his chest. He had a silly half-grin on his face.

"You better not pout, you better not shout," the voice sang.

I shut the door and watched the show.

"Aw geez," said Elmer in a ridiculously high voice. "He's snockered."

"Get on a shirt, Decker. It's time to go," said Bruno.

"Go where? Where go? Where to go?"

Bruno walked over to the closet and grabbed a white short-sleeved button-down and threw it to Pete.

"So what brings you here, paperboy?" Bruno asked me.

"Just checking out a story."

"Well, story time is over. Beat it."

"Jesus, Bruno, who writes your dialogue? Damon Runyon?" I have got to get that mouth fixed.

I looked over at Pete to see if I got a chuckle. He wasn't laughing. Elmer had dragged him to his feet and was stuffing one arm into the shirt. His drunk act was better than Foster Brooks.

Bruno sighed heavily as if he were having a bad thug day.

"I don't got time to teach you lessons. Just get the hell outta here."

I decided that discretion was the better part and opened the door.

"Are you going to be all right, Pete?"

"Fine, fine," Pete said. He waved both arms at me limply. "These guys are my friends," he slurred.

"Yeah, we're your buddies, Pete. He'll be all right. We're just gonna throw some coffee in him and take him to see his boss. Right, Pete?"

"Right." Pete fumbled with his buttons.

"All right," I said. "Bye, Pete."

I walked out the door.

"And kid," I heard Bruno say.

I stopped but I didn't turn around.

"I don't like running in to you like this all the time. It makes me suspicious. You don't want me to be suspicious."

"Sure," I said, my back still toward him.

"No, kid. I run into you again, I'm gonna make like a truck."

I just walked out into the sunlight and closed Pete's door. "Gonna make like a truck?" I asked myself. What was that supposed to mean?

CHAPTER 20

Lj

I sat behind the wheel of Rick's Jeep.

I was frustrated, angry, depressed, horny and feeling more than a little pushed around.

I wanted, I wanted, I wanted. I wanted to punch somebody, preferably someone who wouldn't turn around and shoot me. I wanted to have sex with someone, preferably someone I liked. Jessi. LJ. Even Sarah Brown.

Well, maybe not Sarah Brown.

LJ. I wanted to talk to her. Find out what really happened the other night. Find out if we had a shot at anything, not just sex. Find out who she was, where she was and where was my Corvair, goddammit! I was tired of wheeling around town in a Jeep like Sergeant Fury and his Howling Commandos!

But I couldn't do any of those things so I banged on the steel steering wheel a little. That hurt, so I drove from the Ramada to the paper like a madman. That didn't hurt, but it didn't help either.

I filed my fantasy "Man in the Street" interviews and "Tina's Sunday School Relaxation and Bible Massage" story.

Varnado didn't even read the stories. He handed the sheets to a copy boy and said, "All right, now I want you to go back out to McNeil auditorium and do the beauty pageant story I wanted from you two days ago."

"They're rehearsing the beauty pageant at McNeil Auditorium?" I asked.

LJ, I thought.

"Yeah, the wife is out there and she's been banging on me to get something in tomorrow's paper so let's get it right this time."

"Mrs. Varnado?" I asked.

And LJ, I thought.

"Yeah! What's wrong with you? Get outta here!"

I was moving.

"And take a camera!"

I stopped off at The Mansion and got Rick to give me a ride. I wanted my car back and I was determined to get it.

The Nicholson Academy for Girls, NAG to all its friends and alumni, had one of the most beautiful campuses in the world. It was almost a thousand acres on the east shore of Lake Masterson. It had stately Greek revival class buildings and three soaring brick dorms centered by McNeil Auditorium, which doubled as a chapel.

Rick pulled into the parking lot behind McNeil Auditorium. I didn't see my green Corvair. I saw academy girls going in and out of the stage door at the side of the building carrying bunting and chairs. Rick saw the girls and wanted to help, but I brushed him off. I didn't want that hound within a mile of LJ.

I got out of the Jeep and joined the stream flowing into the building. The stage door led to four steps that led to an offstage storage area that stored a gutted grand piano and a coke machine. From there I went through double doors to the theatre's wings.

The stage was insane. A parade of girls in shorts and jeans and leotards and NAG- plaid skirted uniforms snaked around in a disjointed chorus line, waving and sort-of smiling. Other girls were putting up the patriotic bunting I had seen at the VFW on platforms that formed a "U" shape around the sides and back. Lights were going on and off. Guys from the college and the high school were putting up ramps to the platforms. Musicians were tuning up in the pit. Lots of people were standing around smoking cigarettes and talking.

Mrs. Varnado was standing in the middle, waving her arms and screaming, "Smile, girls, smile! Lift those legs! Smile!"

I walked out on to the stage and waved my huge camera at Mrs. Varnado. She saw me and distractedly waved back and then looked away and then did a double take and screamed at the top of her lungs, "Nooooooooo!"

Everything stopped. Everyone looked at Mrs. V.

"No pictures! Not now! We're not ready! I married a moron!"

She stormed over to me and everyone shifted his and her attention in my direction.

"Later!" she screamed. "Tonight! When we have costumes! When we have makeup! When we have a set!"

"But Mr. Varnado said you wanted it in tomorrow's paper."

"I do!" Every word was a shout even though no one else was making a peep.

"To make tomorrow's paper, I have to take pictures now."

"Football games!" she shouted.

"What?" I asked.

"Football games! Football games are at night. Pictures from football games are in the next day's paper! Tell my idiot husband that we are a football game! Come back tonight! Now everyone, build, practice, rehearse!"

The cacophony resumed.

"I can't be here tonight!" I shouted.

"Of course you can! Are those ramps ready? You work for my husband! Up those ramps, girls! You will be here!"

The girls paraded up the ramps. One guy got his fingers stomped and screamed bloody murder.

"You can't be here tonight, either!" I yelled.

"Of course I will be here tonight! It's my flipping pageant! My dress rehearsal! Why wouldn't I be here?"

"Tonight is Bobby Kennedy's reception."

"Noooooooooooo!"

Everything stopped again.

"Aren't you going to be at the reception?" I asked.

"I am. I am going to be at the reception. I have to be at the reception. Senator Kennedy is coming to town."

My head heard, "You better not pout, you better not shout."

"This is the biggest thing ever. In town. This town. I have to be there. I am the editor's wife. My great, great grandfather was a Gibson. My family founded this town. When dignitaries show up in this god forsaken, flea bitten burg, every hundred years, I have to be there!"

"So . . ."

"So we have to have a dress rehearsal! Now! This afternoon! Girls! Go get your dresses! Go get your bathing suits! Makeup! Makeup! Makeup! Now! Build that set! Drape that bunting! Musicians—get ready to start in a half hour!" People started running off and running on. The musicians wandered off to do whatever they did before they did what they do.

Mrs. Varnado looked off into the house above the balcony.

"LJ!"

"Yes, Ma'am," LJ's electronically amplified voice came back.

"When will our lights be ready?"

"They're ready now, ma'am."

"LJ?" I asked. "Who is LJ?"

"The academy's lighting technician," said Mrs. Varnado. "She's only a sophomore, but she's really good. Californian, I think. Movies."

Only a sophomore?

"Where is she?"

Mrs. Varnado pointed up. "In the lighting booth."

"How do I get there?"

I climbed up a three-story ladder backstage. Walked, crawled and panicked on a dozen narrow catwalks eighty feet above the ground and arrived breathless at the glassed-in lighting booth suspended over the auditorium. The door was locked. I could see LJ in her dodger shirt and hat and cutoffs sitting on a stool over a dimmer board furiously puffing on a handmade cigarette and pushing sliders up and down. The lights in the empty theater were going on and off like a kaleidoscope.

I knocked on the door. She ignored me. I knocked again. She looked at me, smiled, and then flipped me the finger. I made a pathetic face. She flipped me two fingers. Both hands. I got down on my knees and pressed against the glass like Dustin Hoffmann in church.

She came to the door, opened it and looked down at me. "So, you saw *The Graduate.*" A cloud of marijuana smoke escaped and moved toward the ceiling.

"I love movies."

"Who doesn't?" she asked and went back to her stool. "Go away." She put out the joint in an ashtray.

"You love movies, too. I remember that from our conversation." I didn't really remember, but I figured, California girl, lighting, what Mrs. Varnado said . . .

"What else do you remember?"

I moved across the lighting booth floor on my knees. It was made of the same webbed steel as the catwalks. It hurt like hell, but I figured she would have to know that and I might get sympathy points.

I could see in her eyes that I did.

"I remember that I was a drunken asshole and I said some incredibly stupid things."

"I thought you were incredibly honest and vulnerable," she said. The light booth smelled like Bob Marley's birthday party.

"That, too."

"Get up. That can't be comfortable."

"It's not."

I stood up.

"What are you doing here?"

"I came here to find you."

"And take pictures." She brought up a circle of light on where I had left my camera onstage.

"A secondary motivation."

"And get your car."

"A tertiary motivation."

"Tertiary." She smiled again.

"Are you still mad at me?"

"What? About the blonde?"

"What blonde?"

"Good answer. What about the blackout?"

"What blackout?" I looked at her wide-eyed. "I don't remember a blackout."

"You jerk."

"Look, LJ, it was the moonshine and nervousness and trying to impress you, it will never happen again. I usually don't even drink."

"Nothing?"

"Beer sometimes. But no more moonshine. No more hard liquor of any kind. Promise."

"You don't have to promise that."

"I do."

"LJ!" Mrs. Varnado's voice crackled over a small speaker in the booth.

LJ pressed a switch and spoke into a microphone.

"Yes, ma'am." She kept her dark eyes on me.

"I need general lighting."

"Yes, ma'am." She ran up some dimmers.

"Thank you," said Mrs. Varnado.

LJ stood up and took my hand.

"C'mon."

She led me out of the booth.

"Where are we going?" I asked.

"To get you laid."

I stopped stock-still. She looked up at my eyes.

"I'm sorry. I shouldn't kid about that. I guess I'm still a little pissed."

"Okay," I said.

"We're going to get your car."

"Then am I going to get laid?"

She laughed and pulled on my arm.

Behind and to the left of the lighting booth was a metal circular staircase. We went down the stairs, down, down, down the stairs. They descended into a long narrow space between two walls lit by faint blue lights. They ended at a concrete piece of floor about four feet by eight feet next to a steel door. On the other side of the door was the sound of musicians warming up. She pointed.

"That's the auditorium."

I nodded. She walked to a ladder attached to the wall at the far end of the 4X8 space. She got on the ladder and climbed into a dark hole.

"C'mon," she said.

Oh, my God, I thought. She has buried my Corvair. I followed her awkwardly down the ladder. I barely fit.

We descended into darkness and then into light. It was a cavernous room with piles of lumber and canvas flats and anachronistic furniture and other theatrical set pieces. There was a cage with tools and several different kinds of table saws and a huge freight elevator in the far wall, and parked next to a large overhead door, my Corvair.

I hung on the ladder taking it all in. LJ hopped on to the floor.

"Cool, huh?"

"Yeah," I said and climbed on down.

"My own Bat Cave."

She pushed a large green button on the wall. The overhead door lifted opening on a ramp that went steeply up to the parking lot behind the auditorium.

She reached in her pocket and took out my keys and handed them to me.

"Thanks for the Batmobile."

"You're welcome."

She cocked her head and looked at me. Something about the gesture caused my heart to flip like a pancake.

"You're sweet. Kinda slow, but sweet."

She climbed up the ladder a few rungs.

"Now, park your car outside, go take your photos and meet me after dress rehearsal at the boathouse."

"Which boathouse?"

"The academy boathouse. Drive across campus to the lake. Follow the drive along the shore until you come to a house that looks like a boat. I'll be on the roof."

"How will I get on the roof?"

She smiled that smile and said, "You'll figure it out, Ploughboy. Oh, and close the overhead door after you leave. I rigged a remote next to your steering wheel."

And she went up the ladder. I stood staring at her, feeling all warm and giddy and romantic.

But I couldn't take my eyes off of her ascendant butt.

I was pretty sure she was aware of that.

CHAPTER 21

The Boathouse

It didn't look like a boathouse, it looked like a ship, or to be precise, the bridge of a ship. It was a large, sprawled out, white single story with round portholes for windows on the side. The front was glassed in to give a spectacular view of the lake. On the roof was a replica of a pilothouse with long cantilevered walks stretching out on either side with metal stanchions supporting huge chains on the walks around the roof itself. There were even two lifeboats. LJ waved from the front of the roof. The cutoffs and the t-shirt were gone. She was wearing a white two-piece bathing suit with the Dodgers hat. I hadn't realized until then how tan she was.

Oh, boy.

She had been looking through a brass telescope on a stand. I had hoped she had been looking for me, but the telescope was pointed dead-on Mafia Island.

There was no trick to getting up to her. Another metal ladder was placed between the third and fourth porthole. As I walked up behind her, she was still looking through the telescope.

"I think I see your Uncle Pete," she said.

Uncle Pete? How did she know about Uncle Pete?

"Look," she said stepping away from the telescope.

I bent over and looked through it. There was Uncle Pete all right. He was on the dock with Bruno and Elmer and wearing the same clothes they had poured him into this morning. He seemed sober. He was talking earnestly to a tall man wearing black wrap-around sunglasses, a straw fedora and a beige suit.

"See the sunglasses on the guy with the hat?"

"Yes."

"Two thousand a pair."

Two thousand bucks for sunglasses? I thought. How did she know that? I knew nothing about this girl.

Then I felt her lean against my back. I watched Pete shake hands with two-grand sunglasses. I saw the guy hug Pete and kiss him on the cheek. Then Pete got into the boat with Bruno. Elmer stayed on the dock. Then I felt two hands snake themselves into my front jeans' pockets.

This completely foreign gesture was amazingly intimate, amazingly erotic.

"God, you're awfully tall." LJ rubbed her cheek deeply into my back. I didn't move. I didn't breathe. I did not want to break this thing, this posture, this moment, and this spell.

Then LJ sighed and pulled her hands out of my pockets and her body from my back.

"What's happening out there?" she asked

"Pete is in the boat with Bruno heading toward the marina."

"Bruno from the massage parlor?"

I stepped back from the telescope and looked at her.

"You told me all about Uncle Pete and Bruno and Jessi the night of our little party. You forgot about that, too?"

"Yeah, I'm sorry."

"You've already apologized. Come sit with me in the lifeboat."

"The lifeboat?"

"Yeah, we can pretend we are the last survivors from a sunken vessel alone in an empty ocean."

She climbed into a lifeboat. I followed with less climbing and more just lifting one long leg after the other. We sat next to each other in the stern of the boat. She suddenly seemed very nervous. We sat there for what seemed like six hours, rigid and quiet.

"He's not really my Uncle Pete," I finally said.

"No?"

"No. I just call him that. He's my roommate's uncle."

"I have an uncle like that. Uncle John. Close friend of my father's. No relation. John Frankenheimer."

"The movie director?"

"You've heard of him?"

"Are you kidding? *The Manchurian Candidate*? *Seven Days in May*?"

She started to relax.

"I thought, you know, Indiana," she said.

"We have movie theatres in Indiana. Well, two."

"None of my classmates know who he is. I started talking about him in social studies and everyone looked at me like I was from Mars."

"I'm kind of a movie buff."

"Me, too."

Another couple of hours of silence passed.

"Ethan, that man with that guy who is not your Uncle Pete?"

"The two-thousand-dollar sunglasses."

"Yeah. He looked a lot like Sam Giancana."

"The Chicago gangster?"

"Yes."

"How would you know what Sam Giancana looks like?"

"We have newspapers in California. Well, two."

"Still, not many people would recognize . . ."

"My family owns one of those newspapers."

"In Los Angeles."

"I'm expected to keep up with things."

Who is this woman and how did I get so lucky as to be sitting next to her in the middle of an empty ocean?

She inhaled deeply and said, "I know who Sam Giancana is. I know a lot of people think he had John F. Kennedy assassinated. Now I know that he may be in the same town as Robert Kennedy. Ethan, what is going on with you and Uncle Pete and Bobby?"

So I told her about last night and this morning and my father and the teamsters and Mr. Varnado and Jessi and Dallas and the party at The Mansion. I guessed I may have told her some of this before, but I covered all the bases and she didn't interrupt me. I didn't realize how much I needed someone to talk to until I felt this huge relief when I was finished.

"Wow," she said. "No wonder you don't have time to get laid."

"I guess." Lame, but it was all that came out. A fortnight passed and she scooted over next to me. I smelled a very light, but distinctive and intoxicating perfume. She put her hand on my knee as she stared dreamily out at the lake.

"Ever since I got here, I've been wanting to make it with someone on the roof of the boathouse. I just didn't know with whom," she said.

How could I not fall in love with a girl who used "whom" properly when she talked about sex?

I tried to laugh it off. "I hope I'm your first choice."

"You don't get it, do you, Ploughboy? You are my only choice."

"Mrs. Varnado says you're a sophomore."

Lame, lame, lame.

"Uh-huh." She moved off the lifeboat seat and sat down in the bottom of the boat.

"That makes you, what? Fifteen?"

Stupid, stupid, stupid. No wonder I was a virgin.

"Yesterday. Today I am sixteen."

"It's your birthday," was all I could manage to say.

"Uh-huh. Sixteen. Old enough to drive, legally. Old enough to do a lot of things legally in Indiana." She took off her Dodgers hat. Her hair tumbled out to her shoulders.

"But still . . . You're awfully young."

"I'm older than I was the other night when you kissed me."

"I kissed you?" I blurted out.

"Uh-huh," she smiled. "Among other things."

"But we didn't."

"Not yet."

Then she took off her bathing suit top.

"Come down here," she said.

I slid off the seat and lay down next to her. She unbuttoned my shirt as she sang: "Happy birthday to me. Happy birthday to me."

She explained to me everything she needed to have done. She explained thoughtfully and gently and rewarded me subtly with her pleasure and mine. It was, of course, the way I thought lovemaking was supposed to be because I had nothing, outside of magazines and paperbacks, to compare it to and yet it was the only way that lovemaking should have been and was never quite to be again with LJ or anyone else. Never was there a more willing and acquiescent student or a more enthusiastic and patient teacher than on that boat-like building under that full sail of clouds by that northern Indiana lake.

Shortly after, bells started going off all over the building. JC sat up abruptly and started throwing on her bathing suit.

"Chapel!"

"On a Tuesday?"

"Every night at good old NAG. If I miss one more then they are going to boot me out of here. Then where will we be, Ploughboy?"

I started putting on my clothes. Not easy if you are six-six in the bottom of an eightfoot lifeboat.

She clambered over the side. I just had my shirt and underwear on. I stuck my head above the gunwale.

"When will I see you again?"

"Oh, look at that face," she said and kissed me. A long, nice kiss. "Don't worry, Ploughboy. We are now an item. Since I am no longer jailbait, I can be your date tonight at the party."

"Should I pick you up?"

"It's almost eight. You have enough to worry about. I'll get there."

"I'll tell the cops to let you in."

"Are you kidding? I was on the invitation list before you knew there was a list."

And then she kissed me again.

Then she said, "Oh, and my real name is Layla Joan, but if you ever call me that, I will have to kill you."

Then the smile. Then she was gone.

CHAPTER 22

The Party

It was a quarter past nine by the time I got to the house. I had to park at the newspaper because every inch of The Mansion's drive and parking oval were covered with cars and two Copiah County Deputy Sheriffs were keeping people from parking on Main Street.

"Can't I park here?" I had asked one of the guys in a brown uniform and a tan cowboy hat. "That's my house."

"Sorry, kid," said the deputy, who wasn't much older than I was. "No parking on the street. Security."

I wasn't sure what not parking in front of my house had to do with security, but my mama always taught me never to argue with a man who has the legal right to carry a gun so I drove to the newspaper parking lot and walked back.

The grounds of The Mansion looked like Barnum and Bailey lived there. White-coated caterers swarmed in and out of the circus tent like roustabouts. Every city cop in town stood every ten or fifteen feet like stoic clowns. Hundreds of people were milling around in everything from tuxedos to sport jackets to evening gowns to cocktail dresses, each group their own little circus act. Cop cars were parked all over the yard.

The early arrivals were parked in the oval. I saw Mayor Sid's Cadillac parked next to Rick's Mustang and Jeep. And there was Jessi's Firebird. And Mack's truck. What was he doing at Bobby's party? Visions of Teamsters danced in my head.

I was hoping I could slip in through the kitchen and up the back stairs without being noticed, but that was impossible. Mayor Sid and his wife were standing by the pantry screaming at each other as I walked in. Sid was in a brown suit. Mrs. Hamilton was dressed for an evening at the opera. Rick was sitting at the kitchen table looking miserable in a blue pinstripe three-piece. He had a glass of what looked like a Coca-Cola in front of him.

"I distinctly remember telling you black tie," Mrs. Hamilton was yelling at her husband.

"Everyone knows Bobby Kennedy hates black tie," Sid offered weakly.

"I do not care what Bobby Kennedy hates. He is the guest. I am the host. That means I determine what the guests will wear."

"Well, I'm not the only one in a suit," said Sid.

"That's because most all of your friends are as stupid as you!" said Mrs. Hamilton.

When there was a pause in the argument, I asked Rick if he had seen Jessi.

"Got here about an hour ago. She seemed kind of pissed that you weren't around."

"Where is she now?"

"I don't know."

"Bobby?" I asked.

"We are expecting him around ten," Rick said.

"They always wear black tie at the White House," said Mrs. Hamilton.

"Most of the pictures of JFK and Jackie . . ." Sid was still putting up a fight.

"Oh, man," Rick mumbled so only I could hear him. "Not Jackie." He took a swig of his Coke and grimaced.

"And JFK is dead and Jackie is in Greece," said Mrs. H. and then she saw me. "Oh, hi Ethan. How is your momma?"

"She is fine, Mrs. Hamilton. You look terrific this evening."

"Thank you, Ethan, but I feel a tad overdressed thanks to my fashion-numb husband."

"I am sure everything will work out fine. The Senator probably won't even notice."

"Who cares if the Senator notices? I don't give a flying fig about Senator Kennedy or any other Kennedy or any other Democrat in the whole wide world, but the press is here tonight. The *New York Times* and the *Washington Post*. And *Time*. And *Newsweek*. The whole freaking nation is here and the whole freaking nation is going to think that Port Gibson has the fashion sense of a barnyard!"

I couldn't take any more of this. "Yes, ma'am. If you will excuse me, ma'am, I have to get upstairs and change," I said.

"Will you be wearing a tuxedo or a suit?"

"Unfortunately, ma'am, I don't own a tux and no one told me or else I would have rented one." I looked at Rick as though it were all his fault.

"No one told you because no one knew," Rick said.

"I knew," said Mrs. Hamilton. "No one asked."

Rick sat his drink down on the table and I picked it up and took a sip. Just what I thought. Jack Daniels and Coke.

"That Coke tastes kind of funny, Rick. What you got in there?"

"What do you mean?" asked Mr. H.

"Nothing, Pop. It's, uh, not Coke, it's Dr. Pepper."

As Rick was guzzling down the evidence, I slipped out of the kitchen, past a crowd of drinkers in the hall and up the back stairs. As I was hitting the last few steps, I caught a whiff of something, a heavy perfume, Jessi's. My bedroom door was open. So was the door to the attic. I looked inside my room. No one there. The perfume smell was behind me. Over my left shoulder. I went to the attic stairs. The lights were off. I flicked the switch. Nothing happened. I called out. "Anyone up there?" I could hear movement, a rustling sound and some boards creaking, but no one responded. I went into my room and got a flashlight out of my dresser drawer. I turned it on. The batteries were weak, but it would have to do. I returned to the base of the attic stairs. I pointed the faint light upward.

"Hello?" I said. Nothing. But I could smell that perfume. I slowly ascended.

"Jessi?" I asked. Nothing. I moved past the dust-covered landing and turned the corner and up the final flight. "Anyone?" I asked. As I reached the top of the stairs my flashlight flickered out.

"Damn it," I said. It wasn't entirely dark. The lights from the party were reflecting in the four open dormer windows. I looked for deeper shadows in the shadows. I took a couple of steps toward the front window.

"Jessi?" I whispered.

"What?" someone whispered back. My heart stopped. I thought I was going to die.

"Jesus," I managed to say in a remarkably calm voice. "You scared me to death."

Jessi turned on a large flashlight and stuck it under her chin.

"I am the ghost of dentists past."

"Not funny."

"I just wanted to see what kind of man you were, Mack."

"What kind?"

"Not bad. I would have screamed like a banshee." She moved past me toward the front window. I could see her figure outlined against the light. I could tell that she was wearing a dress, but it must have been spray painted on.

"What are you doing up here?" I asked.

"Waiting for the party to fill up. When I first got here there were only a couple dozen people and half of them were my clients. I felt conspicuous."

"Rick's father isn't one of your, uh . . ."

"Sid? No, but he is a sweetheart. I just met him. I don't think Mrs. Hamilton likes me, though." She turned toward me. My eyes had adjusted to the dark and I could see that her dress showed more cleavage than the Grand Canyon.

"I don't see why," I said.

"Honey, if wives start liking me, then it is time to hang up my g-string and move to Salt Lake City."

I moved closer to her. "What's that perfume?"

"L'aire du Temps. Drug store, but top of the line drug store." She sniffed back at me. "Now, that, if I am not mistaken, is Chanel and not the cheap number five crap."

"Really?"

"Yeah, boy, you have been rubbing up against some high-class skin. I think I'm jealous."

I think I blushed.

"It's all right, just take a shower before you head downstairs or else you might find yourself with a boyfriend before the night is done." She headed for the stairs. "I hope she was worth standing me up."

I felt weird, like an adulterous husband. She turned and aimed her flashlight at my face.

"Oh, don't look so sad, newsboy. I'm glad you are getting some. It's good for the complexion. If you want me, I'll probably be downstairs hanging out with your dad."

"Yeah," I said. "What the hell is he doing here?"

"Sid hired him to bartend. Oh, and you might explain to him about the Senator and hyper-sensitive security and all."

"Why?" I asked.

"He's packing." And she winked at me and waved and walked downstairs.

CHAPTER 23

The Gun

For two days I have been wondering what the deal was with the tent. I thought that it was hot enough in the open air without enclosing a couple hundred people in canvas. What I found out when I went looking for Dad was this tent had a door. When I opened the door, I found out that this tent had air conditioning. Air conditioning! A tent! Made you proud to be an American.

I found Jessi talking to Dear Old Dad over by the long institutional tables covered by a white tablecloth that passed for a bar. She was holding a brown drink and smoking a cigarette.

When I came close to her, she took me by the elbow, leaned in and whispered in my ear, "He has it tucked in his belt at the small of his back."

I looked at Dad and wondered what maneuver she used to determine where he kept his gun.

"Hey, boy, what can I fix you?" I heard Dear Old Dad say. Maybe one. Then I thought of LJ and if she saw me drinking again. Where was she?

"Just a coke," I said.

"Ah," said Dad. "The same thing I made for your friends." He filled a glass with Jack Daniels and topped it off with just enough Coke so that it changed color. He handed it to me.

"No," I said. "Just a coke."

"Really? What? Is your mom coming here tonight?"

"No. I just don't feel like drinking."

"Must have been the milkman." He drank down the JD and Coke and refilled the glass with just Coke.

"Can we talk?" I asked him.

"Ain't that what we've been doing?"

"Don't do that redneck thing."

"What redneck thing?"

"Never mind. Can we have a conversation?"

"Sure."

"Outside."

"Depends."

"Depends on what?'

"What we are going to talk about. If we're gonna talk dirty, I want Lacy to hear."

"Please, Dad, it's important."

"Damn, I guess so." Mack turned to Lacy who was working the next institutional table over. "I'm taking a cigarette break with the kid, okay?"

"God, not now, Mack! We are swamped!"

"Thanks. Bye." He was lighting his cigarette and moving toward the tent door. I followed. He went back around the side of the house near where the honeysuckle vines covered a stone fence.

"I love Lacy, but she don't always do what she is told. Cigarette?"

"I don't smoke."

"Good."

"Uh, Dad," I began.

"Uh-oh," Mack said.

"What?"

"That's twice you called me 'Dad'."

"So?"

"You don't call me 'Dad.' I know I have only been back a short time, but in that short time, I have noticed that you never call me 'Dad.'"

"I can call you Dad, can't I? I mean you are my Dad, so what if occasionally I break down and . . ."

"What do you want?"

"You know there are a lot of cops around."

"I know that. Half of them have arrested me at one time or another."

"And when Senator Kennedy shows up, they are probably all going to be pretty high strung."

"Probably."

"So . . ."

"Yeah?"

"It's probably not a good idea to be packing heat."

"What?"

"Packing heat. You know, carrying a gun."

"I know what it means, I just never heard a human being say it in real life."

"So I was hoping that you would give me the gun."

"What makes you think I'm carrying a gun?"

"You were the other night."

"That was when I was at Cisco's."

"So?"

"I always carry a gun at Cisco's."

"But not here?"

"Didn't you notice? Lotta cops here."

"Jessi told me you were carrying. In your belt. Small of your back."

"Damn! And I thought she was feeling me up."

"Dad!"

"That's three times."

"Will you give me your gun?"

"Then won't that mean that you're packing heat?"

"It's my house. I'll put it up. I'll give it back to you tomorrow."

"What if I just put it in my truck?"

"What if I don't trust you?"

He stared me in the eye for a good three count and then he said, "Okay."

"Okay?"

"Okay." And he reached behind his back and then held out his snub-nosed thirty-eight.

"That's it?"

"You don't trust me. You have made that clear on several occasions. I think it is time that you start. I think this might be a beginning."

"Thank you." I almost felt like crying.

"Well, take it, dammit." He was still holding out the gun. I took it and put it in my side coat pocket.

"Be careful, it's loaded," he said.

"I figured."

"Is that it?"

"Well, yeah," I said.

"Then I better get back inside before Lacy starts screaming and pouring whiskey on the floor."

"She does that?"

"Bubba, you don't know." And he smiled and gave me that two-finger salute. I just stood there and watched him go back inside the tent. I was a little stunned.

"I'll be damned! You got it," Jessi said.

I turned around and there she was standing on the other side of the honeysuckle. God, that woman could be everywhere at once.

She looked after Dad.

"That was entirely too easy," she said.

She walked through a gap in the stonewall. She looked at the path Mack had taken back toward the tent.

"So what do you think?" she asked me. "Does he have another gun?"

"You heard the man, it's a matter of trust."

"Yeah," she said. "And I don't trust him."

"Well, I do," I said with some uncertainty. "I have to."

"Yeah, I suppose you do. What are you going to do with the gun?"

"Put it up in my room, I guess."

"You better do it soon. You don't want to be caught with it, either."

"No."

CHAPTER 24

The Congressman

I pushed through the crowd to the house. Just as I reached the stairs in the foyer, a hand grabbed my upper arm. I turned and saw that it was attached to the arm of Congressman Sam Ollestadt.

"There you are," Congressman Ollestadt shouted at me. "I have been looking all over for you!" He was blowing ninety-proof, his eyes were unfocused and he was standing like a sailor in a tempest.

I didn't know what Ollestadt wanted, but whatever it was, I figured it was worth two years of my life to find out.

"Let's go outside!" I shouted back at him. I glanced toward the front room and saw Rick and Sid talking to the Varnados. Mrs. Hamilton had managed to get them both into tuxedos.

With about a dozen "Excuse me's," I managed to get the front door open and slipped out onto the porch. I looked back and Congressman Ollestadt was shaking hands and smiling and moving as quickly and politely and politically as a drunk man could through the body crush.

The front porch was relatively empty. It was a DMZ between the tent and the house. When the Congressman caught up with me, he had somehow acquired another glass of brown liquor. I steered him around the corner of the house to the semicircular part of the porch where the swing hung. I sat on the swing. He more or less collapsed on it next to me.

"Damn fine party," Ollestadt said. "Damn fine. Hate that son of a bitch Kennedy, though. Told him to his face."

"When was that, Congressman?" I asked.

"Just now. Inside. I told him he was a coward. That I fought his damn war in Vietnam. And he was a coward to want to bail out. I told him to his face."

"I don't think so, Congressman. Senator Kennedy hasn't arrived, yet."

"No?" asked the Congressman. "Then who was I talking to?"

"I don't know," I said.

This seemed to worry the Congressman and he pushed the swing back with his feet and let it start swinging. Since I wasn't participating, the swing made more like a tilt-a-whirl rather than a straight back and forth motion. The Congressman didn't like this, so he sort-of jumped/stumbled and flung himself forward out of the swing and grabbed on to one of the Corinthian/Doric columns.

By the time I was able to regain control of the swing and stop its careening motion, the congressman was sitting on the rail with one long arm wrapped around the column like an old war buddy. I sat in the swing, my long legs kept it steady. He shoved his glass toward me as if he were accusing me of murder.

"You know I was in that goddamned war!" he said.

"I heard."

"Yeah, I was. I was damned good at it. War and stuff."

"I bet you were," I said for lack of anything better to say. I was trying to soften him up for the tirade I felt was coming about my conscientious objection.

"Crack shot. Para-jumper-shooter guy. Special Forces. Do you know what the Special Forces are?"

"The Green Berets." Cherchez le Green beret, Uncle Pete had said

"Damn straight. You know what the Special Forces do?"

I could guess a lot of things, but I decided just to shake my head.

"Special stuff. The Special Forces do special stuff. Stuff no one else will do. Stuff that chickenshits like Mr. Attorney General and his star-screwing big cheese brother would never do in a million years but they ordered us to do because we are the Special Forces and you know what we do?"

"Special stuff?" I ventured. CIA stuff, I thought. Is this the guy? Once CIA always CIA?

"Zactly," the Congressman said. "That's why I didn't tell you about all this. I didn't want you to think I was prejudiced against you and your conscientious bullshit just because I was over there doing special stuff."

"Thank you," I said although I had no I idea what I was thanking him for.

"De nada. You know, I don't blame you for not wanting to go over there. Stinking, lousy, shitty war. I was good at it, but I hated it. But we can't quit. Not yet. Can't let all those stinking lousy shitty things we did in that stinking lousy shitty war go for nothing, can we? No! Can't let cowards run things. Tell us what to do while we sit over here and drink cocktails and avoid Mrs. Varnado."

Ah, Mrs. Varnado, I thought. The lady gets around.

"I am a crack shot," the Congressman said again. "Why I could sit on top of the roof of this house here and pick off half of Port Gibson without even budging just like that guy down in Austin, what's his name."

"Charles Whitman," I offered.

"Right. I could, but I won't," Ollestadt said.

"Thank you," I said again.

"I won't because one day, one day I wanna be President just like that sneaking little Kennedy wants to be President only I'm gonna make it on my own not because I got a daddy with a billion billion dollars and the Mafia in my back pocket. Did you know old Joe has the Mafia in his back pocket?"

"No," I said.

"What? Are you contradicting me?" Ollestadt tried to stand up but only succeeded in leaning upright. "Stand up! I am your draft board, you sniveling coward conscientious objector! I hold your life in my hands, dammit. I can send you over there or keep you here cleaning bedpans, you know that?"

"I guess," I said, but I didn't stand up.

"Good for you. Don't stand up. Don't do what I say. You're not a coward, you know. Not really. You may think you're a coward making up all that bullshit about Niebuhr and Sartre and that other bullshit, but you're not. That C.O. thing is not a garden of roses. It will stick to you like dogshit all the rest of your life. You'll never be elected to nothing.

You'll never get a decent job. You'll smell like yellow-dog dog turds the rest of your miserable existence. Your life sucks just because you're different, just because you don't want to go over there and shoot some gooks. You know that don't you?"

"I guess," I said again. Though I hadn't until that moment. It had never occurred to me that anyone would think that my filing conscientious objector would be a bad thing. I guess I never really thought about it at all. Initially, I just thought it was a way to get out of the war. Then I just thought it was just a personal decision, a thing of private conscience. Chop some trees, make a few hospital beds and then go on with my life, but he was probably right. This could be a problem.

"Ah, don't worry about it. I'm not gonna let you screw it up. If the board won't turn you down, I'll see you get what's coming to you." He set his drink down on the porch railing and came back over and sat down on the swing and put his arm around me. I did not like that.

"I like you. You know that?" the Congressman said. "I think you're pretty great. You remind me of me. A go-getter. Your problem is you just don't think things through. Well, that's what I am here for. Your Congressman. Here to think things through for you and for everybody else."

Then he did it. He moved his right hand to the back of my head and held it in an incredibly strong grip, placed his left hand on the side of my neck with his thumb pressing against my Adam's apple so I couldn't move, and kissed me. Kissed me full on the lips: spit, tongue and teeth.

Then he quit. Then he let me go. Then he looked at me as if he had just run over his mom's cat. I suspect I had a similar look on my face.

"Oh, my God," he said. "Oh, my God."

"It's okay," I said though I know I wasn't convincing. For one thing, I could barely talk.

"Oh, my God," was all the Congressman was able to say and then he stood up, suddenly stable, and walked back into the house. I just sat there trying to put some thoughts together. I couldn't find any.

After a while I wandered back around to the front door. Roommate Rick was standing there talking with Mrs. Varnado. Mr. Varnado had evaporated.

"Rick," I said hoarsely. "Can I talk to you for a second?"

I could tell that Rick did not want to leave Mrs. V's considerable attentions, but I must have looked as weirded out as I felt because she told him, "Honey, you just go along with Ethan there and I will just busy myself with freshening our drinks." She took his glass and melted into the crowd.

"This had better be important," Rick said. I just turned and walked down the porch stairs, around the tent, and out into a corner of the front yard where there were no people. Rick followed. When I turned back to Rick, he was holding out a plastic pint flask. His attitude had softened.

"Want a drink?"

"No," I croaked and took the bottle and tilted it back. It was Scotch. Not my favorite, but it was very welcome.

"I have spent the whole afternoon filling up about a dozen of these flasks with expensive booze supplied by Copiah County's finest citizens," Rick said. "What is up with you?"

"Sam Ollestadt just kissed me." My voice was back.

"Sam Ollestadt? My Sam Ollestadt? Republican Congressman Sam Ollestadt?"

I nodded and took another drink from the flask. I held it out to Rick. He shook his head and pulled another flask out of his tux coat pocket.

"What exactly do you mean kissed you?" Rick asked.

"Remember what you did when Jenny Stovall slapped you in ninth grade?"

"Like that? Tongue and everything?"

"Its imprint is on my tonsils."

"Jesus!" Rick unscrewed his bottle and took his own drink. He grimaced. "Tequila," he said. "What are you going to do?"

"I'm not going to cancel my Playboy subscription, if that is what you mean."

"No, I mean are you going to tell anyone?"

"You mean other than you?"

"Yeah."

"Hell, no."

We stood there for a second thinking, not thinking.

"Well, what do you want me to do?" Rick asked.

"Nothing. I just had to tell somebody and I figured you would keep your mouth shut."

"Jesus. I wish you hadn't picked me."

"Why not?"

"My Dad's a Republican. I work for the Republicans. Hell, I work for Ollestadt. He's an up and comer."

I forced the obvious cracks to the back of my mind.

"Just forget it, then," I said and took another drink.

"Okay," Rick said. He started to go.

"You're not going to tell anyone, either?" I asked him. Rick turned back to me.

"Tell anyone about what?" He grinned and slugged me on the shoulder as if to remind me that we were guys and guys didn't kiss congressmen.

"Thanks," I told him, though I had no more idea as to why I was thanking him than I had known why I had thanked Ollestadt. I resolved to quit thanking people. That's when I saw LJ. Or a vision of LJ.

She was wearing a café au lait, empire waist gown that accented her figure and set off her golden California tan. Her black hair was piled loosely on her head allowing sexy tendrils to fall over her ears and brow, at the same time elegant and wanton. Her eye make up was still dark, but softened, but not her eyes. They were narrow, they were fierce, they were very, very pissed off.

Before I could move, she had pivoted abruptly on both feet and moved swiftly away, showing interesting slits on either side of the long dress that allowed the rapid movement and flashed her toned, perfect calves.

I thought of chasing her through the crowd, but she was already disappearing and besides what could I say? She saw me drinking. I had promised upon promise that I wouldn't, especially not tonight, not three hours after we had initiated our physical relationship.

I was immobile in my sadness and self-loathing.

CHAPTER 25

Bobby

So I just stood there in that isolated corner of the front lawn. Something made me want to go talk to Jessi. Something made me want to go talk to my Dad. Something made me want to go find LJ and kiss her harder than the congressman kissed me. But I couldn't do any of those things.

I just stood there and stared across the street. Then it caught my attention. It was moving in the cornfield. It was dark and taller than an animal. I saw a flash of white. It was a man in a dark suit with a white shirt. Jesus, was this it? I looked back toward the house. I didn't see anyone useful, just Mrs. Varnado holding court with a circle of middle-aged Lotharios and Rick moving toward her like a homing pigeon.

I walked parallel to Main Street toward the ancient maple tree by the sidewalk. Its long branches spread out over fifty feet from the trunk, the lowest almost touching the ground, making an effective shield from the lights of the party.

I ducked behind the maple's trunk and looked back across the street. The white shirt was still there and then it turned away, disappearing behind the suit coat. I moved slowly through the covering branches, keeping my eyes on the dark figure almost invisible among the stalks. I made sure his back was still toward me when I dashed across the street and into the rows of corn. Further up Main, I saw a large black sedan, the heavy square shape of a Lincoln Continental or a Chrysler New Yorker, parked on the cornfield side of the street. The cops who had stopped me from parking were gone.

This had to be it. Mafia guys always drove black sedans, didn't they? A sniper was setting up in the cornfield waiting for Bobby to arrive. The complicit cops disappear. The assassin will blow Bobby away and then jump into the black car rushing down Main Street with its lights off, racing to Chicago or Memphis or wherever assassins hang out.

I moved slowly through the cornfield. The tall stalks and thin green shucks made a loud clatter that I was certain could be heard in the next county. I stood still and listened for the sniper. A warm wind played softly across my collar, but it wasn't the blowing air that was causing the hair on the back of my neck to stand up. I heard a slight movement about fifty feet off to my right. I moved slowly forward, trying to step between the rows, edging sideways so as to just barely brush the leaves. I walked up and away from the road and then circled back so I could come up behind the sniper if he was pointing a gun toward my house.

As I closed on the figure, he was facing toward the road. He was not a large man. He seemed even smaller with his stooped posture, not that of a gunman, but the contemplative pose of a philosopher or a college professor. In a flash I knew exactly who I was watching. I spoke to him quietly, but firmly.

"You're Bobby Kennedy, aren't you?" Bobby? I just called Senator Kennedy "Bobby?"

He was not startled. He barely moved. He just turned his head to the side and spoke in an equally quiet voice, as if we were in a library or a church.

"Yeah. Who are you?"

"Ethan Taylor."

"Is this your cornfield?" Bobby asked.

"No, sir," I said. "I live over there." I pointed across the street.

"I thought that house belonged to the mayor. Uh, Hamilton or something."

"It does. I rent it from him."

"Oh, sorry about that."

"Sorry about what?"

Bobby waved his hand in the direction of my house. "All this."

"That's all right. My roommate is busy stealing booze."

"Glad this is doing someone some good."

"Why aren't you over there?"

"I am preparing myself. I hate this sort of thing."

"You have to do this a lot?" I asked.

"Too much." We were still whispering. I wasn't sure why.

"Come on," I told him. "I want to show you something."

I started walking through the cornfield away from the road. Bobby looked quickly over his shoulder at the dark car and then followed me without a word. After we pushed our way through the cornfield, I stopped.

"Are we going far?" Bobby asked. "I will have to make an appearance sooner or later. Corn stalks have ears, but they seldom vote."

"This is it," I said and I pointed to the little church about fifty yards in front of us. A couple dozen cars were parked in the field around it. The tall, clear windows were lit and you could see people waving those funeral parlor hand fans. As we watched, the congregation stood up. An intro was struck on the organ and they began to sing, not the majestic martial music of the white churches I grew up on, but the rocking rhythms of gospel.

"I was told there was not a black community in Port Gibson," Bobby said.

"Not a large one. Probably most of them are there right now."

"Let's go in."

Now that I had him here, despite Turk's invitation, I suddenly had some doubts. "I'm not sure we would be very welcome."

Bobby turned to me and flashed that famous tooth-filled grin. "Maybe <u>you</u> won't be welcome," he said and he walked rapidly out of the corn and toward the church. He stopped at the door so I could catch up with him.

"One thing," he shouted over the music.

"What's that?"

"Don't call me Bobby. I am forty-two years old for God's sake. I'm a United States Senator. I think I've earned Robert or at least Bob."

I opened the door and gestured for him to enter.

I couldn't help it. "Okay, Bobby, I will try to remember," I screamed. And the music stopped just as I said "Bobby." And the entire congregation, as one, turned to look at us.

The minister broke into a huge grin and said, "Ladies and gentlemen, we have an honored guest."

Turk came out of the pews. He was wearing a double-breasted grey suit just a shade lighter than his charcoal skin.

"Thank you, Ethan," Turk said. "I told them you would come through."

Bobby turned to me and smiled and said, "I think I have been set up." Then he held out his hand to Turk. "Hi, Robert Kennedy," he said emphasizing "Robert."

"Yes sir, yes sir," said Turk. He grabbed Bobby's hand in both of his. "I know who you are, sir. My name is Marion Witchell, but my friends call me Turk."

"Nice to meet you, Turk." Then Bobby said in a louder voice. "We don't mean to interrupt your service, here."

There was a chorus of "No, sirs" and "Not at all" and "Never you mind" from the congregation as the minister said in his unmiked booming voice, "No sir, Senator Kennedy, we were rather expecting you."

"I can see that," said Bobby looking at me. I looked away. The minister hurried down the aisle, his purple, fringed silk vestment flowing behind him. He was a large man and he moved like a running back.

"I am the Reverend Thomas Randolph," he towered over Bobby and enveloped his hand.

"How do you do, Reverend Randolph?" Bobby looked down and off to the side as if embarrassed by, what? His height, his color, his Catholicism?

"Sir, would you honor us with a few words?"

Bobby brushed back his hair and looked around at all the black faces staring at him. "Thank you, Reverend," he said. "But I wouldn't presume."

"Please sir, it will give us something to tell our grandchildren." And the Reverend Randolph raised his hands and waved them toward the congregation. They began to applaud, chaotically at first, and then lapsing into a rhythm, like a rock and roll audience calling for an encore.

Bobby looked down and smiled and shook his head, as if he had to put up with this kind of thing every day. Then he lifted his smile to the church people and nodded his head. The applause abruptly returned to the unstructured roar of an ovation as he walked down the aisle. The applause ceased as soon as he stood behind the pulpit. He raised his hands and drifted them down. The audience sat. Forgotten, I moved to the back of the church while the reverend took his seat behind Bobby.

"Thank you," he began, looking down at the podium, his hair falling in front of his face. "This is an unexpected honor." He raised his head and did that trademark brush back of his hair with his right hand. "I really don't know what to say. As you know, I am here in Indiana running in the Presidential Primary. But I am not here tonight to ask for votes."

There was a call of "We will, Bobby" and then "Don't you worry."

"Thank you, but . . . ." He looked around the church. He seemed to be searching the faces for words. "I just want you to know whatever happens, whether I win or lose, whether you choose to vote for me or not, I am one with you. I can never be of you. I am not of your generation. Most of you are either younger or older than I am. I am not of your heritage, your culture. I do not share the terrible bonds you have with the past, with your ancestors, uprooted and taken forcibly to a strange land to be enslaved and later kept in the chains of poverty and prejudice. I do not share your manner of worship, though let me tell you that this is one Irish Catholic who envies your unbridled faith and spirited praise. But I come from a family that came to this continent indentured, if not enslaved. They came poor. They came hungry. They, too, were hated and reviled. Kept out of the best schools. Kept out of the best neighborhoods. Kept out of the best jobs. And they organized and they fought and they worked until their children, their grandchildren, the people of my generation, my brothers were allowed to serve their country, were allowed to lead their country, were allowed to die for their country.

"And as a third generation Irish Catholic I share your pride in the advancements of our countrymen in the last century and the hope that we can go further until one day every American can be seen as only that, an American with all the rights and privileges due for merely being a citizen of this country. That no American will have to burn down his neighborhood to be granted the right to vote. That no American will have to march to be granted the right to a decent education. That no American will have to see his children gunned down in a foreign war or his leaders gunned down in the streets of our cities.

"Martin Luther King did not die just for the Black community. He died for me, for all Americans so that his dream could be every man's dream. As my brother did not die just for Irish Catholics, but he died trying to make his dream of a free and equal America a reality for us all. I promise to you this night, no matter what happens in Tuesday's primary, no matter what happens in this Presidential election or any election, whether I win or lose, or on whatever path my journey takes me, I will dedicate my life to preserving the memory and bringing forth the dreams of those two great Americans, to your generations and my generation and every generation hereafter, so help me God!

"It has been my practice lately that whenever I speak in public I conclude with a quote from George Bernard Shaw, but I think in this place with you people I would like to share a more intimate quote, one that I have carried around in my wallet since my brother's assassination. It helps me to try to understand the tragedies of our times even though it is from a tragedy written thousands of years ago by the Greek playwright, Aeschylus. He wrote, "In our sleep, pain which cannot forget falls drop by drop upon the heart until, in our own despair, against our will, comes wisdom through the awful grace of God."

There was a profound and reverential silence that any actor would have appreciated more than the loudest standing ovation. Bobby seemed a little confused and a touch embarrassed by the soundless audience.

He looked out over the pews and said, "I believe it is customary at this point to ask for an Amen." And then they said it, they shouted it, they chanted it. The choir broke into the famous chorus of it.

"A-a-a-men! A-a-a-men! A-a-men! Amen, Amen!"

Bobby turned and shook hands with Reverend Randolph. Then he went back to the choir and shook hands with each member as they continued to sing and clap. Then he walked back up the aisle, grabbing hands with both of his, the weary smile, the bobbing head, then pausing at the rear of the church to wave.

I was too stunned to open the door for him. I cannot fully describe to you what happened to me in that church that night. For the first time in my life I felt something larger than myself. I felt part of a community. Part of a nation. Part of a world. I was no longer on the outside with my nose pressed against the glass of reality. I was in there. With those people. With this man. This Kennedy. This icon who was too short, too tired, too human to be anything more than just a man, but all the same, a force, an energy, a symbol of the crossroads of a tragic past and a hopeful future.

I felt as if the world had opened in front of me and life had just begun. It was the first time in my life that I ever fully believed in the intangibility of a full and just universe and my place in it.

CHAPTER 26

The Limo

The church was still rocking as we crossed the parking lot.

"So what were you going to do with the gun?" Bobby asked me when we reentered the cornfield.

"The what?" I asked and then I remembered.

"The snub-nosed thirty-eight you have in your Jacket pocket."

I put my hand in my pocket and touched the smooth steel.

"How did you know I had a gun?"

"I recognized the bulge. I bet you didn't know I went on raids with New York City Narcotics officers in the fifties."

"No."

"I saw that bulge a lot. Can I see it?"

"Sure." We stopped in the middle of the stalks and I handed him Mack's pistol.

"Nice. Were you going to pull it on me if I wouldn't go to your church?"

"No. To be honest, I forgot I had it. It's not mine."

"You steal it?"

"No, I confiscated it from my father."

"You people do things different in Indiana. In Massachusetts, it is the fathers that confiscate weapons from their sons."

"Do you think we should leave it in the cornfield?" I asked the Senator.

"Leave what?" he asked.

"The gun," I said.

"Why would we do that?" He handed the gun back to me and we continued walking.

"Won't it make your Secret Service protection nervous?"

"What Secret Service protection?"

"You don't have any Secret Service?"

"Hell, no, if the government paid for protection for every Kennedy who decided he wanted to be President, the country would go broke in a week. All I have is Rodney."

"Who is Rodney?"

"My driver. He is a volunteer, a law student at the University of Indiana. I think a gun would scare him."

"Then what do you do for protection?"

"There is my keen wit and my uncanny ability to scramble when I am forced out of the pocket."

"Seriously."

"Seriously? I have some burly friends that accompany me in dicey situations."

"Where are they now?"

"Up in Indianapolis preparing for a speech I have to make in front of 20,000 people at the Speedway Thursday night. I didn't think I would need them down here. Besides, there is always the local authorities."

"I wouldn't count on them."

"I never do," Bobby said. "My brother was commander in chief of the most powerful military force ever seen on the face of the earth and he had all the Secret Service protection that taxes could buy. If someone really wants to kill me, I'll be dead."

By this time we were walking along Main Street toward the car. I could think of nothing to say. There was nothing to say.

"Listen," said Bobby just before we got to his car. I could see now that it was a dark blue, not black, Continental. "Do you think you could hang on to that gun for the rest of the night?"

"I should be able to manage it."

"How old are you?"

My reflex was to add a couple of years, but I just couldn't form the lie. "Eighteen," I said.

"That's old enough. There is something I have to do after the party, one of those dicey situations only I can't bring along my usual 'friends'."

I distinctly heard the quotes around the word "friends." "Do you think you could go with me and carry that gun? It won't be dangerous. You won't have to use it, but I want the parties involved to see a big guy with that bulge and understand that I am not kidding around."

"You want me to be your muscle?" I asked.

Bobby chuckled. "In a manner of speaking. I want you to be a menacing presence. Have you ever done any acting?"

"High school," I said. "But I watch a lot of tough guy movies." I thought of Bruno and shifted my shoulders like he did.

"That will have to do," said Bobby. We continued walking. As we approached the Lincoln, Rodney bounced out of the driver's side and hustled around to the back door on the off-street side of the car and opened it. Rodney was tall and thin with thick dark- framed glasses. I think Bobby was right about his driver and guns.

Before the Senator got in, he turned to me and said, "Come on, I'll give you a ride to the party."

"It's just across the street," I said.

"The first thing you need to know in your new acting career is how to make an entrance." He slid into the backseat.

"It would be an honor, Senator," I said. Rodney slammed his door and hurried around the back of the car leaving me standing by the curb. I opened the front door and got in.

"Senator is good," Bobby said from the back seat. "Or Mr. Kennedy or even Bob to your close friends. Just don't call me. . . You know, the other."

"Sure thing, Bobby," I said.

CHAPTER 27

The Bomb

Rodney drove all of a hundred yards down to the end of the block where the driveway touched Main Street and did a U-turn back toward the house. He stopped in front of the elaborate concrete stairs that went up the knoll in the front yard. There was no one close enough to see us as we got out of the car. Rodney opened the door for the Senator and once again ignored me.

See if you're gonna get a tip, I thought.

The Senator was moving fast. He was halfway up the concrete steps that led from the sidewalk to the front lawn when it happened. At one moment there was music coming out of the main tent, the dull under-roar of a hundred conversations. The next moment there was the explosion. Off to our right, the top of Henderson Hill erupted in a ball of flame. The neon Ramada Inn sign sparked and crashed to the ground. Bobby instinctively ducked down below the cement railings on either side of the stairs. I turned back to the car as the window on the front passenger side shattered.

"Christ," said the Senator. "What was that?"

I stood staring at the car window. Rodney was down on the ground. Women were screaming at The Mansion. Policemen and Sheriff's deputies were starting up their whirling lights and sirens.

Then Bobby was grabbing my arms and shaking me. I looked down at him.

"What was that? What was that?" he was asking. I shook my head.

"The Ramada Inn," I said.

"Let's go," he said and headed back for the car. I just stood there. Bobby stopped at Rodney and knelt down.

"Are you all-right?" he was asking. Rodney got up on his knees and nodded his head then he threw up on the sidewalk. Bobby helped him stand. Cop cars were ripping up Sid's lawn as they peeled out onto Main Street, bumping over the curb and skidding down the road.

I was still standing there.

"Does it hurt anywhere? Are you bleeding?" Bobby was asking Rodney.

Rodney shook his head and Bobby led him over to the concrete stairs and sat him on the little curlicue base of the railing.

"Stay here!" Bobby commanded him. Rodney nodded again. Bobby came over and grabbed my right arm.

"Let's go!" he insisted.

I still didn't move. I looked past him at the shattered window of the Lincoln. Something about that window bothered me.

"Where?" I managed to ask.

"The Ramada!" he said. "Do you know how to get there?"

"Yes," I said.

"You drive," Bobby commanded.

By the sheer force of the Senator's will, I found myself opening the driver's door. Bobby swept broken glass off the seat and into the gutter and got in the front passenger side.

He slammed his door and shouted, "Let's go! Let's go!" as if he were a cheerleader at a football game.

The keys were still in the ignition. I remember thinking stupidly, "Why not? Who would steal Bobby Kennedy's car?" I turned the huge engine over, flipped on the lights, hit the blinker and slowly pulled out.

"Step on it!" I looked over at Bobby. His eyes were on fire. His hair was falling across his forehead. He was leaning forward, every muscle tensed, his jaw muscles bulging.

Then suddenly I woke up.

"Let's go," I echoed him and I tromped on the gas pedal and pulled a screaming U-turn in the empty Main Street. The Continental took off like a shot as Bobby slammed against the passenger door.

"Now we're cooking!" he screamed. He was like a maniacal teenager, fierce and focused.

I got to the base of Henderson Hill in mere seconds. Two unmarked cop cars, a city police car and a county sheriff's cruiser, blocked the entrance to the drive that led up to the motel parking lot. The deputy was signaling me to go away, but Bobby was shouting, "Drive around! Drive around!"

I started to circle past the police car when the sheriff's deputy pulled his gun and ran toward me. Oh, man, I thought. Shot by a cop. At least Dad will be proud. I slammed on the brakes. The deputy screamed, "What the hell do you think you're doing?"

"Press," I told him, but it didn't stop him from throwing open the door and dragging me out onto the curb. In the meantime Bobby had jumped out of his side of the car and was screaming "Attorney General! Attorney General!" in that familiar Boston accent.

I stood up when my deputy let go of my shoulder.

Bobby was standing there, nose to nose with a pudgy Port Gibson city cop, and waving what looked like a small wallet.

"Jesus," my deputy said. "Is that Bobby Kennedy?"

"Yeah," I told him.

"What's he doing up here?" he asked.

"Ask him!" I screamed over the roar of the fire up on the hill.

"Let them go!" said Bobby's cop and my deputy stepped back. I jumped back in the car as Bobby slid into the seat and slammed his door.

"Attorney General?" I asked as I hit the ignition.

"I kept the badge," said Bobby. "Senators don't get one."

I jerked the steering wheel to the right and bounced up over the curb and around the police car. The rear of the Lincoln slammed against a concrete light pole.

"I hope this isn't your car!" I yelled at Bobby as we tore up the hill toward the fire.

"Borrowed!" he screamed back. "From your rich Republican mayor!" I looked over at him. He was grinning.

At the top of the hill there was a circle of cop cars around the fire. The fire department hadn't shown up yet. I drove around them and parked on a little rise above the motel so we could see what was going on. Bobby and I got out and looked down.

The explosion had to have been a car bomb. Several other cars, pickup trucks and one semi, had been slammed into each other in a semicircle around the burning ball of flame that could have once been a Chrysler Imperial. There was a gaping hole in the row of hotel rooms and flames were darting out of shattered windows.

The center of the hole was where I had spent my afternoon talking to Pete Decker. The ball of fire was where his Chrysler had been parked.

"Room 146," Bobby said. The firelight bounced off his face.

"Yeah," I said and then, "how did you know?"

"I was supposed to be there tonight. After the party."

"You were staying there?"

He shook his head.

"No, I was supposed to meet someone."

"Pete Decker," I said. Bobby looked at me.

"You know him?"

I nodded.

"I was in that room this afternoon. He was my roommate's uncle," I said and then I realized that I referred to him in the past tense.

"You think he is dead?" Bobby asked.

"Yeah," I said. "Him or someone who drove his car."

Bobby nodded again. More sirens were coming down Main Street. I looked back down Henderson Hill and saw the fire trucks.

"Let's get out of here," Bobby said.

I didn't argue. As I drove around the cop cars Bobby looked down into his lap.

"I don't want to go back to the party," the senator said.

I stopped the car abruptly.

"You've got to."

"Why?"

"People will be worried."

"They're not my people."

"They're my people."

"How many of your people are going to vote for me?"

In my head I counted me. And Sam Cooper. Only he was too young to vote.

"That's what I thought. Besides, they're going to be too busy worrying about the explosion to think about another commie pinko Kennedy."

"Ehhhhhh," I said thinking of my father. Then I thought of Jessi.

"I have a friend who needs to talk to you."

"Girlfriend?"

"No."

"Mostly it's a girlfriend or a wife. Some guy wants to impress her." He paused and stared out the window. "I'm starving. Can I meet your friend tomorrow?"

Sure, I thought, we'll just drop in on Jessi at work.

"I guess.

"Good. What's still open this time of night?"

CHAPTER 28

The Pancake House

When we walked into the Pancake House, I thought Harriet was going to have a heart attack. The place was empty, but Bobby still asked for a booth in the back so we couldn't be bothered. Harriet didn't say a word, just poured the coffee and left us with two menus and then ran off to the kitchen to play "guess who is sitting at my table" with the cook.

"Did you know Pete well?" Bobby asked me as we stared at our menus.

I shook my head. "Just a couple of days. He just got into town. You?"

Bobby nodded. "He used to work for my brother."

I didn't get it.

"Pierre's office?"

"Pierre?" Bobby asked.

"Pierre Salinger," I said. "President Kennedy's press secretary."

"I know who Pierre Salinger is. The question is, how do you know who Pierre Salinger is? You're kind of young to have voted in 1960."

"Sam Cooper, one of my friends, is sort of an aficionado."

"Aficionado. A Pierre Salinger aficionado?"

Might as well just jump right in.

"Uh, he is a Kennedy freak," I said.

Bobby exploded into laughter. "A Kennedy freak?"

"Yeah," I said trying not to laugh with him. "He is fascinated with all things Kennedy. Knows everyone in your brother's administration. Birth dates, hobbies, that sort of thing."

"Well, I guess I shouldn't be surprised. Someone has to be buying all those magazines. Tell me, Ethan, are you an aficionado as well?"

"No, not really. I mean, I'd vote for you, but I'm just not as, uh, fanatical."

"But you do know who Pierre Salinger is?"

"Yes."

"Kenny O'Donnell?"

"Special assistant to the President."

"Ted Sorensen."

"Special counsel to the President, chief speechwriter. Wrote 'Ask not what your country can do for you.'"

"Freckles."

"Your golden lab."

"And you're not a 'Kennedy freak?'"

How do you explain Counting Kennedys to a Kennedy?

"A lot of it rubs off," I said.

Bobby looked at me for a while as if sizing me up and then he said, "Pete Decker was the White House liaison to the CIA for the Bay of Pigs."

"Holy crap!" I said.

"You know that meeting I told you about?"

"The one with Pete?"

"Not exactly," said the Senator sipping on his coffee.

I looked past him out the window as a pair of headlights pulled into the parking lot. They stopped. They were pointing right into the café. Behind the headlights was my father's pickup truck. I slumped down below the window sill.

"What are you doing?"

"My father is out there."

"Looking for his gun?" Bobby asked.

"I don't know." The pickup truck backed up and turned and headed to the far corner of the motel. I sat back up. "I guess not." Then it hit me. In all the excitement and racing and screaming at cops, I hadn't put it all together. Daddy made car bombs. How did I know? Pete Decker told me.

"Oh, hell," I said.

"Your parents teach you to talk like that?"

"Half of them. I'm sorry. I just realized something, that's all."

"What?"

"Nothing. About my dad. So Pete was CIA?"

"CIA liaison. He was OSS in the war."

I understood what war. People of Bobby's generation still called World War II "the war" as if Korea and Vietnam never happened.

And my father just blew up a CIA liaison? "Oh, hell," I said again. And then, "I'm sorry."

"No, now you can say it. It is hell and we are up to our necks in it."

Harriet appeared just in time to hear the last of the Senator's sentence. She chose to ignore it.

"Mr. Kennedy, have you decided what you want to eat?"

"Yes, ma'am," Bobby said. "I am sorry about the language."

"Oh, that's all right," Harriet said. "We get truckers in here all the time. I am still gonna vote for you."

"That is awfully nice of you," said Bobby in his best aw shucks, bad little boy tone. "I'd like to have ham and eggs, scrambled, and dry toast."

Harriet then looked over at me. I knew I looked different in my coat and tie, especially in my current company, but I was certain she recognized me.

"Just coffee," I said.

She sniffed and wrote it down.

When Bobby handed her his menu, she hesitated for a moment and then said, "Mr. Kennedy, would you mind signing your menu so I can sort of have it for a keepsake reminder?"

"I would love to," said Bobby. Harriet handed him her green Bic and Bobby scrawled his name across the menu and handed it back to her. She didn't take it. Instead she gave him this sickly smile.

"Could you please write something personal on it? I mean, I want this to go to my grandkids someday and I want them to know that you, well, sort of met me."

"Of course," said Bobby. "What's your name, dear?"

Harriet's face turned into a tomato.

"Harriet."

"To Harriet," he said as he wrote. "My favorite waitress in the state of Indiana."

"Oh, goodness!" Harriet was beside herself. "That is just wonderful! Thank you."

"You're welcome," Bobby said and then she left.

"You have just become a family legend for three generations of waitresses," I said.

"There are worse achievements in a political career," Bobby said. When she was well out of earshot, Bobby continued.

"Did Decker tell you why he was in town?"

I thought about telling him about the assassination story, but I thought better of it. For some reason Bobby seemed to trust me and I didn't want to spook him with crazy conspiracy theories.

"He said he was covering your presidential campaign."

"Covering my campaign?"

"As a journalist."

"Is that what he is calling himself these days?"

"Was."

"We really don't know for sure that he was in that vehicle."

"No."

"But we should probably assume he was the intended victim."

"Unless . . ." I began.

"Unless what?"

Oh, to hell with it, I thought.

"Unless the bomb was intended for you."

"I don't think so."

"Why not?" I asked. "Were you going to ride in Pete's car?"

"I don't know. Maybe. We weren't that detailed in our plans. And if I didn't know I was going to be in that car, how would someone else? We were supposed to go see some gentlemen that Pete knew."

"Important gentlemen?" I asked.

"Yes," said Bobby.

"Important gentlemen who live on an island in the middle of Lake Masterson?"

"How did you know that?"

"It's a small town. There are few secrets."

"Come on."

"Pete had me meet him on a boat in the lake. Later, I saw him take that boat to the island. And this afternoon two men took Pete back to that island."

"What two men?"

In for a penny, in for a pound. "Two hoods. Probably connected with organized crime."

"Good God, how do you know all this?"

And I told him about Pete's cocktail party and my afternoon at the girl's academy. I left out LJ.

"So the last place you saw Pete was leaving that island?"

"Yes."

"So maybe he wasn't in that car?"

"Maybe not, but who else would have a key to his car?"

"If it was his car."

"I saw it parked there."

"Okay, his car. But one of your goons could have gotten the key from Pete."

"Why?"

"I don't know," said Bobby and suddenly he looked tired. I signaled him to be quiet as Harriet came up behind carrying the plate of ham and eggs and my coffee.

"Here you are, Senator," she said. I guess the kitchen help had instructed her on the proper way to address Bobby. She set my coffee down without a comment. "Anything else?"

"More coffee, please, Harriet." Bobby gave her the smile. She quickly retrieved the coffeepot and refilled our cups. I caught a movement out in the parking lot. My dad was throwing something in the back of his pickup and then he got inside the cab.

"And Harriet," Bobby was pouring on the charm. "Mr. Taylor and I have some serious political strategy to discuss and I would appreciate it if you would make certain that we will not be disturbed."

"Sure will, Senator. No one will know you are here."

As she left, I watched Dad back his truck up, turn and peel out of the parking lot. Bobby turned to look out the window.

"Somebody is in a hurry," he said.

"My dad," I said.

"Busy man," said Bobby.

"Yeah," I said. How busy? Did he see me with Bobby? Did he kill Pete? Was he here to kill Bobby? This week? Just now? Did he put it off because I was with him?

"So you think Pete's friends were connected?" Bobby was speaking between mouthfuls of eggs. He looked up when he noticed me staring. "I haven't eaten since yesterday."

"I'm sorry. I was thinking of something else. What were you saying?"

"Do you think Pete's island-friends were connected to organized crime?"

"Don't you know?"

"I kind of got that impression from Pete. He said it was important that I meet with them. Just him and me."

"And the muscle."

Bobby grinned. "Right."

"And you agreed? To meet with gangsters on the eve of your first primary?"

"Pete could be very persuasive."

I thought of Pete and his cannon. It didn't seem to have done him much good.

"What did he have on you?"

The fork with a piece of ham stopped a few inches from his lips.

"What makes you say that?"

"Isn't that what "persuasive" means in politics? Blackmail?"

"Pete knew where the elephants are buried, let me leave it at that."

"And Pete's friends?"

"I believe they know as well."

"So you were going to meet them to make a deal, to keep them quiet," I said. I tried to keep the sarcasm out of my voice. I failed.

Bobby dropped his fork on his plate. His eyes flashed. He shook back his hair and leaned forward. He spoke in an intense whisper.

"I was going to find out what they knew and what they wanted and then I was going to shove it up their ass. I do not make deals with those kinds of people."

I locked eyes with him. I was tired of bullshit. Too many people had screwed with me in the last forty-eight hours. "Not even to be President?"

"No."

"Not even to make your brother President?"

"No. Not even then. Not me."

"There were others who did?"

"Not that I know of." He said it too carefully.

"Not that they told you about," I said.

"You have read too many magazines."

"I live in Indiana," I said. "I have been to Chicago. Richard Daley supported your brother. Richard Daley will support you."

"Mayor Daley is not the Mafia," Bobby said. Then he smiled. "Why would he want to be demoted?"

"So you weren't going to sell out to the mob?"

The smile went away.

"Who the hell do you think you're talking to?"

"Just checking."

"You got brass balls, kid."

"I've been told."

Bobby leaned back and folded his arms, sizing me up. Then he leaned forward, placing his crossed arms on the table.

"Let's go find out if Uncle Pete is still alive."

"How do we do that?"

"I think we will keep my appointment on Lake Masterson. You do know how to drive there, don't you?"

"In my sleep."

"You don't by any chance have a boat, do you?" Bobby stood up.

"No."

"Do you know where we can borrow one?"

"Yep."

CHAPTER 29

The Island

Wednesday May 1, 1968

"Sit down. I am not going to let you row," Bobby whispered. He was sitting between the oars of my dinghy and taking off his Jacket.

"Well, I sure as hell am not going to let <u>you</u> do it!" I whispered back. I was stupidly standing up in the back of the little boat in dramatic defiance. I had been right. All the other boats in the marina were chained and padlocked, but they didn't care about my little dinghy.

"Why not?"

"You are Bobby Kennedy. United States Senator. Brother to our slain president. The hope of the future. It wouldn't be right."

"Yeah, well, this hope of the future wants to row, so sit down before you tip us over."

I sat down. And almost tipped us over.

"Jesus, you don't even know how to sit in a boat. What makes you think you could row?"

"I rowed the other day when I met Pete." God, yesterday with Pete seemed a hundred years ago.

"And how many times did you end up in the water?"

I didn't say.

I looked up at the sky. Clouds were closing in on the moon. It looked to be about three-quarters.

"I thought so," Bobby said. He used one oar to push away from the dock, the same way I had done, and then put the oar into the lock and began rowing.

"You don't like being told no," I observed.

"What makes you say that?"

"Every time someone asks you to do something, go to the church, go to the pancake house, sign my menu you're right there. Every time someone tells you don't do something, don't row, don't go to the island, don't go meet with Pete's friend, you get determined."

"Maybe."

"Who told you not to run for President?"

Bobby smiled. His teeth fairly glowed in the dark.

"Pretty much everybody, at first. Then, toward the end, it was just that tall Texan son of a bitch."

"Lyndon."

"That was enough."

"Why do you hate him so much?"

"I don't hate him. I hate his war."

"Bobby, we're all alone in the middle of a lake, rowing toward put our lives on the line."

Bobby stared at me and let go of a breath.

"I hate him because he is stubborn. I didn't want him for Vice President. My brother didn't want him for Vice President. We asked him for the sake of party solidarity. The stupid son of a bitch was supposed to say 'No'."

"Why didn't you take back the offer?"

"I tried to. Texas bastard wouldn't budge. Politics. And now Lyndon Johnson is President of the United States, exactly what he wanted all along."

"What a coincidence," I said.

"Yeah," said Bobby.

"So basically you hate him because he is stubborn, he doesn't like it when you tell him 'no,' and he wanted to be President. Who does that remind you of?"

"I think we are supposed to be silently creeping up on the bad guys."

So I was for about five seconds.

"Why didn't the Attorney General of the United States launch a full-fledged investigation into the assassination of the President?" I wanted to know, but I regretted asking him the question immediately. Bobby suddenly stopped rowing and a mask of the most incredible pain came over his features. The tragedy mask you see in theaters was cheerful compared to the face I saw on Robert Kennedy's face at that moment. I didn't expect him to answer, but then his mouth opened.

"Who said I didn't?"

"Everybody."

"Well, everybody doesn't know every goddamned thing."

"Then you did investigate the assassination."

"Of course."

"For the Warren Report?"

"God, no."

I leaned forward. The boat sloshed up and down.

"What did you find out?"

"Not enough."

"So you gave up?"

He shook his head. "What the hell do you think we are doing here?" And he started rowing again.

The next ten minutes or less is a blur. I remember Bobby rowing furiously for the island. I remember jumping out of the boat into ankle deep water to pull it up on the beach. I remember heading up the beach toward the trees. I remember taking out my pistol and waving it at Bobby like those company commanders in war movies signaling their troops at Omaha Beach. I remember reaching the pitch-blackness of the woods and looking back to see that Bobby was only about ten yards behind me.

That's all I remember until I woke up in a large wooden chair in the front hall of the chalet looking across at Bruno who was sitting in an identical chair and holding my Dad's .38 in his bear-size paw.

"Who are you, kid? Really."

"Local muscle," I said.

"Local muscle," Bruno repeated. "Jeez, the way you talk. Where did you get this pop gun, newsboy?" he asked. "On the back of a box of Rice Krispies?"

"No," I told him while I tried to sit up. It felt like there was a rubber band pulling my head down to the floor. "My Dad gave it to me."

"How sweet. Daddy gave junior a pop gun for his birthday."

"Maybe you know my Dad."

"Maybe I don't care," said Bruno. He was dangling the .38 from his finger and twirling it.

"Mack Taylor," I said.

Bruno stopped twirling.

"Boom," I said.

Bruno stood up without a word and walked down a short hall of dark reddish wood and knocked respectfully on a set of double doors at the other end. One of the doors opened a crack. There was a muffled conversation and then the door opened to allow Bruno to enter and then it closed again.

Evidently, I had said something interesting.

My head throbbed. I know it is a cliché, but I never really knew what that meant before. I could feel the pounding of my heart on the back of my head and with every beat there was excruciating pain. I touched the back of my head gingerly with two fingers of my right hand. I could feel the sticky matting of hair and blood.

Man, I thought, I've really done it now. I examined my final resting-place. It looked like Cecil B. De Mille's version of a Bavarian hunting lodge. It had high ceilings supported by huge wooden beams making an intricate latticework of triangles above my head. Everything was that dark reddish wood. Floor, walls, furniture, doors and not a carpet in sight. And dead animal heads. Lots of dead animal heads in the hall leading to the double doors. No human heads. I took that as a good sign.

The front door to the place was just a few feet to my right. It was huge and arched. Everything looked thick, solid, masculine, and bulletproof. I was thinking about getting up and just walking out that front door when both double doors slammed open simultaneously.

"He still giggles like a little girl," Bobby said as he stormed down the hall. He stopped at my chair. There was still a ringing in my ears.

"Come on! Get up! We're going, bomb boy," Bobby said.

I stood up on wobbly legs.

"My gun," I said, though I am not sure why. I mean, I wanted the gun, but I don't know why it seemed so important. Getting out alive should have been my first priority.

"Oh, good God!" Bobby said and pivoted on his right foot and left heel and stomped back through the double doors. He returned in less than a minute holding my father's pistol.

"Here," he tossed me the gun. I juggled it for a second, but held on.

"It's empty," I said.

"Yeah, well, they thought about letting you shoot everyone before we left, but I talked them out of it. Now can we go?"

We went outside. It was unnaturally quiet. A thick fog had rolled in and it seemed to be muffling all sound. There was no one around the house. There was no one on the dock. It smelled like it was going to rain.

We walked to the edge of the dock. Bobby put out his hand to keep me from walking off the end. With the fog and the dark I couldn't see two feet in front of me.

"Was Pete in there?"

"Don't you know?" Bobby snapped.

"No, why would I know?"

"We will talk about it later."

"No, let's talk about it now."

"You didn't tell me you were a reporter."

"It never came up."

"You didn't tell me that you worked for a fascist like Ray Varnado."

"I didn't think you would like the idea."

"Good thinking. And most of all, most important of all, you didn't tell me you were the son of the most likely candidate to have blown Pete Decker into oblivion."

"We don't know that he did that."

"But it did cross your mind."

"Yes."

"But it didn't cross your mind to mention it to me."

"Evidently not."

"What part of this evening were you planning on putting in your Grand Dragon Daily News?"

Okay, the man was making some good points, but now he was pissing me off.

"Look, Senator . . ."

"I think this is our boat." He hopped in the dinghy and took up the oars.

I slipped on the wet dock and kind of fell over the gunwale and rolled over on to the aft seat and just lay there.

CHAPTER 30

The Attic

It was just before dawn when Bobby got me back to The Mansion. He insisted on driving.

"Give me the goddamned keys," he had told me when he docked the boat at the marina.

"I'll drive," I said. "I know the way."

"Just give me the goddamned keys," Bobby repeated. He held his hand out like a petulant twelve-year-old demanding his allowance.

I flipped him the keys and he turned and walked down the dock toward the Continental.

"What did I do?" I asked reflexively to no one.

I could hear the engine of the Continental starting.

I sprinted down the dock. As I ran around the corner of the marina shack, I shouted, "Wait!" The large car stopped. I caught up with it and tried to open the front passenger door. It was locked. I reached in where the window used to be and unlocked it. I got in.

"Left or right?" Bobby asked me.

"Senator, I don't know . . ."

He cut me off.

"Left or right?" he asked again.

"Left," I said and other than the one syllable "left" and "right" for directions until we hit Main Street. I saw my house on the right. He didn't slow down.

"Here it is, Senator." His foot stayed on the accelerator.

He stared straight ahead and asked me, "Is there a whorehouse in this town?"

"A what?" I heard him I just couldn't believe what I heard.

"A whorehouse. A house of ill-repute."

I couldn't help it. He was pissing me off. "Missing Ethel?"

Bobby slammed on the brakes. The large battered car screeched to a stop in the middle of the street.

"I never want to hear you mention my wife's name again."

"All right," I said.

"I need to see someone who works at a whorehouse. A particular person. She has information for me."

Jessi, I thought. Dallas. Jesus Christ she wasn't lying.

"Who told you this?" I asked him. He sat there silently staring at the fog shrouded street just beginning to light like an old television set warming up. "That is the woman I told you about earlier, the one at the party."

He looked down for a few seconds then he looked at me.

"Were you planning on writing anything about tonight?"

"Just a puff piece about the party."

"None of the rest of it."

"God, no."

"Did you know your father was going to kill Pete?"

"No. I still don't think he did."

"But he could have."

"It's possible."

"All right. Then who is this woman?"

"Her name is Jessi. She was at the party. I invited her. She wanted to meet you."

"That was not the name I was given."

"She has a stage name. Jeanette Baudelaire."

Bobby laughed quickly, a tension release.

"No," he said.

Then I remembered. Dallas.

"Katrina."

"That's it. Who is she?"

And I told him all I knew about Jessi, about Tina's, about Dallas. I left out the part about the bra and panties on the roof.

"And Bruno at the whorehouse was the same guy on the island?"

"Right," I said. Right, I thought.

"All right," he said and he put the Lincoln into gear. "Are we going in the right direction?"

"To go where?"

"This 'massage parlor'."

"Yes," I said. "It's probably closed, though."

"That's okay," he said. "I just need to know the way." So I showed him. When he saw it, all he said was, "Fine."

We didn't speak on the way back to The Mansion.

He pulled up in front of the concrete steps that led up from Main Street. He seemed to have lost some of his anger but he still didn't answer my "Good bye" and I barely got the door closed when he sped away. I just stood there watching his taillights disappear.

Even through the fog I could see that The Mansion was once again just a house. The tent, the cars, the whole brouhaha had miraculously disappeared. The only signs of Bobby's welcome party were the ruts the cop cars had dug in the lawn when they took off for the Ramada Inn.

I stood there with an empty head for a while, staring up at The Mansion. The first few drops of rain hit my forehead and I looked down. I stared at the pieces of shattered car window Bobby had brushed into the gutter and on the sidewalk.

Then, for no reason other than I was standing there in a gray dawn with an empty head almost in the exact same place I was when Pete's car blew, it occurred to me that there was no reason for the window on the Lincoln to shatter. It had seemed natural at the time. Huge explosion followed by a shattered window. But now, in the still of the early morning light, it didn't make any sense at all.

All the other windows remained intact. All the other windows on the Continental, all the windows on all the other cars, all the windows on The Mansion. As far as I knew, none of them shattered, only the passenger window of the Lincoln just past where Bobby ducked when he heard the explosion. I looked up at the house again. More raindrops were falling, but I ignored them. All the windows seemed to be intact, but it was hard to tell. They were all dark. All except the attic window. The light was on. The window was open. I walked up the concrete stair to where Bobby had stood.

I looked back at Main Street. If someone had taken a shot at Bobby from the attic and missed, the bullet would have hit the Lincoln's window. And with the explosion and the screaming and the sirens, who would have noticed?

And so I ran. I ran up the steps. I ran through the rain up the walk to the porch. I ran up the porch steps. I ran into the house, up the front hall stairs, down the upstairs hall to the door to the attic and then up the attic stairs.

And that is where I found Rick and Mrs. Varnado. Dead.

CHAPTER 31

The Fbi

I was sitting alone at the kitchen table drinking a Pepsi when Police Chief Holman showed up with an army of other cops, a couple of ambulances and a guy in a brown suit.

I know that it was the sixties and college students were supposed to hate cops, that we were supposed to call them "pigs," and we were supposed to sit in the Chancellor's office until some guys in blue uniforms and white helmets came and split our heads open, but this was my sixties, the sixties of a small town in northern Indiana and some of us never got around to getting beat up by cops, so I liked Chief Holman.

I had interviewed him when Sid had hired him out of Kansas City last year. He was a round, jowly, savvy police officer with twenty years on the KC force. He looked a lot like Orson Welles in *Touch of Evil*, and he had Welles' basso profundo, but there wasn't an evil or mean fiber in his body. Oh, I am sure he could and did break an occasional arm if he had to, but only if it were absolutely necessary.

The chief was wearing his dress uniform. I guess it was left over from last night and Bobby's non-arrival. He had, however, neglected to shave and his eyes were dark-rimmed with a lack of sleep, which made him look all the more like Orson Welles.

"You got any coffee, son?" the chief asked as brown suit sat directly across from me without a word. I waved in the general area of kitchen cabinets. He opened cabinet doors while he spoke.

"This is Special Agent Simmons. He's with the F.B.I. If you don't mind, he would like to ask you a few questions about all this." I looked at Simmons. He did a curt little nod. I wasn't sure at the time exactly what the word "sallow" meant, but somehow it leapt into my mind when I looked at the agent. Everything about him seemed yellowed, faded, like old newspapers or new phone books. His eyes were a dark blue. His hair was cut so short I wasn't sure what color it was trying to be. He sat erect and that seemed to emphasize the bony, sharp angles that made up his face and body.

"Ah-hah!" said Chief Holman and he waved the jar of instant we kept behind the corn flakes. "Is this all you got?"

"I'm afraid so."

The chief turned to fill the teakettle with water. I got up and got another Pepsi out of the refrigerator.

"When was the last time you saw your father?" Simmons began.

"Last night," I said. I hated the way I said it. An actor giving the wrong reading. I could hear the defensiveness in my tone.

"Where?"

"Here, at the party." I decided to leave Bobby, Mack and the Sands Motel out of it. Wrong.

"Senator Kennedy said you saw your father at a motel later."

"Oh, yeah," I said. "I forgot. I didn't really talk to him there."

"But you did see him."

"Yes."

"Did you know your father killed people?"

"Hey, now," said Chief Holman.

"That he blew people up in their cars like he blew up Pete Decker?" continued Simmons.

"I know he has been accused of killing people," I said. "No one ever proved anything."

"Did your father know your roommate?"

"Barely. I think he fixed him a drink last night."

"Why would he do that?"

"Because he was bartending here. Didn't someone tell you that?"

"What about Mrs. Varnado?"

"What about Mrs. Varnado?"

"Did your father know her?"

"A lot of people knew Mrs. Varnado."

"Like your father?"

"I guess. I'm not sure."

"Was your father having an affair with Mrs. Varnado?"

"My father didn't kill Mrs. Varnado. My father didn't kill Rick."

"How do you know that?"

"I know. Rick was my friend. My father wouldn't kill my friend."

"Would he kill Senator Kennedy?"

"No."

"Did he like Senator Kennedy?"

"No. My father was a Teamster. Teamsters don't like Bobby Kennedy."

"Did your father ever tell you that?"

"Not in so many words."

"Then how do you know?"

"I read a lot of newspapers."

There was another snort behind me. The teakettle began to scream. Then it stopped. I could hear Chief Holman pouring water into a cup. Simmons was staring at me.

"Coffee, Simmons?" the chief asked.

"No," Agent Simmons said. He didn't take his eyes off of me. I was tired. I was pissed off. I refused to look away.

"You want me to tell you what happened up in your attic?" Agent Simmons asked.

"Not particularly."

"You don't want to hear?"

"I already know."

Agent Simmons looked surprised. Agent Simmons looked away, over my shoulder, and up at Chief Holman. Made you blink, I thought. Agent Simmons looked back at me.

"So what happened?" Agent Simmons asked.

"Someone set up in that window with a high-powered rifle to pick off Senator Kennedy when he arrived at the party. He shot at the Senator just as Pete Decker's car exploded. He missed Senator Kennedy and shattered the front passenger window of Senator Kennedy's Lincoln Continental. If you haven't already, you will find the bullet in that car. Ethan and Mrs. Varnado walked into the room just as the shooter was firing. The shooter didn't want witnesses. The shooter shot and killed Ethan and Mrs. Varnado." Chief Holman placed his coffee on the kitchen table and sat down next to me.

"How do you know all that?" Chief Holman asked me in a quiet voice.

I told him about the sidewalk. I told him about the Lincoln. I told him about the explosion. I told him about the pieces of glass in the gutter. I told him about finding the bodies.

"And you don't think your father was the trigger man?" asked Holman.

"No," I said.

"Then who do you figure did it?" Chief Holman asked.

"Congressman Sam Ollestadt," I said.

I expected someone to laugh. No one did. The Chief looked over at Agent Simmons. Agent Simmons looked over at The Chief.

"What makes you say that?" Chief Holman asked, again with the quiet voice.

Because he's a whacked out rightwing son of a bitch that grabbed me and kissed me on the lips, I wanted to say, but I didn't.

"He's an expert marksman," I said.

"So are half the deer hunters in this county," Chief Holman said.

"He is a conservative. He hates Robert Kennedy."

"Same hunters. Same county."

I took a sip of my Pepsi. I took a leap.

"He worked with the CIA while he was over in Vietnam with Special Forces and the CIA wants Bobby dead because Bobby has plans to disband the CIA because of their possible association with the assassination of his brother. Once CIA, always CIA."

Daddy wasn't the only one who could set off bombs.

"Where did you get all that?"

"Pete Decker," I said. "Pete told me and now Pete is dead." Then I told them about Pete's abduction to the island only I decided to embellish and made the island guys sound more like Langley, Virginia than South Side Chicago. I was tired and I wanted them to stay away from Dear Old Dad and I wanted Ollestadt's head in a noose. I am not homophobic, but I particularly don't like homosexuals masquerading as righteous patriotic Christian reformers. I didn't know who Roy Cohn was at the time, but if I did, I wouldn't have liked him either.

"Anybody else you would care to implicate?" asked the FBI man. "Perhaps President Johnson?"

"Perhaps Mr. Varnado," I said. This also caused a storm of silence. "He's a little right of Genghis Kahn. He hated Pete Decker who was trying to get the goods on him for killing Pete's partner down in Mississippi and God knows he hates Bobby and what do you think Rick and Mrs. Varnado were going to do in that attic? Raise pigeons?" The word pigeons came out a little fuzzy, but other than that, I think I was having an impact.

"Okay," I continued, "maybe dear old Dad did build a bomb now and then for Jimmy Hoffa to scare off some scabs here and there, but he is not the only one good for this thing." I was beginning to slip into my Steve McQueen.

"Where do you think your Dad was heading when he left the motel last night?" Agent Simmons asked.

To the fish camp, to the fish camp, to the fish camp, my head began to sing. I shook my head trying to lose the thought. This was the FBI. They can read minds.

"I don't know," I said.

CHAPTER 32

The Fish Camp

All the way out to the fish camp I wondered what the hell I was doing. I had just spent a huge hunk of my time lying to the FBI about Mack Taylor, a man who may have murdered one of my best friends and my other best friend's uncle. I was pretty sure that was against the law.

Why would I do that? Why would I risk my freedom? Why would I save a father I barely knew and hated most of my life? Was it a blood thing? Is there such a thing as a blood thing? Or was it just that I was so toasted and exhausted from being up for two days that I had no idea what I was doing?

I had been to Mack's fish camp about a half-dozen times when I was a kid. Once we stayed out there for almost a whole summer. It was when Dad and Mom were having one of their infrequent prolonged honeymoon periods when Mom decided that getting drunk right alongside of the old man was the only way to save the marriage. And the last time I was there, right before his final departure, I was about eleven. It was when he grabbed me out of my sleep and hauled me out to the fish camp for a forty-eight hour abduction.

No fishing. No camping.

He was drunk the whole time. He tried to explain exactly what kind of a demanding worthless bitch my mother was and why I shouldn't hold it against him if he abandoned the family and found himself another woman.

Good times.

But at least that last time impressed on me the route to the place. Just a couple of days before my abduction, I had read one of those

Weekly Reader stories about a kid who had been kidnapped and I had learned that it was important to memorize the route to the kidnapper's lair. Somehow, I had done that even though it was pitch dark and I was traveling through unfamiliar country. Now I felt like I was re-creating that horror story of that weekend as I looked for landmarks in the fog that would lead me to Dear Old Dad so I could ask him if he was a murderer as well as a crappy father.

I parked the Corvair next to Dad's pickup. The temperature was cooler out here in the woods and an unpleasant mist combined with the fog. Even though I had changed into jeans before I left The Mansion, it never occurred to me to throw a jacket over my olive-green t-shirt. I picked that shirt on purpose. It was a gift from Rick. He had bought it at an Army Surplus store and presented it to me shortly after I told him I had filed conscientious objector. He told me I might as well get used to it because when they turned down my application, they were sure to "send your sorry ass to the deepest, darkest most dangerous jungle in 'Nam" where he assured me I would get my head blown off.

Even though it was almost noon, the dense fog made it seem like early evening. There were no lights on in the cabin and there wasn't a human sound over the soft roar of Panther Creek. The water was up with the spring rains and it was moving fast. Dad had built a rope bridge that swung from the two trees on this side of the creek to a pair of posts he had planted in the ground just to the left of the cabin.

It was the only way to get to the cabin from the road when the creek was up. I used to scramble across it like a monkey when I was a kid, but now through my exhausted eyes in that dreary day, it seemed very formidable.

My initial impulse was to shout for someone, but somehow the fog and the rushing water gave me the sense that any kind of noise would be useless, so I just stood there and shivered and waited for something, absolutelu clueless as to exactly what that might be.

It was a voice.

"We thought you'd be here."

I froze. It was a familiar voice, but not Mack's. It was a voice that didn't belong here, a voice out of the fog like a voice out of a dream where time and space get all run together and people living away appear with people I see every day and nothing and everything make sense.

I turned around and there he was, slumped shoulders, grey cotton suit and matching fedora and that toothless grin.

I didn't say a word. I couldn't. I felt as if talking would break some sort of magic spell; wake me from the dream.

"What are you doing here?" I finally managed to say.

"I live here," he said simply and then waited for me to reply. I didn't. There was a fog-filled silence and then he said, "We was expecting you. Your pappy and me."

"You were?"

"Yep. We figured you would have to come out here sometime. Didn't expect you so soon, though. Figured you'd sleep some. Looks like you ain't slept a'tall."

He waited again for me to say something. Again, I didn't.

"Well, if you ain't gonna talk, you might as well walk. Come on, let's go see your pappy." He hitched up his stained trousers and walked off toward the river. I followed as far as the bridge. He just hopped right up to the rope bridge and skittered across like a grey Orangutan. When he got to the other side, he hopped back down next to the two poles and turned back to look at me.

I guess my standing there looking petrified at that latticework of ropes and knots must have been the funniest thing he had seen in a long time. He laughed, he pointed, he doubled over. He performed this jig as though pounding his little legs into the ground would stop his giggles and screams. It didn't. Then he turned his little dance toward the woods and jiggled off into the trees and fog until I could hear his peals and shrieks but I lost all sign of movement.

I inhaled deeply and put my left foot on the first rung and grabbed the rope ladder hooked to the trees. The whole thing shook like an earthquake. I felt my stomach heave up toward my nose. I tasted that Pepsi again, but I managed to keep it in my mouth.

I climbed to the top to where the bridge was tied to the two trees. I grabbed on to the stubs of limbs on either tree. I looked across. I looked down.

The bridge consisted of one large rope, about three inches thick, loping across the river with a hundred short ropes connecting two thinner ropes that acted as sort of railings, if anything as delicate and shaky as noodles could be considered railings.

This is what I had to cross to find Dear Old Dad. This is what I had to cross to find out if he was a murderer, and if there was somehow, through him, a murderer in me. That was it, I realized. I wasn't looking for him, I was looking for me, and the first clue to the real me was somehow in this rope thing, this tremulous bridge. I was encouraged by this self-revelation, but then it started to rain.

Crap.

But I crossed it. To this day, I cannot clearly remember how I did it. It was as if I had my eyes closed the whole time, but that would have been absolutely impossible instead of just merely impossible. I do remember looking directly down at the white tufted Panther Creek beneath my inching feet and I do remember my t-shirt getting soaked with both the rain and my nervous sweat, but exactly what I forced my hands and feet and legs to do to get across is still a mystery to me.

On the other side, leaning up against one of the supporting poles was something I found even more unsettling than the fact of the bridge itself. There was an ax there. A red handled, silver and black, barely been used, keenly sharpened ax. I understood its purpose immediately. It could quickly collapse the rope bridge to prevent unwanted guests to visit the far shore, possibly even with the unwanted guest falling mid-stream.

Maybe that is what the grey man found so hysterical. He knew about the ax and I didn't. Maybe he contemplated severing the ropes after I got out on the bridge and the thought of me plunging into the icy river below and being swept off into oblivion just made his feet dance and his eyes water with joy.

I tasted the Pepsi rising again only this time I spit some of it out.

Good thing I didn't know about that ax, I thought. Good thing I hadn't cheated Quasi on our moonshine deals.

I leaned against the ax pole and breathed deeply. Now what? I looked off in the direction I thought the old guy had gone. Trees and fog. How was I going to find anything or anyone out there? I thought I could hear a distant thrashing through the underbrush, but all sound blended in with the river noises and I couldn't be sure of anything.

Damn, damn, damn, I thought, and then I said it aloud.

"Damn! Damn! Damn!"

Then my last "Damn" came back to me, almost like an echo, but not in my voice and followed by a "Right!"

It was my Dear Old Dad. The thrashing noise got louder and then he appeared between the oaks and cedars.

"Damn right!" he repeated and walked up to me and gave me another one of those hugs.

And this time I hugged him back. And this time, for some reason, I started to cry. And I hugged and cried and shook all over and he hugged me back and then he started to cry and if I hadn't been leaning up against that tree I would have fallen down, pulling him on top of me which I am sure would have shook me to my Freudian roots but I didn't. We stayed upright and after a while loosened our grip, it seemed like at the exact same moment, and he stepped back to look at me.

"Damn, boy. You look like hell!"

"Thanks," I said. "I pretty much feel like it."

The rain had let up some, but there was still a steady drizzle. Mack was wearing this olive-green parka that matched my t-shirt and he took it off and handed it to me.

"Here, put this on," he said. "You're gonna catch pneumonia."

I took the jacket, but I said, "What are you going to wear?"

"I got another coat back at the still," he said.

"Still?" I asked. I put on the jacket. It was as warm and comforting as his hug.

"Yeah," he said grinning. "Where do you think your grandpappy gets that moon he sells?"

"Grandpappy?" I asked, but he was already walking off through the woods so I ran to catch up with him.

CHAPTER 33

The Still

"I thought my grandfather was dead."

We trudged through the woods.

"So does everybody else," Mack said. "Marty says he likes it like that. Cuts down on the junk mail."

We were walking through the woods on what seemed like a path. It was narrow, so I was walking just behind Mack.

"Marty? That old man is my grandfather and his name is Marty?"

"Well, not really. Oh, he is your grandfather, but his real name is . . . Well, it really doesn't matter. Marty is what he has called himself ever since he saw that movie with Ernest Borgnine."

"I think I want to know his real name."

"Then you will have to ask him. He gets pissed off every time I tell someone."

"Did mom know about him?"

"Hell, no. That's when I first started telling everyone that he was dead. I loved your mother on first sight. I think I told you that. But she was a lot different from me, especially back then, more refined. I figured I couldn't say to her: 'Hi, Connie, my name is Mack Taylor and I'm in love with you and I am going to marry you, but first I want you to meet my Daddy, you know, that toothless old crazy son of a bitch who wanders around town talking to himself and selling bootleg whiskey.'"

"So you really built this fish camp for him."

Mack stopped to shake his head and laugh. I could now hear a resemblance in the grey man's high-pitched squeals and my father's lower, mellower tones. There was a similar rhythm, a similar shaking of the chin.

"Hell no. I didn't build nothing. That was another lie I told your mother. He did the whole thing. Chopped every tree, chinked every log."

"What happened to my grandmother?"

"She run off just like your mom." I let that go. "We moved out here when I was about two years old. She didn't like living in the woods."

"Where is she now?"

"Dead. I read about it in *The Chicago Tribune* a few years back. She had married a banker of some renown. I told Marty. He just spat and asked me what the hell he was supposed to do about it."

"Jesus."

"Yeah. Your grandmom evidently was something. Beautiful. Rich."

"Rich? I thought the old guy—Marty—hates rich people."

"So you got the 'revenge of the poor people' speech?"

"It was a good one."

"Yeah, the first time you hear it. It wears thin after twenty or thirty years. Your grandpappy was a rich man growing up, educated, too. Your grandmother wouldn't have touched him otherwise."

"What happened?"

Mack stopped walking again but he didn't turn around.

"Life happened, Ethan, my boy. Life happened. Here we are."

And there we were. The rain had completely stopped but the fog was still present. Mack stood at the edge of the trees. A circle about a hundred feet across had been cleared out and in the dead center of that circle, as if the spot had been carefully measured from the surrounding forest, was the damnedest thing I have ever laid eyes one.

It was a moonshine still; a real one and nothing I had ever seen in the movies matched it for its inherent drama and stoic beauty. The central and most distinguishing part of the apparatus was a large round copper pot that had been hinged and clamped shut. It was golden and shiny and later I found out that Marty polished it every day when it wasn't being used.

"Polishin' her up don't do nothing to keep her hid," he later told me. "But a man has got to be proud of his workin' tools."

Underneath the copper behemoth, Marty had dug a fire pit and then elevated the pot above the pit with cinder blocks. When Mack and I had emerged from the forest Marty was wiping down the centerpiece. When my tour began, Mack excused himself and went inside a smaller version of the fish camp cabin on the far edge of the clearing.

"You pour the fermenting mash into that-there copper tub and then clamp it shut and it commence to boil," Marty explained to me.

"Uh-huh," I said and then I asked him. "Are you really my grandfather?"

"You know, your pappy has one big mouth on him. Then the steam from the mash goes out'n this copper pipe and down here to this barrel," he tapped a large wooden barrel near a small creek that neatly cut the clearing in half, "called a doubler where the impurities fall out so it can go on to the branch worm," he pointed down to the stream where what looked like a truck radiator was submerged in the water, "where the steam is condensed and come out over here as pure whiskey," he pointed to a pipe emerging from the radiator and then running to a ditch where a spout emptied out into another wooden barrel.

"Of course that ain't all there is to it. There is the cleaning and feeding the fire and watching and the aging and sometimes the coloring and the flavoring for those folks that want their shine to taste like something more familiar, but that ain't what I sold you. No, sir. Nothing but the purest and the best for you."

"Because I'm your grandson."

"Goddammit! What else did that loose-lipped son of a bitch tell you?"

"That you were once wealthy and educated and my grandmother died in Chicago."

"And what name did he give me?" Granddad started that little dance again, the one I had seen by the bridge. Only this time he wasn't laughing and I suddenly understood the phrase "hopping mad." "What name? What name? What name?" He danced and shouted, danced and shouted.

"I called you Marty, you old prick," Mack called from the cabin door. "Now bring the boy inside before both of you fall down dead from exposure. Jesus, neither one of you has enough sense to come in out of the rain."

And it was raining again, pouring, and yet we hadn't noticed, as if only by Mack's mentioning it, it had become real. I ran toward the cabin, but Marty didn't follow me.

"Stubborn old goat," Mack said as he stepped aside so I could duck in the doorway. The cabin was only one room. The blaze in the large stone fireplace gave the place a flickering, comfortable glow and warmed it. There was a gas stove in one corner with a pair of butane tanks and the walls near it were lined with intricately carved cabinets. A tin pot steamed over a lighted burner. I smelled coffee. Deerskins covered a lot of the walls, acting, I suspected, as a kind of insulation as well as decoration. Along the back wall was a large, handmade bed similarly covered in deer pelts. And above the bed was a painting. It looked old. It looked authentic. It looked like a Van Gogh.

A huge table dominated the center of the room. It was at least seven-foot by three-foot. The top of the table was finished and stained, but the knots and gouges of the wood remained as if this had been a door somewhere out in the weather. There were six chairs, four of them at the table, one in the kitchen area and the other by the fireplace.

"Sit down," Mack said. I did. "Coffee?"

"Sure," I said. "Is this where Marty stays?"

"Usually," Mack said as he poured coffee into two mugs. He opened a cabinet and pulled out a bottle of Jack Daniels. "I am staying here for the time being. It is more secluded and right now I am in more trouble than he is." He laced the coffees with the bourbon without asking me. I didn't mind. I didn't expect to run into LJ.

He came over and placed a mug in front of me and sat across the width of the long table. I sipped the coffee delicately. It was exactly what my system needed and I could feel a soft glow grow within almost immediately.

There was a long silence. I tried to think of a delicate way to begin the conversation and failed.

"Did you kill Pete Decker?" I asked him.

"I guess there's not much point in talking about the weather."

"Did you?"

"Is that what they're saying?"

"Did you?"

"What do you think?"

"I think you didn't like Pete. I think you know how to blow things up."

"Do you think I killed Pete Decker?"

I took a larger sip of coffee and actually considered the question.

"Yes," I said.

"Well, you would be wrong."

"You didn't?"

"Nope."

"Do you know who did?"

"Nope."

"Why should I believe you?"

"No one says you should. But one thing you should know before you start your believing or disbelieving."

"What's that?"

"Pete Decker ain't dead."

"What?"

"Simple sentence. Four words. What part is confusing you?"

"But he got blown up in his car last night."

"Wasn't him."

"How do you know?"

"Jessi saw him."

"When?"

"After."

"Where?"

"In her Sands Hotel room. Right before I showed up. Probably while you were having pancakes with the Senator."

"Ham and eggs."

"What?"

"Bobby had ham and eggs. I had coffee."

"Same difference. While you were chowing down, Jessi was discussing politics with ole Pete."

"Did you see him?"

"Nope, but I saw his boots."

"His boots?"

"The ones he wore at Cisco's. You remember those fancy things with the rattlesnake on it."

"He left them with Jessi?"

"He changed his shoes. Then he lit out."

"In what?"

"In another pair of shoes, I reckon."

"No. If that was his car that got blown up . . ."

"It was."

"Then how did he 'lit out'."

"He took Jessi's car."

"She gave him her car?"

"Not according to her. According to her, he just took it."

"Where did he go?"

"Don't know. I expect he is trying to hide somewhere for a while."

"And you didn't try to blow him up?"

"Nope. If I wanted him blowed up, he would be blowed up."

"Did you kill Ethan and Mrs. Varnado?"

"God, no. Are they dead?"

"Yes. They were shot last night. Same guy who shot at Senator Kennedy. They walked in on him. He shot them dead."

"Then that would be Pete."

"Pete?"

"Jessi says he's the one who wants to kill Bobby. Says he wants to do it for the CIA and Cuba."

"And the Teamsters?"

"Son, if the Teamsters wanted Bobby Kennedy dead, they would have done it a long time ago."

"So you don't want Bobby Kennedy dead?"

"I wouldn't send roses to his funeral, but I am not of a mind to bother with killing him, no."

"Jessi told you that Pete Decker shot at Bobby Kennedy from my attic last night?"

"She did. Said he slipped up there when nobody was looking. I don't think she knew about the other two. We figured the son of a bitch probably blew up his own car so the cops would blame the whole thing on me."

"And how did she find this out?"

"You know men like to brag. After."

"Jessi had sex with Pete Decker?"

"That is what Jessi does. She saw him at the party. She took him home from the party. They made a financial arrangement."

"Why would Pete Decker leave Jessi alive? I mean, she was the only one to see him, and with everyone thinking he was dead, he would be Scot-free."

"I guess that is something you are going to have to ask Pete."

I stood up. "Then let's go find him."

Dear Old Dad stayed seated.

"Son, why don't you just hang out here with me and your new grandpappy and let the professionals sort this out."

"It would seem to me that you would want to clear this thing up."

"Why?"

"To get you off the hook."

"I have been on the hook so long I am beginning to feel like beef jerky."

"Well, I want to get the son of a bitch who killed my roommate."

"Like I said, let the pros handle it. You're just likely to get yourself shot. There's a whole lot of meanness involved in this mess and I don't think you really want to get in the middle of it."

I sat back down.

"I'm already in the middle of it."

"What do you mean?"

And I told him about Bruno and Pete's room and Bobby and the island. At the end of it he stood up and poured us some more coffee and Jack Daniels, only this time without the coffee.

"Yep, you're pretty much screwed. The Chicago boys don't much like people nosing around their business. And Pete has to figure that you know too much, too." He emptied his mug and stood up. "Ah, hell, I guess I better go with you." He grabbed a deer pelt and put on a denim Jacket with sheepskin lining.

I stood up and drained my mug.

"Do you know where we can find Jessi?" I asked.

"The Sands I guess or the cathouse. Why?"

"Maybe she has heard from Pete since you last saw her."

"Maybe. Or maybe Pete thought better of it and knocked her off, too."

"Then we better hurry."

"Yeah, I hate to see that girl get killed. Best lay I had since your mom."

I stood at the door in incredulous shock. Mack opened a drawer and took out a huge automatic pistol and a couple of clips. He slipped one clip in the handle of the gun and put the other in his pocket, and then he looked up at me.

"Oh, sorry," he said. "Too much info."

I pulled myself together and opened the door and then I remembered the snub-nose.

"Uh, one thing," I said. "Do you have any more bullets for the .38?"

"What happened to the ones that were in it?"

"Bruno took them away from me."

He shook his and said, "Sonny, sonny, sonny," as if I was five and I had just lost my third pair of mittens. He went back into the drawer and took out a box of shells and flipped them to me. I caught them without doing my usual juggling act.

"Try not to lose these. I don't think I will be able to walk into Ace Hardware and buy some more."

CHAPTER 34

The Auditorium

We stopped off at The Sands and I knocked on Jessi's door while Dear Old Dad slumped in the backseat. He tried hiding under the deer pelt, but after a few miles decided it wasn't his style.

Jessi wasn't home. I checked with the front desk and the dumpy bald guy watching *I Love Lucy* reruns told me Jessi had checked out.

So we went on to Tina's Massage and Relaxation. Mack came in with me "for old time's sake."

Inside we met Margot. Not her real name. I remembered her from junior high school when she was Barbara Hendricks.

"Jessi is not here. In fact, no one is here. In fact, I am not expecting anyone. In fact, the whole town is at that beauty pageant speech thing. Some big political guy is speaking. In fact, I was just about to lock up and go home."

"Won't your bosses get upset if you just go?" Mack asked.

"They got no problem with it. In fact, they just called and told me to call it a day."

We went back to the Corvair. This time he grumbled "To hell with it" and sat in the front seat.

"Given up on not getting caught?" I asked.

"Given up on caring. Besides, by now they have probably found that bullet in Senator Ratface's Lincoln and every cop in five counties is at that beauty pageant looking for me and a deer rifle."

I backed up the Corvair and turned it down Martin Street.

"And that is exactly where we are heading."

"Whoa, I said I didn't care, I didn't say I was crazy."

"Look, if Jessi wants to get that grassy knoll photo to Bobby, she has to be at the pageant. If Pete wants to knock off Bobby, he has to be there. If we want to save Jessi and catch Pete . . ."

"Hell. Pull over so I can crawl under some a deer hide."

"Don't worry. I've got a better idea."

Any other building in Copiah County and it would have been impossible for me to sneak the most wanted man in Indiana past a cordon of city, county, state and federal cops, but I knew something that no cop on such short notice would know.

I knew about the Bat Cave. And I had still had the remote control.

We were both out of breath when we finally reached the catwalks of the lighting grid. We simultaneously slumped down against the poles just above the second balcony and watched two-dozen or so high school beauties on the stage below engage in the baton twirling choreography that I had seen them rehearsing Sunday morning.

The orchestra was playing a Sousa number and there was a steady low roar from the packed house in the auditorium, so Dear Old Dad had to talk directly in my ear to make himself heard.

"So this is where we expect to find Pete?" he asked.

I nodded my head.

"Pete must be in better shape than I thought."

"There's an elevator on the other side, behind the stage," I said into his ear.

"Thank God we didn't come that way," Mack said.

When the orchestra stopped and at least half the girls on the stage dropped their batons, I looked out over the grid of lighting instruments and cross bars.

There was something wrong. There was a black spot where a stage light should be. I pointed to it.

Down below, Congressman Ollestadt, of all people, was announcing the three finalists for the pageant. As if he would give a crap.

Mack looked down my arm and whispered, "What?" I stood up and took out my gun and waved it toward the left and did this little head gesture like the Cisco Kid telling Pancho to go around one side of the barn while he went around the other.

Dear Old Dad stood up.

"What?" he said again, only this time louder.

"I think I see someone up here," I whispered.

"And that was what all that gun-waving crap was about?" he asked.

"It meant that you were supposed to go to the left and I would go to the right and we would come up on him from two sides."

"And I was supposed to get that from," and he did an exaggerated version of my gestures making him look like a spastic rag doll.

"Just do it."

"Okay, but where is this guy?"

"There!" I pointed again and whispered with dramatic emphasis.

He looked down my arm and squinted his eyes.

"I still don't see crap."

"That's the point. The person is dressed all in black."

"If you say so."

"Just walk on the catwalks that way and I will go this way and meet you on the other side."

"Okey doke," he said. "Just remember," he said opening his Jacket so I could see his t-shirt. "Good guys wear white."

"What is that supposed to mean?" I asked.

"Don't shoot me," he said and grinned and took out his automatic and headed silently off to his left.

As I moved to my right, I could definitely make out the outline of a human figure curled up in the light rigging above the catwalks. It was bent and focused on what was happening on the stage where Ollestadt was trying to act as hetero as possible.

This was not Pete. This was too small to be Pete. I held my gun pointed up next to my right ear like they do on *Adam-12* and looked across and saw Mack coming up on the other side. He was moving carefully and had his gun lifted in front of his eyes. I guessed either he saw the guy or he decided to believe me.

About eight feet away, I pointed my silver revolver at the center of that black mass and hissed in my best stage whisper, "Don't move!"

The figure tensed. Slowly the head moved. It spoke.

"Jesus, Ethan!" LJ said. "Don't shoot me."

She was wearing the same outfit I had seen her in at the VFW, only with a long sleeve leotard. I dropped my gun and whispered across to Mack as LJ climbed down on to the catwalk.

"Mack Taylor, meet LJ Goldman. LJ, Mack."

LJ extended a hand to my father. The leotard left little to the imagination.

"My, my, my," Dear Old Dad said has he raised her hand to his lips.

I almost puked.

I tried to kiss her. She moved away.

"You told me you were going to quit drinking."

"I haven't been drinking," I said reeking of Jack Daniels and coffee.

"At the party. I know you saw me see you."

"For God's sake. I had just been kissed by a Congressman!"

"Congressman Ollestadt?"

"Yes!"

She giggled.

"It wasn't funny."

"You should be seeing what I am seeing in my head. On the lips? Tongue and everything?"

"Tonsil hockey," I said.

"That would take some drinking."

"It did."

"You haven't been drinking since.

"Just coffee."

"Taste," she said. She kissed me. Once, twice. Either she missed the JD or she didn't care. She smelled like the evil weed, but I decided not to bring it up.

Dad finally did this throat-clearing thing and we broke.

"What are you doing up here?" he asked.

"Best seat in the house."

"For a sniper."

"I know. I thought I might catch him."

Dad smiled. "And what were you going to do if you caught him?"

LJ smiled back. "Scream like a little girl. Let's go to the light booth."

"What are we going to do in the booth?" I asked.

"Regroup. Talk as loud as we want. Smoke."

Dad pulled out a cigarette and led the way.

We got to the booth as the audience applauded. Mack offered cigarettes. LJ shook her head and levered through a lighting change. Some bimbo onstage was getting crowned Miss Northern Indiana.

"I always wanted to do that!" shouted LJ above the orchestra playing, for lack of imagination, the Miss America theme.

"Why?" I asked.

"It would mean that I am taller and dumber. I always wanted to be taller and dumber."

"Why?" I asked again.

"It's a California thing," she said.

"Can we go home now?" Mack asked.

"Don't you want to hear the senator speak?" LJ asked back.

"I'd rather hear bull farts," Mack said. The teary-eyed beauty queen was hustled off the stage and LJ brought the houselights up. She produced a water pipe and lighted it as Ollestadt began his introduction.

"My, my, my," my Dad said again and grinned.

"I may be a Republican, but I still remember that dark day in Dallas five years ago when the heart of a nation was ripped from its chest . . ." the congressman began.

"Listen," I said to Mack and LJ who were actually listening to my kissing partner below, "LJ is probably going to turn down the houselights when Bobby starts speaking so I suggest that you and I go to the catwalks over the stage and see if we can spot Pete. We'll meet back here when the houselights go down."

"I thought Pete was dead," LJ said.

"Evidently not," I said. "We think he faked his death so he could get a shot at Bobby."

"Why?" she asked.

"Why not?" grumbled Dear Old Dad.

"LJ, cover the center of the house from here. Dad, you go stage left." I pointed to the right. "And I'll go stage right." I pointed to the left.

"I thought you wanted me to go stage left," Mack said.

"Right," I said.

"Which is it?" he asked.

"What?" I asked.

"Right or left?" he asked.

"Left," I said pointing right.

LJ cut to the chase.

"That way," she said, pointing to the right.

"God, no wonder the knucklehead needs you," Dear Old Dad said and moved off to stage left.

I found a more or less comfortable place sitting behind the wire meshed safety rail and had a clear shot of the left side of the house without being seen by anyone who might look up. I saw Turk and the crowd from the church taking up the whole left half of the second balcony. I saw Sam Cooper in the mezzanine. This should have been the happiest day of his life, but he just looked distracted and sad. He was sitting with Rick's parents. They were all dressed in black.

I saw classmates and old girlfriends and schoolboy bullies and shopkeepers and the guy who takes tickets at the Rialto movie theater and Mrs. Walters, my third-grade teacher who sent me to the principal when I called her a fat slob. I had this sensation of watching my entire life sitting before me, a rerun of my days in Port Gibson. It was not a pleasant sensation.

But I did not see Pete Decker.

Then a phalanx of city and state cops came out of the wings and moved across the front of the stage forming two lines on either side of the podium. They stood staring out at the audience. They were so busy looking fierce and determined that none of them looked up.

I was right, I thought. This would have been a perfect place to nail Bobby. Then the houselights dimmed and three lighting instruments formed a single spot on the speaker's podium. I scrambled back to the booth. LJ and Dear Old Dad were waiting for me. LJ was happily puffing on the pipe. They both shook their heads as I sat down beside them. "I did see your blonde girl friend," LJ whispered in my ear in the eerie silence of a huge and noiseless audience.

"Who?" I whispered back.

"Jessi."

"Where?" I asked. LJ misinterpreted the excitement in my voice.

"Front row center, asshole. She must have screwed an usher."

I leaned over her and whispered to Mack. "Jessi's here."

"I saw her," Mack said. The orchestra started playing "Happy Days Are Here Again" and Bobby walked out of the wings to stand next to Ollestadt at the podium. Whatever the congressman said next was drowned out when the audience rose to its feet in a roar. The applause was thunderous even in the glassed-in lighting booth. Port Gibson may be a Republican town, but a Kennedy was a Kennedy. These Hoosiers were as star-struck as the rest of the nation.

I am not sure why, but I started to cry. LJ put her arm around my back and touched her cheek to mine.

Through my tears I saw Ollestadt hand Bobby a folded piece of paper. Bobby opened it and read it and looked at the congressman with surprise. Ollestadt just nodded his head and moved away from the podium.

Bobby leaned into the microphone and said, "Thank you, thank you." The applause continued. The orchestra stopped playing. The applause continued. Bobby raised his hands and gestured to the audience to be seated. The applause continued. He said, "Thank you" again and then "Please." The applause continued. Finally he just stood there and took it and slowly, reluctantly, the audience sat down and the applause died out. The ovation must have lasted ten minutes.

I don't remember the speech. I remember LJ listening intently, her arm draped across my back the whole time. I remember even Mack listening as he leaned over a guardrail and smoked Pall Malls. I remember thinking that Bobby's speech wasn't nearly as good as the one he gave at Turk's church, but that was because this one came from the pages in front of him and the other had come straight from his heart.

I do remember the end because it was how he ended most of his speeches in 1968 with a quote from George Bernard Shaw's play *In the Beginning*.

"Some men see things that are and ask why," Bobby said looking straight out at the rapt audience. "I see things that never were and ask, why not?"

Then the orchestra began with "Happy Days" again and then the audience jumped to its feet and then Bobby stood there and smiled and then he did something that no one expected, especially the cops on either side of him. He walked around the podium, crossed to downstage left and jumped off the stage on to the auditorium floor.

Then he started shaking hands with the people down front. The row was like a centipede with fingers and knuckles grabbing at him as he moved to his right. Then he moved up the aisle, grabbing hands on either side of him. The crowd from the first rows followed behind him forming a wall between Bobby and his police escort.

And just behind him, just over his left shoulder, I saw Jessi's neon-white blonde head.

"There she is!" LJ pointed at Jessi. "The bitch!"

I grabbed LJ's hand and stood up, pulling her to her feet. "Come on," I shouted over the roar of the crowd and I headed for the spiral staircase. I could barely hear Mack screaming something about an elevator as LJ and I started down the long spiral of steel stairs.

CHAPTER 35

The Whorehouse

Even though we had to climb down essentially six stories of stairs and a ladder and then had to raise the loading door, I still managed to get the Corvair out into traffic before the parking lots got jammed up.

Mack had flopped in the back seat, too out of breath from running down the stairs to ask me any stupid questions and LJ was unusually quiet as I maneuvered like a maniac to get off campus without attracting a cop or causing a four-car pile up.

When I finally got clear and we were cruising down the side streets of faculty housing, when LJ calmly asked, "Now tell me. What are we doing?"

"We are going to a massage parlor," I replied.

"Of course," she said. "And why are we going to a massage parlor?"

"To stop Pete from killing Jessi and Bobby."

"Of course," she said.

Dear Old Dad got enough breath to ask, "What makes you think he is going there?"

"I know Jessi and Bobby are going to the massage parlor. If you think about it, you know Jessi and Bobby are going to the massage parlor. The Mafia has sent Margot home so they know Jessi and Bobby are going to the massage parlor. Why wouldn't Pete know, too?"

"You know, boy, sometimes I don't follow a word you say," my Dear Old Dad told me.

I didn't care. As soon as I got out of suburbia and hit Main Street, I floored the Corvair and raced down toward the river. There was not

~ 215 ~

another vehicle in sight. I swung a hard left on to Broadway throwing LJ against the door.

"Sorry," I said and raced for The Flats.

The tires squealed as I swung the Corvair into Tina's parking lot next to Jessi's Firebird.

"See!" I screamed at LJ and Mack. "The Firebird! Pete is here!" I jumped out of the car and raced toward the front door with Mack's .38 in my right hand. It occurred to me that I should have a plan, but I decided just to bust in and use the element of surprise.

I heard two car doors slam behind me as I hit the locked front door with my left shoulder. My six-foot-six, two-sixty body did the rest. The door crashed open. In the dim light I could see Bobby and Jessi. She was pulling out a gun as Bobby was turning to look at me. I fired wildly as Bobby was diving to the floor. Jessi shot me twice in the stomach and was aiming at Bobby when Dear Old Dad put three bullets in her head.

CHAPTER 36

St. Francis

Friday, May 3, 1968

The next thing I saw was a bright light. Oh, man, I thought, this is it, the final light at the final end of the final tunnel. Then I looked away from the bright light and there was Dear Old Dad grinning at me at the foot of the bed. "Grandpappy" was behind him in his grey suit and holding a Mason jar filled with clear liquid and decorated with a red ribbon. Someone was holding my hand. I looked to my left. It was LJ. I looked back toward the light and figured out where I was.

"How are you feeling?"

"Messed up." And I was. I was slightly aware of some pain around my mid-section but mostly I was still stoned out of my gourd from medication.

"Which hospital?" I asked.

LJ squeezed my hand. "The St. Francis," she said.

Ah. Port Gibson's Catholic hospital. Nothing but the best.

"How is the Senator?"

"The little prick is fine," my father said.

"Jessi?"

"Dead," Dad said. "She killed Pete and Ethan and Mrs. Varnado."

"I guess they didn't arrest you," I told Mack.

"No, but if it ever gets out that I saved Bobby Kennedy's life, the Teamsters are gonna hang me up by my thumbs."

"Ever gets out . . ." I began. Then the room started to spin a little and I had to close my eyes. That just made it worse and I opened them again and there was Bobby standing where Dad had been. LJ was still there, but my father and Marty were gone.

"How are you?" Bobby was asking me.

"Dizzy," I said.

"Listen, I can't stay long. I still have a primary to win. I just wanted to drop in and say thanks and I'm sorry."

"Sorry for what?"

"For not believing in you."

"It's all right, Bobby. Ask not what your Kennedy can do for you," I said.

He smiled. You can get away with a lot of crap if you take a couple of bullets for a guy.

"There is something you can do for this Kennedy, something else."

"What is that?"

"We are kind of keeping this whole thing quiet."

"What?"

"It's easier on everyone. Your father has a record and a trial might get complicated and, well, I swore that I would not be elected president on the blood of my brother's assassination, I'll be damned if I am going to be elected just because you got shot. Besides, can't you just see the headlines? 'Bobby attacked while visiting whorehouse'."

"Massage parlor," I corrected.

"That is not what *The National Enquirer* will call it."

"What about Jessi?"

"Police shot her when she resisted arrest for murdering your friend and the mayor's wife."

"And me?"

Bobby's grin got larger. "Hunting accident. I hear it happens often around here."

I groaned. "Hunting accident. Like some idiot redneck."

LJ smiled, "I have called you worse."

"What about you, Senator?" I asked.

"Jesus, Ethan, go ahead and call me Bobby. I can't seem to stop you, anyway."

"Okay, Bobby. What about you? Did you find out about those men on the island? About Dallas?"

"I have just about everything I need. The meeting on the island was to convince me that, contrary to all the evidence I had been gathering over the last five years, organized crime had nothing to do with Dallas, that it was a Castro plot, revenge for The Bay of Pigs and some rather ill-conceived CIA attempts to assassinate Fidel."

"Who was on the island?" LJ asked.

"The All-star team of organized crime. Carlo Gambino from New York, Carlos Marcello from New Orleans, and my personal favorite, that giggling little gigolo from Chicago, Sam Giancana. They were afraid that if I became President, I would finally have enough power to nail them for Jack's assassination. When I was unconvinced, they told me that if I only met with this woman, this woman who was in Dallas in '63, that she would have incontrovertible, photographic proof that the Cubans were responsible. They told me to meet her at the, uh, massage emporium. Right before I began my speech, Congressman Ollestadt handed me a message to lose my entourage and go with the blonde in the front row. So I did."

"Congressman Ollestadt was with the Mafia?" I asked. I really wanted to believe that one. True Confessions: I was assaulted by a gay gangster.

"No. Evidently he was just one of Jessi's clients."

"Yeah, right," I said.

"She provided him with young men from Chicago. He was being blackmailed. Oh, and he said to tell you that you made it. Made what?"

"I filed conscientious objector."

"Good for you."

"So Jessi wasn't . . . anything she said she was."

"Jessi told you the truth about Dallas. Only she was not carrying a camera. She carried a rifle. All this time I was looking for a gunman. It never occurred to me to look for a gun woman. They killed my brother and then they tried to set me up."

"What are you going to do?" I asked.

"Nothing, now. I'll wait until I'm in the White House and then nail their butts to a tree."

"We're going to California, Ethan," LJ said. "When you get better, Bobby is going to fly us out for the primary. You can meet my parents."

I am afraid I groaned reflexively.

"No, you'll like it. Beaches, sunshine, palm trees," Bobby said. "Best cure in the world for a 'hunting accident'."

"I can't wait."

The next time I opened my eyes, the room was dark, but LJ was still holding my hand.

"I love you," I said and she laid her head on my chest and cried.

CHAPTER 37

The Ambassador

Tuesday, June 4, 1968

Los Angeles, California. Bobby was right. Beaches. Sunshine. Palm trees. And monster houses. I had never been out of the Midwest. I was impressed with everything

We stayed with LJ's parents. A monster among monster houses. The Mansion could have fit in their living room. They gave us separate bedrooms but we had the run of the place most of the day. The servants ignored us. We did it a lot in the swimming pool. LJ thought it was funny that I couldn't get enough of that.

And then it was June 4th.

Bobby got me a room at the Ambassador Hotel just down the hall from his campaign headquarters suite. We were all in the suite that night watching the returns. There were a lot of us. Athletes Rosie Grier and Rafer Johnson and a bunch of the best and the brightest including Pierre Salinger and Ted Sorensen and journalists like Jimmy Breslin from *The New York Daily News* and Karl Fleming from *Newsweek*.

Bobby didn't want to be there. He had been staying at John Frankenheimer's house in Malibu and Ethel was pregnant with number eleven and he was tired and he didn't want to leave the beach, but the news cameras were at the Ambassador and where the news cameras are, so goes the candidate.

Frankenheimer brought him to the Ambassador around 2:00 PM. So there we all were and by 11:30 we knew we had won and we all left the suite cheering and singing and talking all the way down to the ballroom where the walls were covered in red, white and blue bunting and Kennedy posters and Kennedy hope plastered on every conceivable surface. Waterford Crystal Chandeliers, network TV lights, flashbulbs, flashed smiles, all brighter than the Second Coming. They were singing, "Here we go Bobby, here we go" like at a football game and "Sock it to 'em Bobby, sock it to em" like on *The Rowan and Martin Laugh-In*. And they were singing "This man is your man/ this man is my man/ from California to the New York Island/ to the Redwood Forests/ to the Gulfstream Waters/ this man is Robert Kennedy."

What he said was:

"What I think is quite clear is that we can work together in the last analysis, and that what has been going on within the United States over the period of the last three years, the division, the violence, the disenchantment with our society; the divisions, whether it is between the blacks and the whites, whether between the poor and the more affluent or between the age groups or on the war in Vietnam -- that we can start to work together. That we are a great country, an unselfish country and a compassionate country and I intend to make that my basis for running over the period of the next few months."

And he said:

"I want to express my gratitude to my dog Freckles who has been maligned. As Franklin Roosevelt would say, I don't care what they say about me but when they start to attack my dog!"

"I am not doing this in the order of importance, but I would like to thank my wife Ethel and, uh, her patience during this whole effort is, uh, fantastic. So, uh, my thanks to all of you and it's on to Chicago and let's win there."

Then the thumbs-up sign and the flash of the peace sign. In the newsreel you can see LJ in a red scarf just above his right shoulder. He was to go to the waiting press in another room but at the last moment his route was changed.

"Get the gun! Get the gun!" someone screamed. "Get the gun. Get his thumb. Get his thumb. Get his thumb. Let's break it if you have to."

Then I heard, "Senator Kennedy has been shot. Is that possible? Is that possible?" Is that possible?

Yes. It was.

Made in the USA
Columbia, SC
20 March 2023